THE EAGLE'S WING

THE EAGLE'S WING

B. M. BOWER

WILDSIDE PRESS

TO THE AMERICAN EAGLE

Fighting always the Vultures of the earth; whose protective wing extends even into the desert lands; whose shadow has fallen upon the great river, this story of the Colorado is loyally inscribed.

B. M. B.

INTRODUCTION

B.M. Bower was the pseudonym of Bertha Muzzy Sinclair (or Sinclair-Cowan,) *née* Muzzy (1871–1940), an American author who wrote novels, short stories, and screenplays about the American Old West. Her works, most of which feature cowboys of the Flying U Ranch in Montana, reflected her interest in real ranch life, and she populated her tales with working cowhands going about everyday life on the range.

Her fiction was based on real life. Born in Minnesota, she moved with her parents to a homestead near Great Falls, Montana in 1889. That fall, she took employment as a schoolteacher in nearby Milligan Valley—the "school" being a log building with all of 12 pupils. She gave up after one term and returned to the family homestead. However, the experience shaped the characters of teachers who appeared in her later work.

In 1890, she eloped with her first husband, Clayton J. Bower. They moved to Great Falls, then to Big Sandy, where Bertha came into close contact with cowhands and began to gain first-hand knowledge of range life.

Eventually they moved to a lonely cabin with their three young children. To help make ends meet, they took in a 22-year-old cowhand, Bill Sinclair, as a boarder. Bertha and Sinclair became friends, and as she began to teach him to write, he taught her about cowboy life.

To, as she put it, "save my sanity," Bertha began to write, sending stories to magazines. She published her first story in a local publication in 1901, and sold her first novel (*Chip, of the Flying U*) for magazine publication in 1904. (It would eventually appear in book form in 1906.)

In the meantime, her marriage to Clayton Bower deteriorated. He drank, and when he returned home in a rage one day, it proved the final straw. Using the book advance money from *Chip of the Flying U*, and with Bill Sinclair's help, she fled to Tacoma, Washington to stay with her brother and his wife.

The divorce was finalized in 1905. Clayton took custody of two children, Bertha Grace and Harry, while Bertha moved back to Great Falls and took custody of son Roy. Throughout this difficult time, Bower's career progressed nicely, and *The Popular Magazine*—a successful pulp magazine that mostly published short stories—signed her to a short-story writing contract in January 1905.

Despite their age difference, Bertha and Bill Sinclair married on August 13, 1905, at the Great Falls Methodist-Episcopal Church. They rented a home in town and focused on their writing careers. After a blizzard destroyed their herd of breeding horses, which they had planned to build into a separate business, they left Montana and settled in Santa Cruz, California. Both Bertha and Bill Sinclair continued to pursue successful careers as writers. However, by late 1911, Bertha separated from Bill and rented her own house in San Jose, California. She also changed publishers, signing with the prestigious Boston publishing house Little, Brown & Company.

The 1920s led to more success, as Bertha moved to Hollywood and married her third husband, Robert "Bud" Cowan, a cowboy who she had met in Big Sandy. In 1921, they reopened a silver mine in Nevada and operated it for several years until the Great Depression forced them to move again, this time to Oregon. Their marriage lasted until Cowan's death in 1939. Bower did not remarry.

According to Elmer Kelton in his article "Granddad's Guilt," published in *Montana: The Magazine of Western History*, Bower's sales dropped when it was revealed that she was female. Even so, she carved out a lasting niche in the Western genre. She eventually published 57 novels that sold more than 2 million copies.

Although largely forgotten today, her work captures an authentic slice-of-life of ranch life in Montana.

Enjoy.

—John Betancourt
Cabin John, Maryland

CHAPTER 1

KING, OF THE MOUNTED

On the wide south porch of the house where he had been born, Rawley King sat smoking his pipe in the dusk heavy with the scent of a thousand roses. The fragrant serenity of the great, laurel-hedged yard of the King homestead was charming after the hot, empty spaces of the desert. Even the somber west wing of the brooding old house seemed wrapped in the peace that enfolds lives moving gently through long, uneventful months and years. The smoke of his pipe billowed lazily upward in the perfumed air; incense burned by the prodigal son upon the home altar after his wanderings.

The old Indian, Johnny Buffalo, came walking straight as an arrow across the strip of grass beside the syringa bushes that banked the west wing. Rawley straightened and stared, the bowl of his pipe sagging to the palm of his hand. As far back as he could remember, none had ever crossed that space of clipped grass to hold speech with the Kings. But now Johnny Buffalo walked steadily forward and halted beside the porch.

"Your grandfather say you come," he announced calmly and turned back to the somber west wing.

Sheer amazement held Rawley motionless for a moment. Until the Indian spoke to him, he had almost forgotten the strangeness of that hidden, remote life of his grandfather. From the time he could toddle, Rawley had been taught that he must not go near the west wing of the house or approach the brooding old man in the wheel chair. As for the Indian who served his grandfather, Rawley had been too much afraid of him to attempt any friendly overtures. There had been vague hints that Grandfather King was not quite right in his mind; that a brooding melancholy held him, and that he would suffer no one but his Indian servant near him. Now, after nearly thirty years of studied aloofness, his grandfather had summoned him.

The Indian was waiting in the shadowed west porch when Rawley tardily arrived at the steps. He turned without speaking and opened the door, waiting for Rawley to pass. Still dumb with astonishment, a bit awed, Rawley crossed the threshold and for the first time in his life stood in the presence of his grandfather.

A powerful figure the old man must have been in his youth. Old age had shrunk him, had sagged his shoulders and dried the flesh upon his bones; but years could not hide the breadth of those shoulders or change the length of those arms. His eyes were piercingly blue and his lips were firm under the drooping white mustache. His snow-white hair was heavy and lay upon his shoulders in natural waves that made it seem heavier than it really was—just so he had probably worn it in the old, old days on the frontier. His eyebrows were domineering and jet black, and the whole rugged countenance betrayed the savage strength of the spirit that dwelt back of his eyes. But the great, gaunt body stopped short at the knees, and the gray blanket smoothed over his lap could not hide the tragic mutilation; nor could the great mustache conceal the bitter lines around his mouth.

"Back from Arizona, hey?" he launched abruptly at Rawley, and his voice was grim as his face.

Rawley started. Perhaps he expected a cracked, senile tone; it would have fitted better the tradition of the old man's mental weakness.

"Just got back today, Grandfather." Instinctively Rawley swung to a matter-of-fact manner, warding off his embarrassment over the amazing interview.

"Mining expert, hey? Know your business?"

"Well enough to be paid for working at it," grinned Rawley, trying unsuccessfully to keep his eyes from straying curiously around the room filled with ancient trophies of a soldier's life half a century before.

"Not much like your father! I'll bet he couldn't have told you the meaning of the words. Damned milksop. Bank clerk! Not a drop of King blood in his body—far as looks and actions went. Guess he thought gold grew on bushes, stamped with the date of the harvest!"

"I remember him vaguely. He never seemed well or strong," Rawley defended his dead father.

"Never had the King make-up. Only weakling the Kings ever produced—and he had to be *my* son! Take a look at that picture on the bureau. That's what I mean by King blood. Johnny, give him the picture."

The Indian moved silently to a high chest of drawers against the farther wall and lifted from it an enlarged, framed photograph, evidently copied from an earlier crude effort of some pioneer in the art. He placed it reverently in Rawley's hands and retreated to a respectful distance.

"Taken before I started out with Moorehead's expedition in '59. Six feet two in my bare feet, and not an ounce of soft flesh in my body. Not a man in the company I couldn't throw. Johnny could tell you." A note of pride had crept into the old man's voice.

"I can see it, Grandfather. I—I'd give anything to have been with you in those days. Lord, what a physique!"

The fierce old eyes sparkled. The bony fingers gripped the arms of the wheel chair like steel claws.

"That's the King blood. Give me two legs and I'd be a King yet, old as I am—instead of a hunk of meat in a wheel chair."

"It's the spirit that counts, Grandfather," Rawley observed hearteningly, his eyes still on the picture but lifting now to the old man's face. "The picture's like you yet."

The old man grunted doubtfully, his eyes fixed sharply upon Rawley's face. His fingers drummed restlessly upon the arm of his chair, as if he were seeing in the young man his own care-free youth, and was yearning over it in secret. Indeed, as he stood there in the light of the old-fashioned lamp, Rawley King might have been mistaken for the original of the picture with the costume set fifty years ahead.

"Johnny, get the box." Grandfather King spoke without taking his eyes off Rawley.

The old Indian slipped away. In a moment he returned with a square metal box which he placed on the old man's knees. Rawley found himself wondering what his mother would say when he told her that Grandfather King had sent for him, was actually talking to him, giving him a glimpse of that sealed past of his. He watched his grandfather fit a key into the lock of the metal box.

"You're a King, thank God. I've watched you grow. Six feet and over, and no water in *your* blood, by the looks. You're like I was at your age. Johnny knows. He can remember how I looked when I had two legs. Here. You take these—they're yours, and all the good you can get out of them. Read 'em both. Read 'em till you get the good that's in 'em. If you're a King, you'll do it."

He held out two worn little books. Rawley took them, eyeing them queerly. One was a Bible, the old-fashioned, leather-bound pocket size edition, with a metal clasp. The other book was smaller; a diary, evidently, with a leather band going around, the end slipping under a flap to hold it secure.

"I will—you bet!" Rawley made his voice as hearty as his puzzlement would permit. "Thanks, Grandfather."

"I meant 'em for your father—but he wasn't the man to get anything out of 'em worth while. A milksop—wore spectacles before he wore pants! His idea of success was to shove money out to other people through a grated window. Paugh! When he told me that was his ambition, I came near burning the books. Johnny could tell you. He stopped me—only time in his life he ever stuck his foot through the wheel of my chair and anchored me out of reach of the fire. Out of reach of my guns, too, or I'd have killed him maybe! Johnny said, 'You wait. Maybe more Kings come—like Grandfather.'

"So I did wait, and after a while I could watch you grow—all King. I could tell by the set of your shoulders and the tone of your voice and the way you went straight at anything you wanted. So there's your legacy, boy, from King, of the Mounted. Ask any of the old veterans who King, of the Mounted, was! You read those books." He lifted a bony finger and pointed. "There's a lot in that Bible—if you read it careful."

"You bet, Grandfather!" Rawley undid the clasp and opened the book politely. The old man twisted his lips into a sardonic smile. His eyes gleamed, indigo blue, under his shaggy black brows. Then, as if reminded of something forgotten, he dipped into the box, fumbled a bit and held out his hand to Rawley.

"You're a mining expert; maybe you can tell me where I picked them up." His eyes bored into Rawley's face.

Rawley bent his head over the three nuggets of gold. He weighed them in his hand, turned them to the light of the lamp which Johnny Buffalo had lifted from the table and held close.

"Greenhorns think that gold is gold," Rawley grinned at last. "And so it is—but you left a little rock sticking to this one, Grandfather. So I'll guess Nevada."

"Hunh!" The old man's eyes sparkled. "What part?"

Rawley glanced up at him with the endearing King smile. "Say, I'm liable to fall down on that! But I reckon King, of the Mounted, will put me flat against the wall before he quits, anyway. So—well, how about Searchlight?"

"Hunh! I guess you know your job." The old man smiled back at him, a glimmer of that same endearing quality in the smile and the eyes. He waved back the gold when Rawley would have returned it. "Keep it—you've earned it. No use to me any more." He settled deeper into the chair and gave a great sigh as his head dropped back against the cushions. "Fifty years ago I picked 'em up—and I've lived to see a King turn them over twice in his hand and tell me within a few miles of where I got them. That shows what I mean by King blood. Fifty years ago! It's a long time to live like a hunk of meat. I'm seventy-nine—"

"Get out! You'd have to prove it, Grandfather. That's a good ten years more than you look."

"Don't lie to me, boy." But King, of the Mounted, failed to look censorious. "You read that Bible. Remember, that's the legacy old King, of the Mounted, leaves to the next King in line. It don't lie, boy. Read it faithful and heed what it says, and some day you'll say the old man wasn't so crazy after all."

"Why, Grandfather—"

But the old man waved him away with a peremptory gesture. Johnny Buffalo glided to the door, opened it and held it so, waiting with the inscrutable calm of his race.

"Well, good night, Grandfather. I'm—glad to have had this little talk. And I hope it won't be the last. I always wanted to pioneer, and I've always felt as if I'd like to talk over those times—"

Rawley was finding it rather difficult even yet to bridge the silence of a lifetime.

"You grew up thinking I was crazy, most likely. Easy to say the old man's touched in the head—when they don't want to bother with a cripple. You're a King. Maybe you can guess what it means to be a hulk in a wheel chair. And the Kings never ran after anybody; nor the Rawlinses, your grandmother's people. Two good names—glad you carry 'em both. If you live up to 'em both you'll go far. Take care of those two books, boy. Remember what I said—they're your legacy from King, of the Mounted. Good night."

The old man snapped out the last two words in a tone of finality and reached for his pipe. Johnny Buffalo opened the door an inch wider. Rawley obeyed the unspoken hint and straightway found himself outside, with the door closed behind him. He waited, listening, loth to go. Now that the feud was broken, he tingled with the desire to know more about his grandfather, more about those wonderful old fighting frontier days, more about King, of the Mounted.

"Crazy? I should say not!" Rawley muttered as he made his way slowly across the strip of grass by the syringas. "I only hope my brain will be as keen as Grandfather's when I am his age."

He stood for a few minutes breathing deep the night air saturated with perfume. Then, with the spell of his grandfather's vivid personality strong upon him, he went in to where his mother sat gently rocking beside a rose-shaded lamp, looking over a late magazine.

"I've just been having a talk with Grandfather," Rawley announced bluntly, sitting down opposite his mother and studying her as if she were a stranger to him. Indeed, those few minutes spent in the west wing had dealt a sharp blow to his unquestioning faith in his mother. Mrs. King dropped the magazine and opened her lips—artificially red—and gave a faint gasp.

"Grandfather's mind is as clear as yours or mine," Rawley stated challengingly. "A bit old-fashioned, maybe—a man couldn't live in a wheel chair for fifty years or so, shut away from all companionship as he has been, and keep his ideas right up to the minute. If you ask me, I'll say he'd make a corking old pal. Full of pep—or would be if he weren't crippled.

It's a darned shame I never busted through the feud before. Why, fifty years ago he was all through Nevada—think of that! I'd give ten years of my life to have lived when he did, right at his elbow."

He felt the sag in his pockets then and brought out the two little books.

"I always thought, Mother, that Grandfather King was a particularly wicked old party. Well, that's all wrong—same as the idea that he's weak in the head. He gave me this Bible, and made me promise to read it. He said—"

"*Bible?*" Rawley's mother sat up sharply, and her mouth remained open, ready for further words which her mind seemed unable to formulate.

"You bet. He said if I read it faithfully and got all the good out of it there is in it, I'd thank him the rest of my life—or something like that. He meant it, too."

"Why, Rawley King! Your grandfather has always been an atheist of the worst type! I've heard your father tell how he used to hear your grand-father blaspheme and curse God by the hour for making him a cripple. When he was a little boy—your father, I mean—he was deeply impressed by your grandmother asking every prayer-meeting night for the prayers of the church to soften her husband's heart and turn his thoughts toward God. Your father has told me how he used to go home afterwards and watch to see if your grandfather's heart was softened. But it never was—he got wickeder, if possible, and swore horribly at everything, nearly. Your father said he nearly lost faith in prayer. But he believed that the congregation never prayed as it should. I wouldn't believe, Rawley, that your grandfather would have a Bible near him. Are you sure?"

"Here it is," Rawley assured her, grinning. "He said it was my legacy from him."

"Well, that proves to my mind he's crazy," his mother said grimly. "Your father always felt that Grandfather King had sinned against the Holy Ghost and *couldn't* repent. Anyway," she added resentfully, "that's about all you'll ever get from him. When he deeded this place to your father for a wedding present—that was a little while after your grandmother died—he reserved the west wing for himself as long as he lived. It's in the deed that he's not to be interfered with or molested. When he dies, the west wing becomes a part of this property—which is mine, of course. He lives on his pension, which just about keeps him and that awful old Indian. Of course the pension stops when he dies. So he was right about the legacy, at least. But I'll bet he put a curse on the Bible before he gave it to you. It would be just like him."

Rawley shook his head dissentingly. "It's darned hard to sit in a wheel chair for fifty years," he remarked somewhat irrelevantly. "I'd cuss things some, myself, I reckon." And he added abruptly, "Say, Grandfather's got the bluest eyes, Mother, I ever saw in a man's head. I thought eyes faded with old age. Did you ever notice his eyes, Mother?"

His mother laughed unpleasantly. "Your Grandfather King never gave me any inducement to get close enough to see his eyes. Seeing him on the porch of the west wing is enough for me."

"He laid a good deal of stress upon his past," said Rawley. "I suppose because he hasn't any present—and darned little future, I'm afraid. He gave me some nuggets. Would you like a nugget ring, Mother?"

His mother glanced at the nuggets and pushed away Rawley's hand that held them cupped in the palm.

"No, I wouldn't. Not if your Grandfather King had anything to do with it. He's been like a poison plant in the yard ever since I came here, Rawley; like poison ivy, that you're careful not to go near. I don't want to touch anything belonging to him—and I hope I'm not a vindictive woman, either."

Rawley was rolling the nuggets in his hand, staring at them abstractedly.

"It's queer—the whole thing," he said finally. "I feel a sort of leaning toward Grandfather. It was something in his eyes. You know, Mother, it must be darned tough to have both legs chopped off at the knees when you're a young husky over six feet in your socks and full of pep. I—believe I can understand Grandfather King. 'A hunk of meat in a wheel chair'— that's what he called himself. And those amazing blue eyes of his—"

His mother glanced curiously into his face. "They can't be any bluer than yours, Rawley," she observed.

Rawley looked up from the nuggets, his forehead wrinkled with surprise.

"Oh, do you think that, Mother?" He stood up suddenly, still shaking the nuggets with a dull clink in his hand. "Well, I hope Grandfather's passed on a few more of his traits to me. There's a few of them I'm going to need," he said drily and kissed his mother good night.

CHAPTER 2

JOHNNY BUFFALO BEARS
ANOTHER MESSAGE

In his room, Rawley switched on the light and slid into the big chair by the table. Not to his mother could he confess how deeply those few minutes with Grandfather King had stirred him. In spite of her attitude toward the silent feud that had endured for nearly thirty years, he was conscious of the dull ache of remorse. Without meaning to judge his parents or to criticize their manner of handling a difficult situation, Rawley felt that night that he had been guilty of a great wrong toward his grandfather. He at least should have ignored the invisible wall that stood between the west wing and the rest of the house. He was a King; he should not have permitted that reason-less silence to endure through all these years.

As a matter of fact, Rawley's life since he was twelve had been spent mostly away from home. First, a military academy in the suburbs of St. Louis, with the long hiking trips featured by the school through the summer vacations; after that, college—with a special course in mineralogy. Since then, field work had claimed most of his time. Home had therefore been merely a place pleasantly tucked away in his memory, with a visit to his mother now and then between jobs.

The first twelve years of his life had thoroughly accustomed Rawley to the sight of the fierce old man with long hair and his legs cut off at his knees, who sometimes appeared in a wheel chair on a porch of the west wing, attended by an Indian who looked savage enough to scalp a little boy if he ventured too close; a ferocious Indian who scowled and wore his hair parted from forehead to neck and braided in two long braids over his shoulder, and who padded stealthily about the place in beautifully beaded moccasins and fringed buckskin leggings.

Nevertheless, there had been times, as he grew older, when Rawley had been tempted to invade the west wing and find out for himself just how bitterly his grandfather clung to the feud. It hurt him to think now of the old man's isolation and of the interesting companionship he had cheated himself out of enjoying.

He pulled the two old books from his pocket, handling them as if they were the precious things his grandfather seemed to consider them. The Bible he opened first, undoing the old-fashioned clasp with his thumb and opening the book at the flyleaf. The inscription there was faded yet distinct on the yellowed paper. The sloping, careful handwriting of Rawley's great-grandmother sending King, of the Mounted, forth upon his dangerous missions armed with the Word of God—and hoping prayerfully, no doubt, that he would read and heed its precepts.

> To my beloved son,
> George Walter King,
> from his
> Affectionate Mother.

The date thrilled Rawley, aged twenty-six: 1858 was the year his great-grandmother had inscribed in the book. To Rawley it seemed almost as remote as the Stamp Act or the Mexican War. The thought that Grandfather King, away back in 1858, had been old enough to join the Missouri Mounted Volunteers—even to have been made a sergeant in his company and to make for himself a reputation as an Indian fighter—gave the old man a new dignity in the eyes of his grandson. It seemed strange that Grandfather King was still alive and could talk of those days.

The book itself was strangely contradictory in appearance. While the outside was worn and scuffed as if with much usage, the inside crackled faintly a protest against unaccustomed handling. The yellowed leaves clung together in layers which Rawley must carefully separate. Now and then a line or two showed faint penciled underscores; otherwise the book did not look as if it had been opened for many, many years. Nowhere was it thumbed and soiled by the frequent reading of a man living under canvas or the open sky.

"Looks to me like the old boy has simply passed the buck," Rawley grinned. "Maybe he felt as if some one in the family ought to read it. His mother had it all marked for him, too; wanted to give him a good start-off, maybe. No, sir, the old book itself is pinning it onto King, of the Mounted! Mother must be right, after all, and Grandfather never had enough religion to talk about. But he sure gave me a Sunday-school talk; funny how a book can stand up and call you a liar."

He smiled as he closed the book, whimsically shaking his head over the joke. Then, just to make sure that his guess was correct, Rawley opened the Bible again. No, there could be no mistake. Crackly new on the inside—though yellowed with age—badly worn on the outside, the book itself proclaimed the story of long carrying and little reading. The evidence against the sincerity of the old man's pious admonitions was conclusive. Rawley laid the Bible down for a further consideration and took up the worn old diary.

Here, too, Grandfather King had betrayed a certain lack of sincerity. Reading the faded entries, Rawley decided that King, of the Mounted, must have been an impetuous youth who had learned caution with the years. Dates, arrivals, departures—these remained. Incidents, however, had for the most part been neatly sliced out with a knife. And with a stubborn disregard for the opinion of later readers the stubs of the pages elided had been left to tell of the deliberate mutilation of the record. So Rawley read perfunctorily the dry record of obscure scouting trips, and the names of commanders long since dead and remembered only in the records.

Rawley learned that his grandfather had taken part in the making of much frontier history. He spoke of Captain Hunt in a matter-of-fact way and mentioned the date on which a certain Captain Hendley had been killed by Indians somewhere near Las Vegas, in Nevada. On the next page Rawley found this gruesome paragraph:

From a young Indian captured in the battle of last week, I learned the secret of the devilish poisoned arrows, which are black. The black arrows are poisoned in this manner, he tells me, and since I have befriended him in many small ways I do not doubt his word. To procure the poison, an animal is slain and the liver removed. A captured rattlesnake is then induced to strike the liver again and again, injecting all of its poison into the meat. The arrow-points are afterwards rubbed in the putrid mass and left to dry. Needless to say, a wound touched by this poison and decayed meat surely causes death. The young Indian tells me that a certain desert plant has been successfully used as an antidote, but he did not tell me the name of the plant. He declared that he did not know, that only the doctors of his tribe know that secret.

I think he lied. He was willing to tell me the horrid means of making the poison. But is too cunning to let me know the antidote. So the tobacco I've given him is after all wasted. The information merely increases my dread of the black arrows. Rattlesnake venom and putrid liver—paugh! I shall—

A page was missing. Followed several pages of brief entries, with long lapses of time between. Then came a page which gave a glimpse into that colorful life:

June, 1866. On board the "Esmeralda." Arrived at El Dorado (*Deuteronomy*, 2:36) today. This is the first boat up the river.

The Scriptural reference had been inserted in very small writing above the name of the place. Evidently Grandfather King had been reading some Bible, if not the one his mother had given him.

A town has sprung up in the wilderness since I was here last, cursing the heat and stinging gnats in '59. A stamp mill stands at the river's edge and houses are scattered all up and down the river, while a ferry crosses to the other shore. A crowd came down to the landing for their mail and to see what strangers were on the boat. As yet I do not know whether our company will be stationed here or at Fort Callville, a few miles up the canyon. The Indians are quiet, they say. Too quiet, some of the miners think. On the edge of the crowd I saw a young squaw—or perhaps she is Spanish. She has the velvet eyes and the dark rose blooming in her cheeks, which speaks of Spanish blood. By God, she's beautiful! Not more than sixteen and graceful as a fairy. I leaned over the rail—

Several pages were cut from the book just there, and Rawley swore to himself. When one is twenty-six one resents any interruption in a romance. The next entry read:

July 4th. Great doings at the fort today, with barbeque, wrestling, target practice and gambling. Miners and Indians came out of the hills to celebrate the holiday. In the wrestling matches I easily held my own, as in the sharp-shooting. Anita received my message and was here—el gusto de mi corazon. What a damned pity she's not white! But she's more Spanish than Indian, with her proud little ways and her light heart. Jess Cramer tried again to come between us, and there was a fight not down on the program. They carried him to the hospital. A little more and I'd have broken his back, the surgeon said. If he looks at her again—

More elision just when the interest was keenest. Rawley wanted to know more about Anita—"the joy of my heart", as Grandfather had set it down in Spanish. The next page, however, whetted Rawley's curiosity a bit more:

July 15th. To-morrow we march to Las Vegas to meet a party of emigrants and guard them to San Bernardino. The Indians are unsettled and traveling is not safe. A miner was murdered and scalped within ten miles of the fort the other day. No mi alebro—Anita wept and clung to me when I told her we had marching orders. Dulce corazon—God, how I wish she was white! But in any case I could not take her with me. I shall return in a month's time—

August. In hospital, after a hellish trip in a wagon with other wounded. Mohave Indians attacked our wagon train, one hundred miles northeast of here, on the desert. While leading a charge afoot against the Indians I was shot through both legs. Gangrene set in before we could reach this place, and the doctor will not promise the speedy recovery I desire.

My Indian boy, Johnny Buffalo, refuses to leave my side. He hates all other whites. On the desert I picked him up half dead with thirst, and set him before me on the saddle because he feared the wagons. I judge him to be about ten. If I live, I shall keep the boy with me and train him for my body-servant. A faithful Indian is better than a watch-dog—

A lapse of several months intervened before the next entry. Then a brief record, which told of the closing of one romance and the beginning of another:

November 15th. This day I married Mary Jane Rawlins. Was able to stand during the ceremony, supported by two crutches. My Indian boy slipped away from the others and stood close behind me during the service, one hand clutching tightly my coat-tail. Mary has courage, to wish to marry a man likely to be a cripple the rest of his days.

Nothing further was recorded for several years; four, to be exact. Then:

Returned today from hospital. After all this suffering, both legs were taken off above the knee. The poison had spread to the joints. What a pity it was not my neck.

On the next page was one grim line:

December 4th, 1889. My wife, Mary Rawlins King, was buried today.

That ended the diary. In a memorandum pocket just inside the cover, a folded paper lay snug and flat. Rawley drew it forth eagerly and held it close to the lamp. His face clouded then with disappointment, for nothing was written on the paper save a list of Bible references.

So that was the legacy. An old diary just interesting enough to be tantalizing, with half the pages cut out; Bible references probably given to King, of the Mounted, by his mother. And a worn old Bible that had never been read. Rawley stacked the books one upon the other and leaned back in his chair, staring at them meditatively while he filled his pipe. He took three puffs before he laughed silently.

"He was a speedy old bird, I'll say that much for him," he told himself. "I'll bet those pages he cut out fairly sizzled. And I'll bet he cut them out about the time he married Grandmother. Also, I think he left one or two pages by mistake. Well, I'll say he lived! As long as he had two good legs under him he was up and coming. I don't suppose there's a chance in the world of getting him to talk about Anita. '*El gusto de mi corazon*—' There's nothing like the Spanish for love-making words. And that was in July—and he married Grandmother in November. Poor little half-breed girl who should have been white! But then, I reckon he'd have gone back to her if he could. But they sent him home—crippled for life. You can't blame Grandfather, after all. And I notice he mentioned the fact that Grandmother wanted to marry him. Sorry for the handsome young soldier on crutches, but it's darned hard on Anita, just the same. And I don't suppose he could even get word to her."

He smoked the pipe out, his thoughts gone a-questing into the long ago, where the black arrows were dipped in loathsome poison, and young Indian girls had the fire and grace of the Spaniards.

"She'd be old, too, by now—if she's alive," he thought, as he knocked the ashes from his pipe and yawned. "I wonder if she ever forgot. And I wonder if Grandfather ever thinks of her now. He does, I'll bet. Those terrible, blue eyes! They *couldn't* forget."

He went to bed, his imagination still held to the days of the fighting old frontier; still building adventures and romances for the dashing, blue-eyed King, of the Mounted.

He was dreaming of an Indian fight when a sharp tapping on his window woke him to gray dawn. He sprang out of bed, still knuckling the sleep out of his eyes, and saw Johnny Buffalo standing close to the open screen. The Indian raised a hand.

"You come quick. Your grandfather is dead."

CHAPTER 3

"MY HEART IS DEAD"

It was the evening after the funeral, and Rawley was sitting again on the porch, staring out gloomily over a cold pipe into the yard. His grandfather's death had hit him a harder blow than he would have thought possible. The shock of it, coming close on the heels of his first keen realization that Grandfather King was a vivid personality, left him numbed with a sense of loss.

His mother's evident relief at the removal of an unpleasant problem chilled and irritated him. Her calm assumption that the Indian must also be removed from the place, now that his master was gone, seemed to Rawley almost like sacrilege. The place belonged to his mother only by right of his grandfather's generosity. To rob the Indian of a home he had enjoyed since boyhood was unthinkable.

He turned his head and glanced toward the west wing, his eyes following his thoughts. A dimly outlined figure stood erect upon the porch of the west wing. Pity gripped Rawley by the throat; pity and half-conscious admiration. Even the greatest grief of his life could not bow the shoulders of Johnny Buffalo. With no definite purpose, drawn only by the kinship of their loss, Rawley rose, crossed the grass plot by the syringas and sat down on the top step of the west porch.

Johnny Buffalo stood with his arms folded, the fringe on his buckskin sleeves whipping gently in the soft breeze that rose when the sun went down. He was staring straight out at nothing—the nothingness that epitomized his future. Rawley slanted a glance up at him and began thoughtfully refilling his pipe. By his silence he was unconsciously bringing himself close to the soul of the Indian, the traditions of whose race forbade hasty speech.

Half a pipe Rawley smoked, staring meditatively into the dusk. In that time Johnny Buffalo had moved no more than if he were a statue of brown stone. Then Rawley tipped his head sidewise and looked up at him.

"Sit down, Johnny. I want to talk."

"Talk is useless when the heart is dead," said Johnny Buffalo after a long pause. But he came down two steps and seated himself, straight-backed, head up, beside Rawley.

"The man I love is cold. His spirit has gone. So I am left cold, and my heart is dead. I shall wait—and be glad when my body is dead."

Rawley felt a sharp constriction in his throat. For one moment he almost hated his mother who would drive this stricken old man out into a world he did not know. A gun against his temple would be kinder. He drew a long breath.

"Would you like to wait here, where he lived?" Intuitively he crystallized his thoughts into the briefest words possible to express his meaning.

Johnny Buffalo shook his head slowly, with a decisiveness that could not be questioned. He folded his arms again across his grief-laden breast.

"It is your mother's. In the fields I can wait for death, which is my friend. I shall walk toward the land of my people. When death finds me I shall smile."

Rawley turned this over in his mind, seeking some point where argument might break down bitter resolution.

"Cowards wait for death when life grows hard," he said at last. "The brave man meets life and faces sorrow because he is brave and will overcome. The brave man fights death which is an enemy. He does not run away from life and welcome his enemy. My grandfather found life very hard. For fifty years my grandfather faced it because his spirit was strong."

"Your grandfather's spirit was strong. His body was broken. My body is strong. My spirit is broken. Can a strong body live with a broken spirit inside?"

Rawley had to smoke over this for a while. Johnny Buffalo, he conceded privately, was no man's fool. Rawley tried to put himself in the Indian's place and discover, if he could, something that would make life worth the living.

"Your people are scattered," he said quietly. "Few are left. The Mohaves are a broken tribe."

"The Mohaves are not my people," the Indian corrected him calmly. "I am Pahute. In the mountains along the river you call the Colorado, my people lived and hunted—and fought. My uncle was the chief, and I was proud. One day my mother beat me with a stick. I took my bow and my arrows and some dried meat, and that night I left my people, for I was angry and ashamed. With my bow I had killed two mountain sheep. With my bow I had hidden in the rocks and had wounded a white man who was digging in the hillside. I thought I was a warrior and not to be beaten by a squaw.

"The great thirst found me as I was walking toward the mountains where all my life I had seen the sun go down. With my bow and arrow I could get meat, but I could not get water. All my life I had lived near the river. The great thirst I did not know.

"I fell in the sand. When I awoke, water was in my mouth. I looked, and I was lying in the arms of a white man. He was big and strong and very handsome. He was Sergeant King. Your grandfather. I looked into his eyes and I was not afraid. There was no hate in my heart for him, but all other whites I hated. He lifted me and carried me in his arms and laid me in a wagon with white women and children. I hated them. I was weak from the thirst and from much walking, but I bit deep into the arm of a woman who put her hand on me.

"There was much yelling in that wagon. The woman struck me many times. A horse came galloping. Your grandfather lifted me out of the wagon and put me on the horse with him. So we rode together in one saddle. I loved him.

"The Mohaves attacked the whites when we had gone many days. My sergeant left me with his horse by the wagons. He crept behind bushes and killed many. He was a great warrior and I was proud when his gun brought death to a Mohave. I watched him, for I loved him. When I saw him fall from his knees and lie on his face in the sand, I jumped from the horse and went creeping through the brush. He was not dead. I took his gun and killed Mohaves. Pretty soon my sergeant looked at me and smiled while I killed. When there were no more Mohaves, the captain came. They put my sergeant in a wagon and I sat beside him. I gave him water, I gave him food. With my fists I beat back those who would take from me the joy of serving him.

"A long time he was sick in the town we entered. I was with him. Every day and every night he could open his eyes and see that I was with him."

The sonorous voice ceased its monotone and the Indian sat silent, staring into the past. After a while he turned his head and looked full at Rawley.

"I was a boy when he took me. Now I am an old man. Since he took me there has been no night when my sergeant could call and get no answer. There has been no day when my sergeant could look and could not see me. Now my sergeant is gone. My heart is gone with him."

Enthralled by the picture vividly painted with bold strokes by the Indian, Rawley sat hunched over his pipe, cuddling the cooling bowl in his fingers.

"Your sergeant was my grandfather. At the last I loved him, too. I am a King. I need you." His tone stamped the lie as truth. Later he would find some way of making it the truth, he thought.

Johnny Buffalo eyed him sharply in the deepening dusk.

"You have read the book?" he asked after a minute. "If you have read, then I will go with you. The spirit of my sergeant will go. My heart may live again."

"What book?" Rawley's eyes widened.

"Your grandfather gave you the book. Your grandfather commanded that you read." Reproach was in the voice of Johnny Buffalo.

"I have read the diary—the book where he wrote of his travels. Do you mean that book?"

Johnny Buffalo gave a grunt that was pure Indian and signified disgust.

Rawley frowned over the puzzle and his very evident defection. It must be the Bible that was meant, he decided. But he could see no reason why he should read the Bible and then go somewhere. Still, the thing seemed to have pulled Johnny Buffalo out of his slough of despond, and that was what Rawley had been working for.

"If you mean the Bible," he said tentatively, "I read it a little, that night."

Johnny Buffalo peered at him. "Read that book more. Your grandfather commanded that you should read. I heard the promise you gave. You said, 'You bet.' It was a promise to obey your grandfather."

"I mean to keep the promise," Rawley replied defensively. "I haven't had time. Things have been pretty much upset since that night."

The Indian meditated. "You read," he admonished after due deliberation. "Your grandfather never talked to make words. I think he would have told you more. But his spirit went. I will stay in a tent by the river. When you have read, you come. We will talk more when you have read."

Rawley felt the dismissal under the words. He offered the Indian money, which was refused by a gesture. Then, conscious of a certain vague excitement in the back of his mind, he went back to his own part of the house.

CHAPTER 4

RAWLEY READS THE BIBLE

In his room again, Rawley unlocked his desk and got the two books which were his "legacy." He was young, and for all his technical training the spirit of romance called to his youth. There was something particularly important, something urgent in the admonition that he should read the Scriptures. Rawley's training was all against vague speculations. Your mining engineer fights guesswork at every stage of his profession.

He sat down with the books in his hand and began to reason the thing out cold-bloodedly, as if it were a problem in mineral formations. He undid the clasp of the Bible, opened it and looked through all the leaves, seeking for some hidden paper. He spent half an hour in the search and discovered nothing. There was no message, then, hidden in the Bible. His grandfather must have meant the actual reading of the text itself.

Then he remembered the paper filled with references, hidden in the pocket of the diary. There might be something significant in that, he thought. He opened the diary, took out the paper and glanced down the list of references. They were scattered all through the book and there were sixty-four of them.

He opened the Bible again and began to look for the first one—I Kings, 20:3. The leaves stuck together, they turned in groups, they seemed determined that he should not find I Kings anywhere in the book. Daniel, Joshua, Jeremiah, Zechariah and Esther he peered into; there didn't seem to be any Kings.

He muttered a word frequently found in the Bible, laid the book down and went to the living room, to the big, embossed Family Bible that had his birth date in it and the date of his father's death; and pictures at which he had been permitted to look on Sunday afternoons if he were a good boy. His mother had gone out to some meeting or other. He had the room to himself and he could read at his leisure.

It struck him immediately that this Bible had not been much read either. But the leaves were thick enough to turn singly, the print was large, and if I Kings were present he felt that he had some chance of finding it. With pencil and paper beside him, and with the list of references in one hand, he therefore set himself methodically to the task. And he was twenty-six, and the blood of the adventurous Kings beat strongly in his veins. So when he had found the book and the chapter which headed the list, he ran his finger down the half-column to the third verse; and this is what he read:

Thy silver and thy gold is mine; thy wives also and thy children, even the goodliest, are mine.

Rawley was conscious of a slight chill of disappointment when he had written it down in his fine, beautifully exact, draftsman's handwriting. But he went doggedly to work on the next reference nevertheless:

Psalms, 73:7. Their eyes stand out with fatness; they have more than heart could wish.

This was no more promising, but he had promised to read, and this seemed to him the most practical method of getting at his grandfather's secret purpose and thoughts. So he settled himself down to an evening's hard labor with book and paper.

He was just finishing the work when he heard his mother's footsteps on the porch. Rather guiltily he closed the Bible and folded his notes, so that his mother, coming into the room, found Rawley standing before a large window, thoughtfully gazing out into the dark while he stuffed tobacco in his pipe. His mother was a religious woman and a member of the church, but she took her religion according to certain fixed rules. Reading the Bible casually, apparently for entertainment, would have required an explanation—and Rawley did not want to explain, least of all to his mother.

He listened with perfunctory interest to her account of the evening's edifications (a Swedish missionary having lectured in his own tongue, with an interpreter) and escaped when he could to his room. He wanted to be alone where he could try and guess the riddle his grandfather had placed before him.

That there was a message of some kind hidden away in the Scriptural quotations, Rawley felt absolutely certain. In the first place, they did not seem to him such passages as a devout person would cherish for the comfort they held. Moreover, certain verses had been repeated, although the text itself did not seem to justify such emphasis. Precious metals, and journeyings into rough country, he decided, was the dominant note of the citations and the net result was confusing to say the least. If his grandfather really intended that he should discover any meaning in the jumble, he should have furnished a key, Rawley told himself disgustedly, some time after midnight, when he had read the quotations over and over until his head ached and they seemed more meaningless than at first.

But his grandfather had told him emphatically that there was a lot in the Bible, if he read it carefully enough. There might have been in the statement no meaning deeper than an old man's whim, but Rawley could not bring himself to believe it. Somewhere in those verses a secret lay hidden, and Rawley did not mean to give up until he had solved the problem.

At daylight the next morning Rawley awoke with what he considered an inspiration. He swung out of bed and with his bathrobe over his shoulders made a stealthy pilgrimage into the old-fashioned library where the conventional aggregation of "works" were to be found in leather-bound sets. Squatting on his haunches, he inspected a certain dim corner filled with fiction of the type commonly accepted as standard. He chose a volume and returned to bed, leaving one of his heelless slippers behind him in his absorption in the mystery.

He crawled back into bed and read Poe's "Gold Bug" before breakfast, giving particular attention to the elucidation of the cipher contained in the story. The general effect of this research work was not illuminating. Poe's cipher had been worked out with numbers, whereas Grandfather King had carelessly muffled his meaning in many words; unless the book, chapter and verse numbers were intended to convey the message in cipher similar to Poe's.

This possibility struck Rawley in the middle of his shaving. He could not wait to put the theory to the test, but hastily wiped the razor, and the lather from one side of his face, opened his grandfather's old Bible at the index and began setting down the number of each book above its name in the reference list. Thus, I Kings, 20:3 became the numerals 11-20-3.

He was eagerly at work at this when his mother called him to breakfast. His mother was a woman who worked industriously at being cultured. She had a secret ambition to be called behind her back a brilliant conversationalist. Breakfast, therefore, was always an uncomfortable meal for Rawley whenever his mother had attended some instructive gathering the evening before.

While he ate his first muffin, Rawley listened to a foggy interpretation of the Swedish lecturer's ideas upon universal brotherhood. Rather, he sat quiet while his mother talked. Then he interrupted her shockingly.

"Say, Mother, do you know whether Grandfather ever read Poe?"

A swallow of coffee went down his mother's "Sunday throat." It was some minutes before she could reply, and by that time Rawley had decided that perhaps he had better not bother his mother about the cipher. He patted her on the back, begged her pardon for asking foolish questions, and escaped to his own room, where he spent the whole day with "The Gold Bug" opened before him at the page which contained Poe's rule concerning the frequency with which certain letters occur in the alphabet.

That evening there was a fine litter of papers scribbled over with letters and numbers, singly and in groups. Rawley could not get two words that made sense. The thing simply didn't work. If his grandfather had ever read Poe's "Gold Bug", he certainly had not used it for a pattern.

He went back to his sixty-four Bible verses and began studying them again. But he could not see any reason why Grandfather King should claim any one's wives and children, whose "eyes stand out with fatness." The third and fourth verses were intelligible;

Proverbs, 2:1. My son, if thou wilt receive my words, and hide my commandments with thee.

II Chronicles, 1:12. Wisdom and knowledge is granted unto thee; and I will give thee riches, and wealth, and honor, such as none of the kings have had that have been before thee, neither shall there any after thee have the like.

Even the next three lent themselves to a possible personal meaning:

Psalms, 2:10. Be wise now therefore, oh ye kings; be instructed, ye judges of the earth.

I Chronicles, 22:16. Of the gold, the silver, and the brass, and the iron, there is no number. Rise, therefore, and be doing and the Lord be with thee.

Deuteronomy, 11:11. But the land, whither ye go to possess it, is a land of hills and valleys, and drinketh water of the rain of heaven.

After that, he was all at sea.

He picked up the little Bible and opened it again. It must be there that the message was hidden; and Rawley felt very sure, by now, that the Bible quotations held the secret. The book opened at the eleventh chapter of Deuteronomy. Here was a verse marked—a verse made familiar to Rawley in his hours of exhaustive study. Only a part of the verse was marked, however, by a penciled line drawn faintly beneath certain words.

With a sudden excitement Rawley seized a fresh sheet of paper and wrote down the marked passage, "The land whither ye go to possess it is a land of hills and valleys."

Painstakingly then he began at the beginning of the reference list and worked his way once more through book, chapter and verse. But this time he used his grandfather's Bible and copied only such parts of the verse as were underscored. Now he was on the right track, and as he wrote his excitement grew apace. From a hopeless jumble, the verses conveyed to him this message:

... Gold is mine ... more than heart could wish. My son, if thou wilt receive my words and hide my commandments with thee ... I will give thee riches, and wealth ... such as none of the kings have had that have been before thee. Be wise now, therefore, be instructed. Of the gold ... there is no number. The land whither ye go to possess it is a land of hills and valleys. Do this now, my son. Go through ... the city which is by the river in the wilderness ... yet making many rich. In the midst thereof ... a ferryboat ... which is by the brink of the river. Take victuals with you for the journey ... turn you northward into the wilderness ... to a great and high mountain ... cedar trees in abundance ... scattered over the face of ... the high mountain. In the cliffs ... there is a path which no fowl knoweth, and which the vulture's eye hath not seen. Come to the top of the mount ... pass over unto the other side ... westward ... on the hillside ... a very great heap of stones ... joined ... to ... a dry tree. Go into the clefts of the rocks ... into the tops of the jagged rocks ... to the sides of the pit ... take heed now ... that is ... exceeding deep. It is hid from the eyes of all living ... creep into ... the midst thereof ... eastward ... two hundred, fourscore and eight ... feet ... ye shall find ... a pure river of water ... proceed no further ... there is gold ... heavier than the sand ... pure gold ... upon the sand. And all the gold ... thou shalt take up ... then shalt thou prosper if thou takest heed ... I know thy poverty, but thou art rich ... take heed now ... On the hillside ... which is upon the bank of the river ... in the wilderness ... there shall the vultures also be gathered ... ye shall find ... him that ... is mine enemy ... his mouth is full of cursing ... under his tongue is mischief and vanity ... be watchful ... the heart is desperately wicked ... He that keepeth his mouth keepeth his life ... I put my trust in thee. Now, my son, the Lord be with thee and prosper thou.

His first impulse was to find Johnny Buffalo. He folded the paper, slipped it safely into a pocket and reached for his hat. He had neglected to ask the Indian just where he meant to make his camp, but he felt sure that he could find him. Indeed, when he stopped in the path halfway to the front gate and looked toward the west wing, he could just discern a figure standing on the porch. So he crossed the grass plot and in a moment stood before Johnny Buffalo.

Again his mood impelled him to the manner that most appealed to the old Indian, nephew of a chief of his tribe. He waited for a space before he spoke. And when he did speak it was in the restrained tone which had won the Indian's confidence the evening before.

"I have read," he stated quietly, "and I know what it is that Grandfather meant. If we can go inside I'll read it to you."

"The door is locked." Johnny Buffalo pointed one finger over his shoulder. "It is a new lock put there by your mother. She does not want me to go in."

Rawley pressed his lips tightly together before he dared trust himself to speak. He looked at the barred door, thought of the room he had seen, its furnishings enriched by a hundred little mementoes of the past that belonged to his soldier grandfather. He had a swift, panicky fear that his mother would call in a second-hand furniture dealer and take what price he offered for the stuff. That, he promised himself, he would prevent at all costs.

"Come into my room, then," he invited. "I want to read you what I discovered."

"No. The house is your mother's. We will go to my camp."

So it was by the light of a camp fire, with the Mississippi flowing majestically past them under the stars, that Rawley first read as a complete document the Scriptural fragments that contained his grandfather's message. Away in the northeast the lights of St. Louis set the sky aglow. Little lapping waves crept like licking lips against the bank with a whispery sound that mingled pleasantly with the subdued crackling of the fire. Across the leaping flames, Johnny Buffalo sat with his brown, corded hands upon his knees, his black braids drawn neatly forward across his chest. His lean face with its high nose and cheek bones flared into light or grew shadowed as the flames reached toward him or drew away. His lips were pressed firmly together, as if he had learned well the lesson of setting their seal against his thoughts.

"There is one point I thought you might be able to tell me," Rawley said, looking across the fire when he had finished reading. "This 'City which is by the river in the wilderness'—and 'In the midst thereof a ferryboat which is by the brink of the river.' Do you know what place is meant by that? Is it El Dorado, Nevada? Because Grandfather's diary tells of going up the river to El Dorado. And I remember, now, there was some kind of Bible reference written over the name. I don't remember what it was, though. I didn't look it up. We'll have to make sure about that, for the directions start from that point. It says we're to go through the city which is by the river, and turn northward—and so on."

The Indian reached out a hand, lifted a stick of wood and laid it across the fire. His eyes turned toward the river.

"Many times, when the air was warm and the stars sat in their places to watch the night, my sergeant came here with me, and I gathered wood to make a fire. Many hours he would sit here in his chair beside the river. Sometimes he would talk. His words were of the past when he was the strongest of all men. Sometimes his words were of El Dorado. It is a city by the river, and a ferryboat is in the midst thereof. It has made many rich with the gold they dig from the mountains. I think that is the city you must go through."

"There isn't any city now," Rawley told him. "It's been abandoned for years. I don't think there's a town there, any more."

"There is the place by the river," Johnny Buffalo observed calmly. "There is the great and high mountain. There is 'the path that no man knoweth.'"

"Yes, you bet. And we're going to find it, Johnny Buffalo. I've got a chance to go out that way this month, to examine a mine. I didn't think I'd take the job. I wanted to go to Mexico. But now, of course, it will be Nevada, and I'll want you to go with me. Do you know that country?"

A strange expression lightened the Indian's face for an instant.

"When I killed my first meat," he said, "I could walk from the kill to the city by the river. My father's tent was no more distant than it is from here to the great city yonder. Not so far, I think. The way was rough with many hills."

Impulsively Rawley leaned and stretched out his arm toward the Indian.

"Let's shake on it. We will go together, and you will be my partner. Whatever we find is the gift of my grandfather, and half of it is yours when we find it. I feel he'd want it that way. Is it a go, Johnny Buffalo?"

Something very much like a smile stirred the old man's lips. He took Rawley's hand and gave it a solemn shake, once up, once down, as is the way of the Indian.

"It is go. You are like my sergeant when he held me in his arms and gave me water from his canteen. You are my son. Where you go I will go with you."

CHAPTER 5

A CITY FORSAKEN

The storekeeper at Nelson stood on his little slant-roofed porch and mopped his beaded forehead with a blue calico handkerchief. The desert wrinkles around his eyes drew together and deepened as he squinted across the acarpous gulch where a few rough-board shacks stood forlorn with uncurtained windows, to the heat-ridden hillside beyond.

"It's going to be awful hot down there by the river," he observed deprecatingly. "You'll find the water pretty muddy—but maybe you know that. Strangers don't always; it's best to make sure, so if you haven't a bucket or something to settle the water in, I'd advise you to take one along. I've an extra one I could lend you, if you need it."

"We have a bucket, thanks." Rawley stepped into the dust-covered car loaded with camp outfit. "El Dorado is right at the mouth of the canyon, isn't it?"

The storekeeper gave him an odd look. "This is El Dorado," he answered drily. "This whole canyon is the El Dorado. There used to be a town at the mouth of the canyon, but that's gone years ago. Better take the left-hand road when you get down here a quarter of a mile or so. That will take you past the Techatticup Mine. Below there, turn to the right where two shacks stand close together in the fork of the road. The other trail's washed, and I don't know as you could get down that way. Car in good shape for the pull back? She's pretty steep, coming this way."

"She's pulled everything we've struck, so far," Rawley replied cheerfully. "Other cars make it, don't they?"

"Some do—and some holler for help. It's a long, hard drag up the wash. And if you tackle it in the hot part of the day you'll need plenty of water. And," the storekeeper added with a whimsical half-smile, "the hot part of the day is any time between sunrise and dark. It does get *awful* hot down in there! I don't mean to knock my own district," he added, "but I don't like to see any one start down the canyon without knowing about what to expect. Then, if they want to go, that's their business."

"That's the way to look at it," Rawley agreed. "I expect you've been here a good while, haven't you?"

The storekeeper wiped a fresh collection of beads from his forehead. He looked up and down the canyon rather wistfully.

"About as many years as you are old," he said quietly. "I came in here twenty-five years ago."

Rawley laughed. "I was about a year old when you landed. Seems a long while back, to me." He stepped on the starter, waved his hand to the storekeeper and went grinding away down the steep trail through the loose sand. Johnny Buffalo, sitting beside him, lifted a hand and laid it on his arm.

"Stop! He calls," he said.

Rawley stopped the car, his head tilted outward, looking back. The storekeeper was coming down the trail toward them.

"I forgot to tell you there's a bad Indian loose in the hills somewhere along the river," he panted when he came up. "He's waylaid a couple of prospectors that we know of. A blood feud against the whites, the Indians tell me. You may not run across him at all, but it will be just as well to keep an eye out."

"What's his name?" Johnny Buffalo turned his head and stared hard at the other.

"His name's Queo. He's middle-aged—somewhere in the late forties, I should say. Medium-sized and kind of stocky built. He'll kill to get grub or tobacco. Seeing there's two of you he might not try anything, but I'd be careful, if I were in your place. There's a price on his head, so if he tries any tricks—" He waved his hand and grinned expressively as he turned back to the store.

"He is older than that man thinks," said Johnny Buffalo after a silence. "Queo has almost as many years as I have. When we were children we fought. He is bad. For him to kill is pleasure, but he is a coward."

"If there is a price on his head he has probably left the country," Rawley remarked indifferently. "Old-timers are fine people, most of them. But they do like to tell it wild to tenderfeet. I suppose that's human nature."

Johnny Buffalo did not argue the point. He seemed content to gaze at the hills in the effort to locate old landmarks. And as for Rawley himself, his mind was wholly absorbed by his mission into the country, which he had dreamed of for more than a month. There had been some delay in getting started. First, he could not well curtail the length of his visit with his mother, in spite of the fact that they seemed to have little in common. Then he thought it wise to make the trip to Kingman and report upon a property there which was about to be sold for a good-sized fortune. The job netted him several hundred dollars, which he was likely to need. Wherefore he had of necessity had plenty of time to dream over his own fortune which might be lying in the hills—"In the cleft of the jagged rocks"—waiting for him to find it.

Just at first he had been somewhat skeptical. Fifty years is a long time for gold to remain hidden in the hills of a mining country so rich as Nevada, without some prospector discovering it. But Johnny Buffalo believed. Whether his belief was based solely upon his faith in his sergeant, Rawley could not determine. But Johnny Buffalo had a very plausible argument in favor of the gold remaining where Grandfather King had left it in the underground stream.

The fact that Rawley was exhorted to "take victuals for the journey" meant a distance of a good many miles, perhaps, which they must travel from El Dorado. Then, they were to go to the top of a very high mountain and pass over on the other side. Johnny Buffalo argued that the start was to be made from El Dorado merely because the mountain would be most visible from that point. It would be rough country, he contended. The code mentioned cliffs and great heaps of stones and clefts in jagged rocks, with a deep pit, "Hid from the eyes of all living," for the final goal. He thought it more than likely that Grandfather King's gold mine was still undiscovered. And toward the last, Rawley had been much more inclined to believe him. He had read diligently all the mining information he could get concerning this particular district, as far back as the records went. Nowhere was any mention made of such a rich placer discovery on—or in—a mountain.

He was thinking all this as he drove the devious twistings and turnings of the canyon road. Another mine or two they passed; then, nosing carefully down a hill steeper than the others, they turned sharply to the left and were in the final discomfort of the "wash." A veritable sweat box it was on this particular hot afternoon in July. The baked, barren hills rose close on either side. Like a deep, gravelly river bed long since gone dry, the wash sloped steeply down toward the Colorado. Rawley could readily understand now the solicitude of the storekeeper. The return was quite likely to be a time of tribulation.

He had expected to come upon a camp of some sort. But the canyon opened bleakly to the river, the hot sand of its floor sloping steeply to meet the lapping waves of the turgid stream. At the water's edge, on the first high ground of the bank, were ruins of an old stamp mill, which might have been built ten years ago or a hundred, so far as looks went.

He left the car and climbed upon the cement floor of the old mill. What at first had seemed to be a greater extension of the plant he now discovered was a walled roadway winding up to the crest of the hill. He swung about and gazed to the northward, as the Bible code had commanded that he should travel. A mile or so up the river were the walls of a deep canyon— Black Canyon, according to his map. Farther away, set back from the river a mile, perhaps two miles, a sharp-pointed hill shouldered up above its fellows. This seemed to be the highest mountain, so far as he could see, in that direction. If that were the "great and high mountain" described in the code, their journey would not be so long as Johnny Buffalo anticipated.

The nearer view was desolation simmering in the heat. A hundred yards away, on the opposite bank of the wash, the forlorn ruins of a cabin or two gave melancholy evidence that here men had once worked and laughed and loved—perchance. He looked at the furnace yawning beside him, and at the muddy water swirling in drunken haste just below. It might have been just here that his grandfather had landed from the steamboat *Gila* and had watched the lovely young half-breed girl in the crowd come to welcome the boat and passengers.

He started when Johnny Buffalo spoke at his elbow. How the Indian had reached that spot unheard and unseen Rawley did not know. Johnny Buffalo was pointing to the north.

"I think that high mountain is where we must go," he said. "It is one day's travel. We can go today when the sun is behind the mountains, and we can walk until the stars are here. Very early in the morning we can walk again, and before it is too hot we can reach the trees where it will be cool."

"We have a lot of grub and things in the car," Rawley objected. "It seems to me that it wouldn't be a bad plan to carry the stuff up here and cache it somewhere in this old mill. Then if your friend Queo should show up, there won't be so much for him to steal. And if we want to make a camp on the mountain, we can come down here and carry the stuff up as we need it. There's a hundred dollars' worth of outfit in that car, Johnny," he added frugally. "I'm all for keeping it for ourselves."

Johnny Buffalo looked at the mountain, and he looked down at the car—and then grunted a reluctant acquiescence. Rawley laughed at him.

"That's all right—the mountain won't run away over night," he bantered, slapping his hand down on Johnny Buffalo's shoulder with an affectionate familiarity bred in the past month. "I've been juggling that car over the desert trails since sunrise, and I wouldn't object to taking it easy for a few hours."

Johnny Buffalo said no more but began helping to unload the car. It was he who chose the trail by which they carried the loads to the upper level, cement-floored, where no tracks would show. He chose a hiding place beneath the wreckage of some machinery that had fallen against the bank in such a way that an open space was left beneath, large enough to hold their outfit.

A huge rattlesnake protested stridently against being disturbed. Rawley drew his automatic, meaning to shoot it; but Johnny Buffalo stopped him with a warning gesture, and himself killed the snake with a rock. While it was still writhing with a smashed head, he picked it up by the tail, took a long step or two and heaved it into the river, grinning his satisfaction over a deed well done.

Rawley, standing back watching him, had a swift vision of the old Indian paddling solemnly about the yard near the west wing. There he was an incongruous figure amongst the syringas and the roses. Here, although he had discarded the showy fringed buckskin for the orthodox brown khaki clothes of the desert, he somehow fitted into his surroundings and became a part of the wilderness itself. Johnny Buffalo was assuredly coming into his own.

CHAPTER 6

TRAILS MEET

By sunrise they were ready for the trail, light packs and filled canteens slung upon their shoulders. The car was backed against the bluff that would shade it from the scorching sunlight from early afternoon to sundown. Beside it were the embers of a mesquite-wood fire where they had boiled coffee and fried bacon in the cool of dawn. As a safeguard against the loss of his car, Rawley had disconnected the breaker points from the distributor and carried them, carefully wrapped, in his pocket. There would be no moving of the car under its own power until the points were replaced. And Johnny Buffalo had advised leaving a few things in the car, to ward off suspicion that their outfit had been cached. Furthermore, he had cunningly obliterated their tracks through the deep, fine sand to the ruins of the stamp mill. Even the keen, predatory eyes of an outlaw Indian could scarcely distinguish any trace of their many trips that way.

They crossed the wash, turned into the remnant of an old road leading up the bank to the level above, and followed a trail up the river. Once Johnny Buffalo stopped and pointed down the bank.

"The ferryboat went there," he explained. "Much land has been eaten by the river since last I saw this place. Many houses stood here. They are gone. All is gone. My people are gone, like the town. Of Queo only have I heard, and him the white men hunt as they hunt the wolf."

Rawley nodded, having no words for what he felt. There was something inexpressibly melancholy in this desolation where his grandfather had found riotous life. Of the fortunes gathered here, the fortunes lost—of the hopes fulfilled and the hopes crushed slowly in long, monotonous days of toil and disappointment—what man could tell? Only the river, rushing heedlessly past as it had hurried, all those years ago, to meet the lumbering little river boats struggling against its current with their burden of human emotions, only the river might have told how the town was born—and how it had died. Or the grim hills standing there as they had stood since the land was in the making, looking down with saturnine calm upon the puny endeavors of men whose lives would soon enough cease upon earth and be forgotten. Rawley's boot toe struck against something in the loose gravel—

a child's shoe with the toe worn to a gaping mouth, the heel worn down to the last on the outer edge: dry as a bleached bone, warped by many a storm, blackened, doleful. Even a young man setting out in quest of his fortune, with a picturesque secret code in his pocket, may be forgiven for sending a thought after the child who had scuffed that coarse little shoe down here in El Dorado.

But presently Johnny Buffalo, leading the way briskly, his sharp old eyes taking in everything within their range as if he were eagerly verifying his memories of the place, turned from the trail along the river and entered the hills. His moccasined feet clung tenaciously to the steep places where Rawley's high-laced mining boots slipped. The sun rays struck them fiercely and the "little stinging gnats" which Grandfather King had mentioned in his diary were there to pester them, poising vibrantly just before the eyes as if they waited only the opportunity to dart between the lids.

The thought that perhaps his grandfather had come that way, fifty years ago, filled the toil of climbing up the long gully with a peculiar interest. Fifty years ago these hills must have looked much the same. Fifty years ago, the prospect holes they passed occasionally may have been fresh-turned earth and rocks. Men searching for rich silver and gold might have been seen plodding along the hillsides; but the hills themselves could not have changed much. His grandfather had looked upon all this, and had divided his thoughts, perhaps, between the gold and his latest infatuation, the half-breed girl, Anita. And suddenly Rawley put a vague speculation into words:

"Hey, Johnny! Here's a good place to make a smoke, in the shade." He waited until the Indian had retraced the dozen steps between them. "Johnny, there was a beautiful half-breed girl here, when Grandfather made his last trip up the river. She was half Spanish. My grandfather mentioned her once or twice in his diary. Do you remember her?"

"There were many beautiful girls in my tribe," Johnny Buffalo retorted drily. "What name did he call her?"

"Anita. It's a pretty name, and it proves the Spanish, I should say."

The old man stared at the opposite slope. His mouth grew thin-lipped and stern.

"My uncle, the chief, was betrayed in his old age. His youngest squaw loved a Spanish man with noble look. I have the tale from my older brothers, who told me. The child she bore was the child of the Spanish gentleman. My uncle's youngest squaw—died." Johnny Buffalo paused significantly. "The child was given to my mother to keep. Her name was Anita. She was very beautiful. I remember. Many visits Anita made with friends near this place. I think she is the same. It was not good for my sergeant to look upon her with love. I have heard my brothers whisper that Anita looked with soft eyes upon the white soldiers."

Rawley's young sympathies suffered a definite revulsion. If his grand-father's *dulce corazon* were a coquette, her fruitless waiting for his return was not so beautifully tragic after all. There were other white soldiers stationed along the river, Rawley remembered, with a curl of the lip. His romantic imagination had not balked at the savage blood in her veins, since she was a beauty of fifty years ago. But he was a sturdy-souled youth with very old-fashioned notions concerning virtue. He finished his smoke and went on, feeling cheated by the cold facts he had almost forced from Johnny Buffalo.

They reached the head of that gulch, climbed a steep, high ridge where they must use hands as well as feet in the climbing, and dug heels into the earth in a descent even steeper. Rawley told himself once that he would just as soon start out to follow a crow through this country as to follow Johnny Buffalo. One word had evidently been omitted from the Indian's English education by Grandfather King—the word "detour." Rawley thought of the straight-forward march of locusts he had once read about and wondered if Johnny Buffalo had taken lessons from them in his youth.

However, he consoled himself with the thought that a straight line to the mountain would undoubtedly shorten the distance. If the Indian could climb sneer walls of rock like a lizard, Rawley would attempt to follow. And they would ultimately arrive at their destination, though the glimpse he had obtained of the mountain from the ridge they had just crossed failed to confirm Johnny Buffalo's assertion that it was one day's travel. They had been walking three hours by Rawley's watch, and the mountain looked even farther away than from El Dorado. But Johnny Buffalo was so evidently enjoying every minute of the hike through his native hills that Rawley could not bear to spoil his pleasure by even hinting that he was blazing a mighty rough trail.

They were working up another tortuous ravine where not even Johnny Buffalo could always keep a straight line by the sun. In places the walls overhung the gulch in shelving, weather-worn cliffs of soft limestone. Bowlders washed down from the heights made slow going, because they were half the time climbing over or around some huge obstruction; and because of the rattlesnakes they must look well where a hand or a foot was laid. Johnny Buffalo was still in the lead; and Rawley, for all his youth and splendid stamina was not finding the Indian too slow a pacemaker. Indeed, he was perfectly satisfied when the dozen feet between them did not lengthen to fifteen or twenty.

The mounting sun made the heat in that gully a terrific thing to endure. But the Indian did not lift the canteen to his mouth; nor did Rawley. Both had learned the foolishness of drinking too freely at the beginning of a journey. So, when Johnny Buffalo stopped suddenly in the act of passing around a jutting ledge, Rawley halted in his tracks and waited to see what was the reason.

The Indian glanced back at him and crooked a forefinger. Rawley set one foot carefully between two rocks, planted the other as circumspectly, and so, without a sound, stole up to Johnny Buffalo's side. Johnny waited until their shoulders touched then leaned forward and pointed.

Up on the ridge a couple of hundred yards before them, a man moved crouching behind a bush, came into the open, bent lower and peered downward. His actions were stealthy; his whole manner inexpressibly furtive. His back was toward them, and the ridge itself hid the thing he was stalking.

"He's after a deer, maybe. Or a mountain sheep," Rawley whispered, when the man laid a rifle across a rock and settled lower on his haunches.

"Still, it is well that we see what he sees," Johnny Buffalo whispered back. "We will stalk him as he stalks his kill."

The Indian squirmed his shoulder out of the strap sling that held his rifle in its case behind him. With seeming deliberation, yet with speed he uncased the weapon, worked the lever gently to make sure the gun was chamber loaded, and motioned Rawley to follow him.

In the hills the old man had somehow slipped into the leadership, and now Rawley obeyed him without a word. They stole up the side of the gulch where the man on the ridge could not discover them without turning completely around; which would destroy his position beside the rock and risk the loss of a shot at his game. He seemed wholly absorbed in watching something on the farther side of the ridge, and it did not seem likely that he would hear them.

A little farther up, a ledge cutting across the head of the gulch hid him completely from the two. An impulse seized Rawley to cross the gulch there and to climb the ridge farther on, nearer the spot which the man had seemed to be watching. He caught the attention of Johnny Buffalo, whispered to him his desire, and received a nod of understanding and consent. Johnny would keep straight on, and so come up behind the fellow.

Unaccountably, Rawley wanted to hurry. He wanted to see the man's quarry before a shot was fired. So, when a wrinkle in the ridge made easy climbing and afforded concealment, he went up a tiny gully, digging in his toes and trying to keep in the soft ground so that sliding rocks could not betray him.

Unexpectedly the deep wrinkle brought him up to a notch in the ridge, beyond which another gully led steeply downward. Immediately beneath him a narrow trail wound sinuously, climbing just beyond around the point of another hill. He could not see the man up on the ridge, but he could not doubt that the rifle was aimed at some point along this trail. He was standing on a rock, reconnoitering and expecting every moment to hear a shot, when the unmistakable sound of voices came up to him from somewhere below. He listened, his glance going from the ridge to the bit of trail that showed farther away on the point of the opposite hill. The thought flashed through his mind that the man with the rifle could easily have seen persons coming around that point; that he must be lying in wait. Whoever it was coming, they must pass along the trail directly beneath the watcher on the ridge. It would be an easy rifle shot; a matter of no more than a hundred yards downhill.

He stepped down off the rock and started running down the steep gully to the trail. He was, he judged, fully a hundred yards up the trail from where the man was watching above. He did not know who was coming; it did not matter. It was an ambush, and he meant to spoil it. So he came hurtling down the steep declivity, the lower third of which was steeper than he suspected. Had he made an appointment with the travelers to meet them at that spot, he could not possibly have kept it more punctually. For he slid down a ten-foot bank of loose earth and arrived sitting upright in the trail immediately under the nose of a bald-faced burro with a distended pack half covering it from sight.

There was no time for ceremony. Rawley flung up his arms and shooed the astonished animal back against another burro, so precipitately that he crowded it completely off the trail and down the steep bank. Rawley heard the sullen thud of the landing as he scrambled to his knees, glancing apprehensively over his shoulder as he did so. There had been no shot fired, but he could not be certain that the small flurry in the trail had been unobserved.

"Get back, around the turn!" he commanded guardedly and drove before him the two women who had been walking behind the burros.

The first, a fat old squaw with gray bangs hanging straight down to her eyebrows, scuttled for cover, the lead burro crowding past her and neatly overturning her in the trail. But a slim girl in khaki breeches and high-laced boots stood her ground, eyeing him with a slight frown from under a light gray Stetson hat.

"Get back, I say! A man on the ridge is watching this trail with a rifle across a rock. It may be Queo—get back!" He did not stop with words. He took the girl by the arm and bustled her forcibly around the sharp kink in the trail that would, he hoped, effectually hide them from the ridge.

"Are you quite insane?" The girl twitched her arm out of his grasp. "Or is this a joke you are perpetrating on the natives? I must say I fail to see the humor of it."

"Climb that gully to the top and sneak along the ridge a couple of hundred yards, and you will see the point of the joke," Rawley retorted with an access of dignity, perhaps to cover the extreme informality of his arrival.

"And why should any one—even Queo—want to shoot us?" True to her sex, the girl was refusing to abdicate her first position in the matter.

"How should I know? He may not be watching for you, particularly. From the ridge he probably saw your pack train around the turn above here, and he may have thought you were prospectors. I don't know; I'm only guessing. What I do know is what I saw: a man with a rifle laid across a rock, up there, watching this trail. It may not be you he's after; but I wouldn't deliberately walk into range just to find out."

"What would you do, then? Stay here forever?"

"Until my partner and I eliminate the risk, you'd better stay here." Rawley's tone was masterful. "I only came down to warn whoever was coming—walking into an ambush."

The girl eyed him speculatively, with an exasperating little smile. "It all sounds very thrilling; very tenderfooty indeed. And in the meantime, there's poor old Deacon down there on his back in the ditch. Do you always—er—arrive like that?"

Rawley turned his back on her indignantly and discovered the old squaw sitting solidly where the lead burro had placed her. She was very fat, and she filled that portion of the trail which she occupied. The red bandana was pushed back on her head, and her gray curtain of bangs was parted rakishly on one side. She was staring at Rawley fixedly, a look of terror in her eyes.

He went to her, meaning to help her up. Now that he recalled that first panicky moment, he remembered that the burro had deposited her with some force in her present position. She might be hurt.

But the old squaw put up her hands before her, palms out to ward him off. She cried out, a shrill expostulation in her own tongue which caused the girl to swing round quickly and hurry toward her.

"No, no! He isn't a ghost! Whatever made you think of such a thing? He doesn't mean to harm you—no, he is *not* a spirit. He merely fell down hill, and he wants to help you up. Are you hurt—Grandmother?" Her clear, gray-brown eyes went quickly, defiantly to Rawley's face.

That young man could not repress a startled look, which traveled from the slim girl, indubitably white, to the squaw whimpering in the trail. She must be trying her own hand at a joke, he thought, just to break even with his fancied presumption in halting their leisurely progress down the trail.

From up on the ridge a rifle cracked. The three turned heads toward the thin, sinister report. They waited motionless for a moment. Then the girl spoke.

"That wasn't fired in our direction," she said, and immediately there came the sound of another shot. "And that's not the same gun," she added.

"That sounds like an old-fashioned gun shooting black powder. Didn't you hear the *pow-w* of it?"

"That would be Johnny Buffalo—my Indian partner," said Rawley. "You folks stay here. I'm going back up there and see what's doing."

"Is that necessary?" The girl looked at him quickly. "I think you ought to help turn Deacon right side up before you go." She leaned sidewise and peered down over the bank. "He's in an awful mess. His pack is wedged between two bowlders, and his legs are sticking straight up in the air."

Rawley sent a hasty glance down the bank. "He's all right—he's flopping his ears," he observed reassuringly. "I'll be back just as soon as I see how Johnny Buffalo is making out. That fellow may have got him. You stay back here out of sight. Promise me." He looked at her earnestly, as if by the force of his will he would compel obedience.

Her eyes evaded the meeting. "Pickles will have to be rounded up," she said. "He's probably halfway to Nelson by this time. And there's Grandmother to think of."

"Well, you think of those things until I get back," he said, with a swift smile. "I can't leave my partner to shoot it out alone."

CHAPTER 7

NEVADA

He ran to the point of rocks, gathered himself together and cleared the trail and the open space beyond in one leap. How he got up the steep bank he never remembered afterward. He only knew that he heard the sharp crack of the first rifle again as he was sprinting up the little gully that had concealed his descent. He gained the top, stopped to get his bearings more accurately and made his way toward the spot where he had seen the man with the rifle.

It occurred to him that he had best approach the spot from the shelter of the ledge where he had separated from Johnny Buffalo. At that point he could pick up the Indian's tracks and follow them, so saving time in the long run.

Johnny Buffalo's moccasins left little trace in the gravelly soil. But here and there they left a mark, and Rawley got the direction and hurried on. Fifty yards farther up the ridge he glimpsed something yellowish-brown against a small juniper. A few feet farther, he saw that it was Johnny Buffalo, lying on his face, one arm thrown outward with the hand still grasping the stock of his rifle.

He snatched up the rifle, crouched beside the Indian and searched the neighborhood with his eyes, trying to get a sight of the killer. In a moment he spied him, away down the deep ravine up which he and Johnny Buffalo had toiled not half an hour before. The man was running. Rawley raised the rifle to his shoulder, took careful aim and fired, but he had small hope of hitting his target at that distance.

At the sound of the shot so close above him, Johnny Buffalo stirred uneasily, as if disturbed in his sleep. The man in the distance ducked out of sight amongst the bowlders; and that was the last Rawley saw of him at that time.

"I must apologize for not taking you more seriously when you warned me," said the girl, just behind him. "Is this—?"

"My partner, Johnny Buffalo. He isn't dead—he moved, just now—but I'm afraid he's badly hurt." Rawley lifted anxious blue eyes to her face.

"We can carry him down to the trail. Then, if Deacon is all right when we get him up, we can put your partner on him and pack him home. It's only a mile or so."

"It might be better to take him to Nelson," Rawley amended the suggestion. "I could get a car there and take him on to Las Vegas, probably. Or some mine will have a doctor."

"It's farther—and the heat, with the long ride, would probably finish him," the girl pointed out bluntly. "On the other hand, a mile on the burro will get him home, where it's cool and we can see how badly he's hurt. And then, if he needs hospital care, Uncle Peter can take him down to Needles in the launch, this evening when it's cool. I really don't mean to be disagreeable and argumentative, but it seems to me that will be much the more comfortable plan for him. And I can't help feeling responsible, in a way. I suppose he was trying to protect us, when he was shot."

Rawley looked up from an amateurish examination of the old man. The bullet wound was in the shoulder, and he was hoping that it was high enough so that the lung was not injured. His flask of brandy, placed at Johnny's lips, brought a gulp and a gasp. The black eyes opened, looked from Rawley to the girl and closed again.

"There! I believe he's going to be all right," the girl declared optimistically. "I'll take his feet, and you carry his shoulders. When we get him down to the trail, I'll have Grandmother look after him until we get the burros straightened out. Queo—or whoever it was—did you see him?"

Rawley waved a hand toward the rocky ravine. "You heard me shoot," he reminded her. "Missed him—with that heirloom Johnny carries. He was running like a jackrabbit when I saw him last. Well, I think you're right—but I hate to trouble you folks. Though I'd trouble the president himself, for Johnny Buffalo's sake."

"It's a strange name," she remarked irrelevantly, stooping and making ready to lift his knees. "He must be a Northern Indian."

"Born in this district," Rawley told her. "Grandfather found him in the desert when he was a kid. I suppose he gave him the name—regardless."

Until they reached the trail there was no further talk, their breath being needed for something more important. They laid the injured man down in the shade of a greasewood, and the girl immediately left to bring the old squaw. She was no sooner gone than Johnny Buffalo opened his eyes.

"It was Queo," he said, huskily whispering. "I thought he was shooting at you. I tried to kill him. But the damn gun is old—old. It struck me hard. I did not shoot straight. I did not kill him. Queo looked, he saw me and he shot as he ran away. The gun has killed many—but I am old—"

"You're all right," Rawley interrupted. "Quit blaming yourself. You saved two women by shooting when you did. Queo was afraid to stay and shoot again when he knew there was a gun at his back. He has gone down the ravine where we came up."

"Who was the white girl?" Even Johnny Buffalo betrayed a very masculine interest, Rawley observed, grinning inwardly. But he only said:

"I don't know. She was on the trail, with an old squaw and two burros. It was they that Queo was laying for, evidently. Don't try to talk any more, till I get you where we can look after you properly. Where's your pack? I didn't see it, up there."

"It is hidden in the juniper. I did not want to fight with a load on my back."

"All right. Don't talk any more. We'll fix you up, all fine as silk."

The girl was returning, and after her waddled the squaw, reluctant, looking ready to retreat at the first suspicious move. Rawley stood aside while the girl gave her brief directions in Indian—so that Johnny Buffalo could understand, Rawley shrewdly suspected, and thanked her with his eyes. The squaw sidled past Rawley and sat down on the bank, still staring at him fixedly. His abrupt appearance and the consequent stampede of the burros had evidently impressed her unfavorably. The look she bestowed upon Johnny Buffalo was more casual. He was an Indian and therefore understandable, it seemed.

The narrow canyon lay sun-baked and peaceful to the hard blue of the sky. With the lightness which came of removing the pack from his shoulders, Rawley walked up the trail and around the turn to where the burro called Deacon still lay patiently on his back in the narrow watercourse below the trail. He slid down the bank and inspected the lashings of the pack.

"We use what is called the squaw hitch," the girl informed him from the trail just above his head. "If you cut that forward rope I think you can loosen the whole thing. The knot is on top of the pack, and of course Deacon's lying on it." A moment later she added, "I'll go after Pickles, unless I can be of some use to you."

Privately, Rawley thought that she was useful as a relief to the eyes, if nothing else. But he told her that he could get along all right, and let her go. The girl piqued his interest; she was undoubtedly beautiful, with her slim, erect figure, her clear, hazel eyes with straight eyebrows, heavy lashes, and her lips that were firm for all their soft curves. But Johnny Buffalo's life might be hanging on Rawley's haste. However beautiful, however much she might attract his interest, no girl could tempt him from the chief issue.

By the time she returned with Pickles, Rawley had retrieved Deacon and was gone down the trail with him. She came up in time to help him lift Johnny Buffalo on the burro and tie him there with the pack rope. She was efficient as a man, and almost as strong, Rawley observed. And although she treated the squaw with careful deference, she was plainly the head of their little expedition—and the shoulders and the brains.

Only once did the squaw speak on the way to the river. The girl was walking alongside Deacon, steadying Johnny Buffalo on that side while Rawley held the other. They were talking easily now, of impersonal things; and when, on a short climb, the burro stepped sharply to one side and Johnny Buffalo lurched toward the girl, Rawley slipped his arm farther behind the Indian. His fingers clasped for an instant the girl's hand. The squaw, walking heavily behind, saw the brief contact.

"Nevada! You shall not be so bold," she cried in Pahute. "Take away your hand from the white man."

The girl turned her head and answered sharply in the same tongue and afterwards smiled across at Rawley, meeting his eyes with perfect frankness.

"Yes, my name is Nevada. I'll save you the trouble of asking," she said calmly. "El Dorado Nevada Macalister, if you want it all at once. Luckily, no one ever attempts to call me all of it. My parents were loyal, romantic, and had an ear for euphony."

"Were?" The small impertinence slipped out in spite of Rawley; but fortunately she did not seem to mind.

"Yes. My father was caught in a cave-in in the Quartette Mine when I was a baby. Mother died when I was six. I have a beautiful, impractical name—and not much else—to remember them by. I've lived with Grandfather and Grandmother; except, of course, what time I have been in school." She gave him another quick look behind Johnny Buffalo's back. "And your autobiography?"

"Mine is more simple and not so interesting. Name, George Rawlins King. Place of birth, a suburb of St. Louis. Occupation, mining engineer. Present avocation, prospecting during my vacation. My idea of play, you see, is to get out here in the heat and snakes and work at my trade—for myself."

"And Johnny Buffalo?"

"Oh, he just came along. Hadn't seen this country since he was a kid and wanted to get back, I suppose, on his old stamping ground. He lived with Grandfather. But Grandfather died a few weeks ago, and Johnny and I have sort of thrown in together. Now, I suppose our prospecting trip is all off—for the present, anyway."

"This country has been gone over with a microscope, almost," said Nevada. "I suppose there is mineral in these hills yet, but it must be pretty well hidden. The country used to swarm with prospectors, but they seem to have got disgusted and quit. The war in Europe, of course, has created a market—" She stopped and laughed with chagrin. "Of course a lady desert rat like me can give a mining engineer valuable information concerning markets and economic conditions in general!"

"I'm always glad to talk shop," Rawley declared tactfully.

But Nevada fell silent and would not talk at all during the remainder of the journey.

CHAPTER 8

"HIM THAT IS—MINE ENEMY"

Their progress was necessarily slow, and Nevada's "mile or so" seemed longer. Johnny Buffalo remained no more than half-conscious and breathed painfully. Nevada invented a makeshift sunshade for him, breaking off and trimming a drooping greasewood branch and borrowing the squaw's apron to spread over it. This Rawley held awkwardly with one hand while he steadied the swaying figure with the other, and so they came at last abruptly to the river he had left at sunrise.

The trail dipped down steeply to a small basin that overlooked the river possibly a hundred feet below. The canyon walls rose bold and black beyond—sheer crags of rock with here and there a brush-filled crevice. Around the barren rim of the basin two or three crude shacks were set within easy calling distance of one another, and three or four swarthy, unkempt children accompanied by nondescript dogs rushed forth to greet the newcomers.

The old squaw waddled forward and drove the dogs from the heels of the burro called Pickles, which lashed out and sent one cur yelping to the nearest shack. The children halted abruptly and stared at the two strangers open-mouthed, retreating slowly backward, unwilling to lose sight of them for an instant.

Rawley stole a glance at Nevada, just turning his eyes under his heavy-lashed lids. A furtive look directed at his face was intercepted, and the red suffused her cheeks. Then her head lifted proudly.

"My uncle's children are not accustomed to seeing people," she explained evenly. "Strangers seldom come here, and the children have never been away from home. Please forgive their bad manners."

"Kids are honest in their manners," Rawley replied, "and that's more than grown-ups can say. I reckon these youngsters wonder what the deuce has been taking place. I'd want an eyeful, myself, if I were in their places."

Nevada did not answer but led the way past the shacks, which did not look particularly inviting, to a rock-faced building with screened porch that faced the river, its back pushed deep into the hill behind it. Rawley gave her a grateful glance. He did not need to be told that this was the quietest, coolest place in the basin.

"We'll make him as comfortable as we can, and I'll send for Uncle Peter," she said, as they stopped before the door. She called to the oldest of the children, a boy, and spoke to him rapidly in Indian. It seemed to Rawley that she was purposely emphasizing her bizarre relationship.

A younger squaw—or so she looked to be—came from a shack, a fat, solemn-eyed baby riding her hip. Her hair was wound somehow on top of her head and held there insecurely with hairpins half falling out and cheap, glisteny side combs. A second glance convinced Rawley that she had white man's blood in her veins, but her predominant traits were Indian, he judged; except that she lacked the Indian aloofness.

"Mr. King, this is my Aunt Gladys—Mrs. Cramer," Nevada announced distinctly. "Aunt Gladys, Queo shot Mr. King's partner, who had discovered him lying in wait for Grandmother and me and was trying to protect us. Mr. King ran down to the trail to warn us, while his partner crept up behind Queo. He fired, after Queo had shot at us, but he thinks he missed altogether. At any rate Queo shot him. So Grandmother and I brought him on home. He saved our lives, and we must try to save his."

Aunt Gladys ducked her unkempt head, grinned awkwardly at Rawley, who lifted his hat to her—and thereby embarrassed her the more—and hitched the baby into a new position on her hip.

"Whadda yuh think ol' Jess'll say?" she asked, in an undertone. "My, ain't it awful, the way that Queo is acting up? Is there anything I can do? It won't take but a few minutes to start a fire and heat water."

They had eased Johnny Buffalo from the burro's back to the broad doorstep, which was shaded by the wide eaves of the porch. Now they were preparing to carry him in, feet first so that Nevada could lead the way. She turned her head and nodded approval of the suggestion. So Aunt Gladys, after lingering to watch the wounded man's removal, departed to her own shack, shooing her progeny before her.

Rawley had never had much experience with wounds, but he went to work as carefully as possible, getting the old man to bed and ready for ministrations more expert than his. In a few minutes Nevada came with a basin of water that smelled of antiseptic. Very matter-of-factly she helped him wash the wound.

"I think that is as much as we can do until Uncle Peter comes," she said when they had finished. "He's the one who always looks after hurts in the family." She left the room and did not return again.

With nothing to do but sit beside the bed, Rawley found himself dwelling rather intently upon the strangeness of the situation. From the name spoken by Nevada, he knew that he must be in the camp of the enemy. At least, Jess Cramer was the name of Grandfather's rival who figured unfortunately in that Fourth of July fight away back in '66, and there was furthermore the warning of the code, "Take heed now ... on the hillside ... which is upon the bank of the river ... in the wilderness ... ye shall find ... him that ... is mine enemy." Rawley had certainly not expected that the enemy would be Jess Cramer, but it might be so.

He was repeating to himself that other warning, "He that keepeth his mouth keepeth his life," when Nevada's voice outside brought his attention back to the immediate exigencies of the case. He had already told her his name—she had repeated it to that flat-faced, hopelessly uninteresting "Aunt Gladys." Nevada had taken particular pains, he remembered, to tell her aunt all about the mishap and to stress the service which he and Johnny Buffalo had rendered her and her grandmother. Was it because she wished to have some one beside herself who was well-disposed toward them? Partly that, he guessed, and partly because the easiest way to forestall curiosity is to give a full explanation at once. In Nevada's rapid-fire account of the shooting, Rawley fancied that he had unconsciously been given a key to the situation and to the disposition of Aunt Gladys. He grinned while he filled his pipe and waited.

Presently the deep, masculine voice he had heard outside talking with Nevada ceased, and a firm, measured tread was heard on the porch. A big man paused for a few seconds in the doorway and then came forward; a man as tall as Rawley, as broad of shoulder, as narrow hipped. He was dressed much as Rawley was dressed, except that his shirt was of cheaper, darker material and the breeches were earth-stained and old, as were his boots. He carried his head well up and looked down at Rawley calmly, appraisingly, with neither dislike nor favor in his face. He was smooth-shaven, and his jaw was square, his lips firm and somewhat bitter. Rawley rose and bowed and stood back from the bed.

"My niece has told me all about the shooting," he said, moving toward the bed. "I'm not a doctor, but I've had some experience with wounds. In this country we have to learn to take care of ourselves. Is your partner unconscious?"

"Dopey, I'd say. I can rouse him, but it seemed best to let him be as quiet as possible. He had over an hour in the heat, and the joggling on the burro didn't do him any good, I imagine." Rawley hoped Uncle Peter would not think he was staring like an idiot, but he could not rid himself of the feeling that somewhere, some time, he had seen this man before.

Uncle Peter bent and examined the wound. When he moved Johnny Buffalo a bit, the Indian opened his eyes and stared hard into his face.

"My sergeant! I did not think to—"

"Out of his head," Rawley muttered uneasily. "It's the first symptom of it he's shown."

Johnny Buffalo muttered again, pressed his lips together and closed his eyes. After that he did not speak, or give any sign that he heard, though Uncle Peter was talking all the while he dressed the wound.

"It's going to take some time," he said. "The bullet broke his shoulder blade, but if the lung is touched at all it was barely grazed. Nevada spoke of my taking him down the river to Needles, but it can't be done. The engine in the launch is useless until I can get a new connecting rod and another part or two." He stared down at Johnny Buffalo, frowning.

"Well, from all accounts the two of you saved the women's lives to-day," he said, after a minute of studying over the situation. "Queo was after the grub, probably—and he's no particular love for any of us. He undoubtedly knew who was coming down the trail—he may have watched them go up, just about daybreak. Common gratitude gives the orders, in this case. You can stay here until this man is well enough to ride, or until I can take you to Needles."

A little more of harshness and his tone would have been grudging. Rawley flushed at the implied reluctance of the offered hospitality.

"It's mighty good of you, but we don't want to impose on any one," he said stiffly. "If he can stay for a day or two, I can get out to Needles and bring up a boat of some kind. It's the only thing I can think of—but I can make it in a couple of days."

The other turned and regarded him much as Nevada had first done, with a mixture of defiance and pride. His jaw squared, the lines beside his mouth grew more bitter.

"We may be breeds—but we aren't brutes," he said harshly. "You'll stay where you are and take care of your partner. The burden of nursing him can't fall on the women." He stopped and seemed debating something within himself. "We've no reason to open our arms to outsiders," he added finally. "If folks let us alone, we let them alone—and glad to do it. Father's touchy about having strangers in camp. But all rules must be broken once, they say."

"I think you're over-sensitive," Rawley told him bluntly. "You're self-conscious over something no one else would think of twice. It's—"

"Oh, I know. You needn't say it. Sounds pretty, but it isn't worth a damn when you try to put it in practice. Well, let it drop. I'll send over some medicine to keep his fever down, and the rest is pretty much up to nature and the care you give him. It's cool here—that's a great deal."

"We'll be turning out your niece, though, I'm afraid. I can't do that." For the first time Rawley was keenly conscious of the incongruity of his surroundings. Here in a settlement of Indians (he could scarcely put it more mildly, with the dogs and the frowsy papooses and the two squaws for evidence) one little oasis of civilized furnishings spoke eloquently of the white blood warring against the red. The room was furnished cheaply, it is true, and much of the furniture was homemade; but for all its simplicity there was not one false note anywhere, not one tawdry adornment. It was like the girl herself—simple, clean-cut, dignified.

"My niece won't mind. I shall give her my own dugout, which is as comfortable as this. I can find plenty of room to stretch out. Hard work makes a soft bed." He smiled briefly. Again Rawley was struck with a sense of familiarity, of having known Uncle Peter somewhere before.

But before he could put the question the man was gone, and Johnny Buffalo was looking at him gravely. But he did not speak, and presently his eyes closed. After that, the medicine was handed in by a bashful, beady-eyed boy who showed white teeth and scudded away, kicking up hot dust with his bare feet as he ran.

After all, what did it matter? A chance meeting in some near-by town and afterwards forgetfulness. Uncle Peter evidently did not remember him, so the meeting must have been brief and unimportant.

CHAPTER 9

"A PLEASANT TRIP TO YOU!"

Rawley chanced to look out of the window. He muttered something then and strode to the screened door.

"Hey! You aren't going back up that trail, surely?" He went out hurriedly and took long steps after Nevada.

The girl turned and looked at him over her shoulder, flinging back a heavy braid of coppery auburn hair. She had Pickles by his lead rope and was plainly heading into the trail to Nelson.

"Why, yes. There's a load of grub beside the trail where Deacon upset. I'm going after it."

Rawley rushed back, seized his hat, sent an anxious glance toward the bed and then ran. He overtook Nevada just at the edge of the basin and stopped her by the simple method of stopping the burro with a strong hand.

"You go back and sit beside Johnny," he commanded. "I'll get that grub, myself. And if you've got a rifle, I'd like to borrow it."

"That's utter nonsense—your going," Nevada exclaimed. "I meant to take one of the boys—I just sent him in to wash his face, first."

Rawley laughed. "Do you think a clean face on a kid will have any effect on Queo? You'll both stay at home, please. I'm going."

"If you're determined, I can't very well stop you," she said coldly. "But I certainly am going. I always do these things. There's no possible reason—"

Rawley looked over at the nearest shack, where Aunt Gladys stood watching them, the baby still on her hip. "Mrs. Cramer, I am going up after the grub we left by the trail. Will you see that Johnny Buffalo is looked after? And will you call Miss Macalister's grandmother, or whoever has any authority over her?" His voice was stern, but the twinkle in his eyes belied the tone.

Aunt Gladys giggled and hitched the baby up from its sagging position. "There ain't nobody but Peter can do nothing with Nevada," she informed him. "Her gran'paw, maybe—but he don't pay no attention half the time. You better stay home, Nevada. Queo might shoot you."

"How perfectly idiotic! Do you suppose he would refrain from shooting Mr. King, but kill me instead?"

"Well, you can't tell what he might do," Aunt Gladys observed sagely. "He's crazy in the head."

Rawley laid his fingers on Nevada's hand, where she held Pickles by the bridle. He looked straight into her eyes, bright with anger. His own eyes pleaded with her.

"Miss Macalister, please don't be obstinate. To let you go back up that trail is unthinkable. I am going, and some one must be with my partner. I can make the trip well under two hours; there is heavy stuff in that ditch which needs a man's shoulder under it, getting it back into the trail. Please stay with Johnny Buffalo, won't you?"

Nevada hesitated, staring back into his eyes. Her hand slid reluctantly from the bridle. Her lip curled at one corner, though her cheeks flushed contradictorily.

"Masculine superiority asserts itself," she drawled. "Since I can't prevent your going, I think, after all, I shall prefer to stay at home. A pleasant trip to you, Mr. King!"

"Thanks for those kind words," Rawley cried, his voice as mocking as hers. "Come on, Pickles, old son!"

A boy of ten, with his face clean to the point of his jaws, came running from the shack with a rifle sagging his right shoulder. Rawley waited until he came up, then took the rifle, spun the boy half around and gave him a gentle push.

"Thanks, sonny. Ladies and children not allowed on this trip, however. You stay and protect the women and babies, son. Got to leave a man in camp, you know. Wounded to look after."

The boy whirled back, valor overcoming his tongue-tied bashfulness. "Aw, he wouldn't come here! Gran'paw'd kill 'im. Gran'paw purt' near did, one time. I c'n shoot, mister. I c'n hit a rabbit in the eye from here to that big rock over there."

"Yes—well—this isn't going to be a rabbit hunt. You stay here, sonny."

"Aw, you're as bad as Uncle Peter!" the boy muttered resentfully, kicking small rocks with his bare toes. "I guess you'll wish I'd come along, if Queo gets after you!"

Rawley only laughed and swung up the trail, leading the burro behind him, since he was not at all acquainted with the beast and had no desire to follow it vainly to Nelson, for lack of the proper knowledge to halt it beside the scene of Deacon's downfall.

As he went, Rawley scanned the near-by ridges and the brush along the trail. There was slight chance, according to his belief, that the outlaw Indian would venture down this far, especially since he could not be sure he had failed to kill Johnny Buffalo. On the other hand, he must have been rather desperate to lie in wait for two women coming home with supplies. Rawley wondered why he had remained up on the ridge; why he had not waited by the trail and robbed them of such things as he needed. Then he remembered Nevada's very evident ability to whip wildcats, if necessary—certainly to meet any emergency calmly—and shook his head. The old squaw, too, would probably do some clawing if the occasion demanded, and she knew just who and why she was fighting. On the whole, Rawley decided that Queo had merely borne out Johnny Buffalo's statement that he was a coward and had taken no chances. And from the boy's remark about his grandfather nearly killing Queo, he thought the outlaw had not wanted his identity discovered.

As for his own risk, Rawley did not give it a second thought. Queo had been well scared, finding two men on the job where he had expected to deal only with women. He had been headed toward the river when Rawley last saw him. It was more than probable that he would continue in that direction.

But it is never safe to guess what an Indian will do—much less an Indian outlaw who must become a beast of prey if he would live and keep his freedom. Rawley remembered Johnny Buffalo's pack and tied Pickles to a bush directly under the spot where the shooting had taken place, while he climbed the ridge to retrieve his belongings. He brought canteen and pack down to the trail and hung them on the packsaddle, feeling absolutely secure. The ridge was hot and deserted, even the birds and rabbits having taken cover from the heat.

He went on around the little bend and anchored the burro again while he carried up a sack of potatoes, bacon, flour and a package wrapped in damp canvas, which he guessed to be butter. The tribe of Cramer had what they wanted to eat, at least, he reflected. Also, the load would have made a nice grubstake for the outlaw. Two such burro loads would have supplied Queo for months, adding what game he would undoubtedly kill.

Rawley had just finished packing the burro and had looped up the tie rope to send Pickles down the home trail, when some warning (a sound, perhaps, or a flicker of movement) caused him to look quickly behind him. He glimpsed a dark, heavy face behind a leveled gun barrel, broken teeth showing in an evil grin. Rawley threw himself to one side just as the gun belched full at him. Something jerked his left arm viciously, and a numb warmth stole into that side.

He dropped forward, his right hand flinging back to his holstered automatic and drawing up convulsively with the gun in his hand.

"Thanks for packing the stuff!" chortled Queo, and the two fired simultaneously.

Both scored hits. The leering, black face sobered and slid slowly out of sight behind the rock. Rawley's head dropped so that his face lay in the blistering dust of the trail. Through his hat crown a small, singed hole showed in front, a ragged tear opposite at the back. Pickles, scored on the leg with the second shot from Queo's gun, kicked savagely with both feet and went careening down the trail toward home, his pack wabbling violently as he galloped.

It was the sight of him trotting down the trail alone that halted Nevada midway between her rock dugout and the shack where Gladys was setting steaming dishes on the table for the three men who were "washing up" at the bench under the crude porch. Nevada gave a little cry and ran to meet Pickles, and the first thing she noticed was the fresh, red furrow on his leg, from which the blood was still dripping. Turning to call, she saw Peter coming close behind her, wiping his face and neck as he walked.

"Oh, Uncle Peter—he's been shot!" she cried tremulously. "It must be Queo again."

Peter's eyes turned to the trail, visible for some distance up the side hill. There was no one in sight, and without a word he turned back to his own house, dug into the hill near Nevada's, and presently returned, passing the girl with long strides. He carried his rifle and struck into the hill trail bareheaded. Nevada looked after him, her eyes wide and dark.

An hour later, Peter returned, walking steadily down the trail with Rawley on his back. Without a word he passed the staring group at the shack and carried his burden into the room where Johnny Buffalo lay in uneasy slumber. A step sounded behind him, and he spoke without turning.

"Have Jess and Gladys bring that spring cot out of my cabin, Nevada. They'll be more contented in the same room. He got Queo—I found him behind a rock not fifty feet from this chap. Now Queo's cousin will take up the feud and get this fellow—if he pulls out of this scrape."

"Is he badly hurt?" Nevada was holding her voice steady from sheer will power.

"Arm smashed and a scalp wound. All depends on the care he gets. Well—" Peter straightened and wiped his forehead, looking thoughtfully at Rawley, half lying in a big chair, his long legs spread limply, his face white and streaked with blood, "—we owe him good care, I guess. He must have killed Queo after he'd been shot in the arm. And he's saved this outfit some trouble. I didn't tell you—but Queo was laying for a chance at us. Well— run and get that cot here."

Nevada pushed back her craning family and sent them running here and there on errands. Her grandfather and Jess, the husband of Gladys, looked at her inquiringly from the porch of the shack. Rawley might have thought it strange that they remained mere bystanders during the excitement. But Nevada did not seem to notice their indifference.

"Queo shot him twice—but he killed Queo," she told them. "Uncle Jess, you're to get his spring cot, Uncle Peter says, and fix a bed in there." Her eyes went challengingly to her grandfather. "Uncle Peter says we owe them the best care we can give," she stated clearly. "He says they have saved some lives in this family."

The tall, bearded old patriarch looked at her frowningly. He glanced toward the rock cabin, grunted something unintelligible to the girl, and went in to his interrupted dinner.

CHAPTER 10

A FAMILY TREE

It seemed as fantastic as a troubled dream. To be lying there helpless, to look across and see Johnny Buffalo staring grimly up at the ceiling, his face set stoically to hide the pain that burned beneath the white bandage, held no semblance of reality. Was it that morning only, that they had left the car and started out to walk to the "great and high mountain"? Perhaps several days had passed in oblivion. He did not know. To Rawley the shock of drifting back from unconsciousness to these surroundings had been as great as the shock of incredulous slipping down and down into blackness. He moved his head a half-inch. The pain brought his eyebrows together, but he made no sound. Johnny Buffalo must not be worried.

"All right again, are you?" Peter moved into Rawley's range of vision. "You had a close squeak. The thickness of your skull between you and death—that was all. The bullet skinned along on the outside instead of the inside."

"I'll be all right then," Rawley muttered thickly. "Don't mean to be a nuisance. Soon as this grogginess lets up—"

"You'll be less trouble where you are," Peter interrupted him bluntly. "I've done all I can for you now, so I'll go back to my work. The Injun's making out all right, too. Head clear as a bell, near as I can judge. I'll see you this evening, and if there's anything you want, either of you, just pound that toy drum beside you. That will bring one of the women."

Rawley looked up at him, though the movement of his eyeballs was excruciatingly painful. Again that sense of familiarity came to tantalize him. What was it? Peter's great, square shoulders, his eyes? He made another effort to look more closely and failed altogether. His vision blurred; things went black again. Perhaps he slept, after that. When he opened his eyes again a cool wind was blowing; the intolerable glare outside the window had softened.

He was conscious of a definite feeling of satisfaction when Nevada appeared with a tray of food such as fever patients may have; tea, toast, a bit of fruit—mostly juice. Behind her waddled her grandmother; Rawley could not yet believe in the reality of the relationship between this high-bred white girl and the old squaw. In the back of his mind he thought there must be some joke; or at least, he told himself, looking at the two closely, Nevada must be one of the tribe by adoption. He had heard of such things.

And there was her Uncle Peter, who was a white man in looks, in personality, everything. Yet Uncle Peter had flared proudly, "We may be breeds—but we aren't brutes." He could only have meant himself and Nevada. He looked at her, his eyes going again to the squaw with her gray bangs, the red kerchief, her squat shapelessness.

Her fear of him seemed to have evaporated upon reflection. Her curiosity concerning him had not, evidently. She set down the tray and stared at him with a frank fixity that reminded Rawley of the solemn regard of the sloe-eyed baby riding astride Aunt Gladys' slatternly hip.

"You feed Johnny Buffalo, Grandmother," Nevada directed. "He used to live in this country when he was a boy. You can't tell—you might be old acquaintances." She smiled, patted the old woman on a cushiony shoulder and approached Rawley, who was suddenly resigned to his helplessness.

"Grandmother rather holds herself above full-blood Indians," she whispered. "She's only half Indian, herself. I don't want her to snub your partner; he looks so lonely, somehow. What is it?"

"He's grieving over my grandfather's death," Rawley told her, his own voice dropped to an undertone that would not carry. "Until I proposed this trip he didn't want to live. He's better, out here."

"I do hope—"

A shrill ejaculation from the squaw brought Nevada's head around. "What is it, Grandmother?"

The old woman started a singsong Indian explanation, and Nevada smiled. "She says they do know each other. She remembers him when he was a boy and was lost. So that's fine. He can hear about all his old playmates and his family." She turned her back on them as if the duties of hostess sat more lightly on her shoulders, since one of the patients could visit with her grandmother.

"I'm wondering what happened, up the trail."

Nevada thoughtfully cooled the tea with the spoon and looked at him speculatively. "Uncle Peter can tell you better than I can—since I was not permitted to go along. Besides, the less talking you do now, I believe, the less danger there is of complications. Neither wound is so bad of itself, Uncle Peter says. It's having your head hurt, along with the broken bone in the arm. Unless you are very quiet for a day or two, there may be fever; and fevered blood makes slow healing. That's Uncle Peter's theory, and it must be correct. He has books and studies all the time—when he isn't working. Then, of course, there's the danger of infection from the outside; but he has been very careful in the dressings. Johnny Buffalo," she added after a minute, "is worse off than you are. His shoulder blade is badly smashed. And then he's so much older."

She was talking, he knew, to prevent him from doing so. And since his head felt like a nest of crickets, all performing at once, he was content to let her have her way. Across the room he could hear the intermittent murmur of the two Indians, the voice of the grandmother droning musically, with sliding, minor inflections as she recounted, no doubt, the history of the old man's family and friends.

He watched Nevada pour and sweeten a second cup of tea and did a swift mental calculation in genealogy. Jess Cramer, he knew, was a white man. The husband of Gladys, bearing the name of Grandfather King's enemy, must be a son of the old man and of this half-breed squaw. Very well, then, old Jess Cramer's children would be one quarter Indian—Peter, Jess and Nevada's mother (granting that Nevada was a blood relative). Nevada's father must have been white—a Scotchman, by the name, and by Nevada's clear skin and coppery hair. Well, then, Nevada was—A knife thrust of pain stabbed through his brain, and he could not think. Nevada set down the cup hastily and laid cool fingers on his temple. He lifted his right hand and held her fingers there. The throbbing agony lessened, grew fainter and fainter. After all, what did it matter—the blood in those fingers? They were cool and sweet and soothing—

He thought Nevada had lifted her hand and was gently removing the bandage from his head. But it was Uncle Peter, and Nevada was not there, and it was dark outside. In another room a clock began to strike the hour. He counted nine. It was strange; he could not remember going to sleep with her fingers pressed against the pulse beat in his temple. Yet he must have slept for hours. He closed his eyes and then opened them again, staring up with a child-like candor into the man's bent face.

"I know. You look like Grandfather," he said thickly. And when Peter's eyes met his, "It's your eyes. Grandfather had eyes exactly like yours. And there's something about the mouth—a bitterness. Gameness, too. Grandfather had his legs off at the knees, for fifty years. Called himself a hunk of meat in a wheel chair. God, it must be awful—a thing like that, when the rest of you is big and strong—but you're not crippled that way. Oh, Johnny! Are you awake?" He heard a grunt. "I've got it—what you meant at first, about seeing your sergeant. Uncle Peter looks like—"

A hand went over his mouth quite unexpectedly and effectually. He looked up into the eyes like Grandfather King's and found them very terrible.

"Fool! Never whisper it. Am I not the son of Jess Cramer? It had better be so! Better not see that I am like his enemy—and rival." He leaned close, his eyes boring into the eyes so like his own. "One word to any one that would slur my mother, and—" he pressed his lips together, his meaning told by his eyes. "She came to me today, chattering her fear. Old Jess Cramer lives with other thoughts, and his eyes are dim at close range. Never come close to him, boy. Never recall the past to him. It would mean—God knows what it would mean. My mother's life, maybe. And then his own, for I'd kill him, of course, if he touched her."

Rawley blinked, trying to make sense of the riddle. Then his good hand went out and rested on Peter's arm, that was trembling under the thin shirt sleeve.

"Uncle Peter!" His lips barely moved to form the words, and afterward they smiled. "The blood of the Kings! I'm glad—"

"Are you?" Peter bent over him fiercely. "Proud of a man who went away and left my mother—"

"He had to go," Rawley defended hastily. "He meant to come back in a month's time. But he was shot through the legs, and in hospital for months, and then sent home a cripple. After that he lost his legs altogether. How could he come back? Johnny can tell you."

Peter pulled himself together and redressed the long, angry gash on Rawley's head. Johnny Buffalo, having slowly squirmed his body to a position that gave him a view of Rawley's cot, watched them unblinkingly, his wise old eyes gravely inscrutable. When he had finished, Peter strode to the door and stood there looking out. Rawley had a queer feeling that he was looking for eavesdroppers.

"What you say will make my mother happier," he told Rawley, coming back and speaking in his usual calm tone of immutable reserve. "She seemed very bitter today when she talked with me. She has always thought your grandfather went away knowing he would never come back. And she has proud, Spanish blood in her veins—"

"Anita, by —!" Rawley's jaw dropped in sheer, crestfallen amazement.

"Did he tell you?" Peter eyed him queerly.

"It's the diary. The beautiful, half-Spanish girl, all fire and life—he described her like that. And—"

"Well, they change as they grow old." Peter's lips twitched in a grin. "The beautiful Spanish señoritas get fat and ugly, and the Indian women are more so. Your grandfather's fiery Spanish girl had nothing to pull her up the hill. Monotony, hardships—one can't wonder if the recidivous influences surrounding her all these years pulled her down to the dead level of her mother's people. Take this Indian here—" he tilted his head toward Johnny Buffalo—"he was taken out of it when he was a kid. Now, aside from certain traits of dignity and repression, I imagine he's more white than Indian."

Rawley nodded. "Lived right with Grandfather all his life and has studied and read everything he could get his hands on. He's better educated than lots of college men; aren't you, Johnny?"

"Yes. I think very much, of many things which Indians do not know. I do not talk very much. And that is wisdom also."

"Mother had nothing from books. When her youth went and she began to take on weight, she dropped her pretty ways and became like the squaws. I remember, and it used to hurt my pride to see her slip into their ways. I was—white." His mouth shut grimly.

Rawley lay looking into his face, trying to realize the full significance of this amazing truth. His grandfather's son, and Anita's. His own uncle. With Indian blood, but his uncle nevertheless. If Grandfather King had known—

"He'd have been proud," he said aloud, "to have a son like you. He always wanted—and my father was a weakling, physically, I mean. He died when I was just a kid. Grandfather called him a damned milksop, because he wanted to work in a bank. Johnny can tell you a lot about Grandfather—your—father." He lowered his voice, mindful of Peter's warning. And then, "Does Nev—does your niece know about it?"

"She does not. The fewer who know it, the better for all concerned. There will be four of us, as it is. There mustn't be five. Why make the lives of two old people bitter? Old Jess—I've a brother, Young Jess—thinks I am his son. He needs me, and Nevada needs me. We've hung together, in spite of the mixed breed you see us. Jess is Injun in looks and ways. Nevada's mother was all white. Jess married a mission half-breed girl, and their kids are Injun to the bone. Belle, Nevada's mother, married a Scotchman—good blood, I always thought, from his looks and actions. Nevada's—Nevada."

He said it proudly, and Rawley felt his blood tingle with something of the same pride.

From the other bed Johnny Buffalo spoke suddenly. "Anita, your mother, is my cousin. The daughter of my aunt. My blood is mingled with the blood of my sergeant's son. My heart is now alive again and life is good. My sergeant has gone where he can walk on two feet, and I am left to care for his son and his grandson. I now see that God is very wise."

"He is?" Peter pulled down his heavy, black brows and the corners of his lips. "I've spent a good deal of time wondering about that. There's Nevada—and one-eighth Indian. Is that—"

"Oh, what the devil difference does that make?" Rawley gave a flounce that made him groan. But in the midst of it he managed to growl, "You said it yourself; Nevada's—Nevada."

CHAPTER 11

RAWLEY THINKS THINGS OUT

At intervals of fevered wakefulness during that night, Rawley went over and over the astonishing state of affairs. The hour and the temperature that was almost inevitable conspired to twist and exaggerate the truth, to give him an intolerable sense of kinship with the slovenly, platter-faced Gladys, the stolid obesity of the old squaw, and of a hopeless abyss between himself and Nevada. They were related, somehow. They must be, since her Uncle Peter was also his uncle. Uncle Peter, he thought, had been terribly wronged, and he must somehow make amends, must remove the handicap of that savage blood. In the morning he must tell Gladys that he was her cousin; why, that made him Indian, too! No wonder his hair was so black, and he loved the wilderness with such a passion. He was part Indian, that was why. Johnny Buffalo was some relation; how Rawley's mother would hate that!

What he did not know was that he talked about it, with Johnny Buffalo awake and listening in the bed against the farther wall, and with Peter awake, too, in a bed he had made for himself on the porch. He remembered that Peter came and gave him a drink, and that it did not seem to matter so much, after that. He slept late into the morning, after the opiate, and awoke to a saner point of view.

As before, Nevada and her grandmother brought trays of food and helped the two helpless ones to eat. With the knowledge Peter had given him, Rawley looked with more interest at the old lady, covertly trying to see the slim little half-caste Spanish girl whom Grandfather King had found "the joy of his heart." On the whole, Rawley could not feel that his grandfather would have gone on loving, in any case. And he could not get away from the fact that Anita had consoled herself with considerable expedition.

"You aren't such a hero, after all," Nevada bantered him, bringing him out of his revery with a laugh. "You're looking abominably well, this morning, for a young man who was brought in dead only yesterday. And after all, you did not kill Queo. Uncle Jess and Uncle Peter went up to the spot last evening, just before dark, to identify him beyond all doubt, and—he'd disappeared. They found where he had lain behind the rock, and they knew he was wounded, by the blood." She shivered involuntarily. "But he wasn't anywhere to be found. Uncle Peter feels quite put out. He looked at Queo when he went up after you, and he felt sure the man was dead. So now, if he lives, he'll be more venomous than ever."

"Then I'm sorry I hit him at all," Rawley declared. "But I had to. He was after the grub, all right. He thanked me for carrying it up to the trail for him. Then he plugged me—I didn't duck quite soon enough. So—I always hate to be killed, like that," he finished whimsically.

"That sounds like Uncle Peter," Nevada observed. "Your voice, I mean. Grandmother, don't you think Mr. King looks and talks like Uncle Peter?"

Rawley tried not to look as startled as he felt. The pillowy (after all, one letter would have called her willowy in the old days, so that not so much had been changed) Anita walked deliberately over to them, advancing one side at a time, like a duck that travels in a leisurely mood. She laid her cushioned knuckles on her bulging hips and regarded Rawley steadfastly.

"Mebby he look—a lil bit," she conceded with a superb indifference. "Peter, he t'inner—a lil bit. More darker. More—like his fadder, Jesse."

"Yes-s—he does look more like Grandfather, of course. But I do think Mr. King looks like them both." Nevada spoke with a perfect sincerity which sent the spirits of three persons up a notch or two.

Rawley laughed. "Well, maybe we're some relation—away back," he said recklessly. "A Cramer, connected with my family, was known to have come West, years ago. I remember reading it in some old record. But I'm afraid I can't claim he was very closely related. In fact, I rather think he wasn't." His eyes met the eyes of old Anita, and he almost thought he saw a gleam of approval in them. He could not be sure.

Of the look in the eyes of Peter, who was standing in the doorway, he was much more positive. The color came into his face as their eyes met. After all, others were sure to notice the resemblance, and there must be some explanation ready.

"I'm sure that's it." Nevada laughed softly. "You're a fourth or fifth cousin, perhaps. Likenesses do travel that way. I wonder if Grandfather would know."

"I wouldn't want to ask him," her Uncle Peter observed in his grim way. "Why stir the old man up for days, just to satisfy idle curiosity?" He laid his hand on Nevada's head, smoothing back a lock of her hair with a gesture inexpressibly tender. "On the strength of the fifth-cousin relationship, seems like we might drop the Mr. King. Father hates to think of his past—a quarrel with his family brought him West, as nearly as I can make out. What do folks call you, young man, when they know you well?"

"Oh, Rawley is what I grew up under. George Rawlins King is my name. I wish you would call me Rawley. Then I could say Uncle Peter, and Nevada, and—Grandmother, maybe, if Mrs. Cramer will let me."

"Uncle me all you please," grinned Peter. "And Nevada is down on all the school maps. If you don't mind, when you do meet father, let it be as George Rawlins. Your last name might or might not recall a family quarrel. But—we spare him excitement as much as possible. And while you're here, the outfit will call you—Rawlins."

"Well, then I'll explain to Aunt Gladys," said Nevada, as if they were planning a secret for fun; and yet there was a certain look of anxiety, too, in her face. "I think I can manage her—but then she never says much to Grandfather, anyway. They don't like each other very well," she explained to Rawley. "Grandfather was angry when Uncle Jess married her, and while they never quarrel, it is merely toleration. Aunt Gladys won't tell."

Rawlins then lay for a long time thinking how strangely the pattern is woven into the woof of Life. With the sun shining and the noise of playing children outside, the unexpected turn of events seemed more natural. So much had happened in the past twenty-four hours that Rawley found himself checking up, as he called it, on events and emotions engendered by the sudden crises. He glanced across at the other bed and found Johnny Buffalo awake and seemingly comfortable; wherefore he made bold to ask a few questions.

"Johnny, I thought I had those women hidden around a bend in the trail. How did Queo manage to spot them so as to try a shot? I've been wondering about that first rifle shot. Are you sure it was fired at us?"

"I am sure. You were not hidden altogether. I, myself, could see heads, though I could not see the trail. Queo was higher. I think that little point was too low."

"Well, that accounts for it. I lost my bearings down there, then. Part of the ridge was hidden, I know. I thought it was the place where he was located. He shot wide, anyway." He lay looking at a Las Vegas merchant's calendar, reviewing still the immediate past.

"There's another thing that just struck me this morning. How did Grandfather know that Jess Cramer was located here on the river? Jess was a soldier at the fort, I thought, when Grandfather saw him last. It's in the diary."

"I think you should read again more carefully, my son. My sergeant spoke to me often of Jess Cramer. He had found gold here at this canyon. He was often at the fort, spending his gold in the games of chance. Jess Cramer played not for sport, but to win. A sergeant's pay was not large, and my sergeant spent many hours in searching for such gold as Jess Cramer brought with him to the fort. My sergeant had won a little. He kept it and searched for more of the same. It was not only for Anita that the two quarreled. A woman and gold make hatreds that do not die. He did not tell me all. He longed for a son who would take up the search. Or so I believed. I did not know that he had found his gold. I thought that the nuggets he gave to you he had won at cards from Jess Cramer. He told you that he picked them up. My sergeant does not lie. So I know that he had found the gold he had sought, and that if you obeyed him you would learn the secret he had kept from me."

"He had a son," Rawley muttered, "and he'd have been proud of him if he had known about him. Johnny, I can't help thinking that Peter is more Grandfather's son than my father was."

Johnny Buffalo meditated, staring at the ceiling.

"There was love," he said softly at last. "My sergeant did not love the mother of your father. I could see in his eyes when he looked upon her that his thoughts were not with her, and that his heart was far away."

They lay for a long time silent. Each thought that the other slept, he lay so still. But of a sudden Rawley reached up his uninjured hand and pushed back the bandage that was slipping over his eye. The movement betrayed not so much protest against a physical discomfort as the impatient mind that seeks in vain for the correct answer to a puzzle.

But Johnny Buffalo did not sleep. He lay staring at the ceiling, his mouth closed firmly with lines beside it which nature draws to show when the soul is weary. But there was no longer any bitterness there, though there was pain. The hollow eyes glowed steadily, as if the old man had found a light ahead somewhere in the blackness of his grief. Once, a gentle snore drew his attention, and he turned his head and stared for a long while at the young, unlined face with the bandage drawn diagonally above it. For Rawley the Great Game had only begun; his stakes were piled before him, to win or to lose. The old Indian wondered gravely how that Game would be played. Wisely? Bravely—he was sure. Honestly—he hoped.

CHAPTER 12

RAWLEY PLAYS THE GAME

How wisely, how honestly, how bravely he would play the Great Game, Rawley unconsciously indicated that evening, when Peter sat alone with the two, after Nevada and her grandmother had given them their supper and gone away. Peter had declared himself rather proud of his surgical skill, and had almost yielded to Rawley's importunities that he might get up and dress in the morning and help take care of Johnny Buffalo. But Peter had his father's firmness, after all.

"I took five stitches in that gash on your head," he explained. "Queo uses slugs to knock over an elephant. I'm not so sure your skull isn't cracked. You talk rather crack-brained, sometimes." (That was Peter's first joke with them.) "Best wait until we're sure, anyway."

Rawley gave an embarrassed kind of laugh and sent an involuntary, inquiring glance at Johnny Buffalo.

"I wish you'd lock the door, Uncle Peter, and then bring me my coat. I've got something on my mind other than a cracked skull and embroidered hide.

"Now, to make the thing clear to you, Uncle Peter, I'll have to say that Grandfather left here expecting to come back—and I hope you told your mother what happened."

Peter nodded.

"Well, there Grandfather was, helpless. It made him kind of proud and bitter, and he sort of held himself away from folks. But he was disappointed because my father was sickly and didn't take to anything outdoors, and I never met him face to face, or spoke a word to him, until the night before he died. Of course nobody dreamed he was going—I don't think he did, or Johnny, even.

"At any rate, he sent for me. And he said I was all King, and he had waited to make sure. He talked a little and gave me his old diary and an old Bible his mother had given him. He told me to read the Bible—that there was a lot in it, if I read it carefully. It was the last talk I had with him. He died in the night.

"Well, the point I'm getting at is this: Grandfather had a secret—about a mine out here. He had it all described, in a kind of code that sure had me guessing blind for awhile. I found a long list of Bible references, you see—no one would ever think of wading through the bunch, unless it was a preacher, maybe; and he wouldn't need to. It took me a while to catch on to the fact that they meant something. Grandfather, you must know, wasn't religious. Anything but. So the crux of the matter was those references looked so darned dry and innocent, and they were the only thing I could find to work on. Johnny, there, made it mighty plain to me that I'd better work on *something*. I tried Poe's cipher, and I looked up all the references. I will say that just reading verse after verse, according to the references, they make snappy reading; murder and bloodshed and bigamy and the wrath of God. And names I couldn't pronounce, of tribes headed out on the warpath. It was great stuff—not.

"But finally I dug into the little old Bible Grandfather had carried around with him—and hadn't read, or the book's a liar—and I got this. I want to read it to you: I dug it out by writing down words and phrases in all the verses, that Grandfather had marked. I'll read it as if it were altogether—which it wasn't, by a long shot:

"Gold is mine, more than heart could wish. My son, if thou wilt receive my words and hide my commandments with thee, I will give thee riches, and wealth, such as none of the Kings have had that have been before thee. Be wise, now, therefore, be instructed. Of the gold, there is no number. The land whither ye go to possess it is a land of hills and valleys.

"Do this, now, my son. Go through a city which is by the river in the wilderness, yet making many rich. In the midst thereof a ferry-boat which is by the brink of the river. Take victuals with you for the journey. Turn you northward into the wilderness, to a great and high mountain; cedar trees in abundance scattered over the face of the high mountain. In the cliffs there is a path which no fowl knoweth, and which the vulture's eye hath not seen. Come to the top of the mount. Pass over unto the other side, westward. On the hillside, a very great heap of stones joined to a dry tree. Go into the clefts of the rocks, into the tops of the jagged rocks, to the sides of the pit. Take heed, now—that is exceeding deep. It is hid from the eyes of all living. Creep into the midst thereof, eastward, two hundred and fourscore feet. Ye shall find a pure river of water. Proceed no further. There is gold heavier than the sand; pure gold upon the sand. And all the gold thou shalt take up. Then shalt thou prosper if thou takest heed. I know thy poverty, but thou art rich.

"Take heed, now. On the hillside which is upon the bank of the river in the wilderness, there shall the vultures also be gathered. Ye shall find him that is mine enemy. His mouth is full of cursing, under his tongue is mischief and vanity. Be watchful—the heart is desperately wicked.

"He that keepeth his mouth, keepeth his life. I put my trust in thee. Now, my son, the Lord be with thee and prosper thou."

Rawley folded the paper, looking up under his bandaged brows at Uncle Peter, and sending a glance past him to the unreadable face of Johnny Buffalo.

"So that's what I dug out of his Bible. He meant it for his son. He told me so himself. But he said my dad wasn't the man to get anything out of it—which was true. When he passed it on to me, he—he didn't know he had another son who *could* make good on the proposition. It's yours, by rights. He just gave it to me because he didn't know of any one else. And—all I ask, Uncle Peter, is that you make some kind of provision for Johnny, over there. I told him we'd go fifty-fifty, and—" he held out the folded paper to Peter—"Johnny's been hands and feet and a loyal friend to Grandfather, all these years. Fifty. Just think of that, Uncle Peter. Grandfather didn't have anything but his pension—and this. He didn't say so, but I know he expected me to look after Johnny. I will, of course. I can make good money at my profession. And I want to say, Uncle Peter," he added boyishly, "that I'm mighty glad Grandfather left something—for his son."

Rawley lay back with a relieved sigh and watched Peter, his eyes smiling a little. He did not think that he had done any unusual thing. Peter was exactly the kind of son whom Grandfather King had longed for, all these years. Rawley guessed that Peter, too, had been defrauded of the father he would have worshiped. It was a foregone conclusion that, had Grandfather King known Peter, he would have sent him, long ago, hunting for the mine. And while Peter had not said so, Rawley guessed shrewdly that Peter did not greatly admire Jess Cramer, in spite of the fact that he had believed the man his father. His nightmare thoughts, that he had somehow defrauded Peter, were wiped out once for all. The code had been written for the son of King, of the Mounted. The son had it. No more was to be said.

Peter opened the paper and read it through slowly, a corner of his lip drawn between his teeth. What he thought, no man could say. He finished the reading and folded the paper slowly, looking at Rawley afterward from under his heavy brows.

"Have you still got the Bible and the references?" he asked.

"Yes. In my safe deposit box, in St. Louis."

"Humph." Peter deliberately twisted the paper into a spill, felt in his pocket for a match, and as deliberately set fire to the paper, turning and tilting it until the creeping flame was about to scorch his fingers. He laid the stub on the floor, bent and watched it go black, then set his foot upon the charred fragments.

"Boy, you keep what was given you. If I've any right in it, I'll sign that right over to you. But never mention that—" he motioned toward the ashes on the floor—"above your breath. Your grand—my father was right. The vultures are perched here by the river, and the old vulture's eye is never shut. While you're here, forget it. Both of you."

"But it isn't mine. It's yours, Uncle Peter. I don't want it—now."

"If it's mine, then it will never be found. I don't need it. When the vultures swoop down and light—the feast will be big enough even for them. But I warn you, remember. Never speak of that again, in this camp." He stood up, gazing down at Rawley much as Grandfather King had looked at him that night. With a quick, impulsive movement he stooped and laid his hand over Rawley's, pressing it warmly. He smiled; and there was that in the smile which made Rawley draw in his breath sharply.

"If Fate had dealt the cards straight to me—I might have had you for *my* son!"

He drew his hand away, turned and walked out.

CHAPTER 13

THE COLORADO

The tribe of Cramer dined. In the shack beside the big mesquite tree was heard the clatter of knives and forks—more knives than forks, one might guess—the dull clink of enameled ware, the high, demanding voices of hungry children more Indian than white. Above all the clamor of feeding, the shrill petulance of Aunt Gladys could be heard rising above all other sounds as she expostulated incessantly with her young. The baby was crying monotonously. Some one kicked a dog, which shot out of the open door ki-yi-ing hysterically.

In the smaller rock dugout, tinkle of glass and silver plate and china betrayed the fact that the white blood held itself aloof from the red at mealtime. In the larger cabin built for Nevada, Rawley had just finished his supper, eaten with Johnny Buffalo in a punctilious regard for the old man's feelings, though he had been invited to join Peter and Nevada at table.

In the matter of recovery, young bones were healing much faster than the old. Rawley had been promoted to a gauze pad held in place by strips of adhesive over the long gash on his head. His arm had settled down to the dull, grinding ache and intolerable deep itching of knitting bone and healing flesh. Johnny Buffalo, splinted and bandaged, was able to sit propped in cushions in a big chair on the porch.

Rawley left him reading deliberately the matchless "Apology" of Socrates, which Peter had lent him that day, and started out for a walk, choosing between his own company and the companionship of Nevada, which seemed always to bring at least half the tribe of Cramer at their heels like the dragging tail of a kite. Rawley reflected disgustedly that as yet he had never had five consecutive minutes alone with Nevada. When her grandmother was not filling the foreground, the offspring of Aunt Gladys formed a snuffling, big-eared background which Nevada sweepingly termed the Little Pitchers. Whether Nevada enjoyed the company of the Little Pitchers on their infrequent strolls to the river bank, or approved the solid chaperonage of the juglike Anita, Rawley had never been able to decide. Nevada's manner toward her dark-skinned kinsfolk was impartially and imperturbably gracious. Indeed, Rawley sometimes suspected that she deliberately encouraged their tagging along. Four goggling kids and three dogs, he considered, might be recommended as a romance-proof chaperonage.

Mechanically he walked straight down to the river, to the spot which Nevada always chose as their destination. A flat rock there formed a convenient place to sit and enjoy the view of the river and the hills beyond. Across the swift-moving, muddy stream, bottom lands covered with cottonwoods gave a refreshing touch of green to the picture. Arizona cottonwoods they were, since the Colorado formed the dividing line. Away to the southwest, he could see the hills made familiar at Kingman. Rough, rather forbidding mountains they had been at close range, but now they were made soft and alluring by the blue haze of distance. Straight down the river he could see the hill that looked down on El Dorado, that "city forsaken." Up the river he could not see, because of the high, granite cliffs that blocked the view.

Because nature had seemed to bar the way, Rawley turned and made his way aimlessly toward the barrier. With his left arm in splints and carried in a sling, he could not do much in the way of climbing; but presently he stumbled upon a well-defined path leading amongst bowlders just under the rim of the basin. The path led up the canyon, and Rawley followed it with a desultory interest in seeing where it led—and for the exercise it promised. Perhaps, had he given the matter thought, he would have owned that a strange trail never failed to tempt his feet to follow. At any rate, he held to the pathway.

Now the river was hidden completely from him, though he could hear it complaining over the bowlders in the canyon and hurrying through as fast as if indignation lent it speed. The path went on, finding the easiest places to worm through the jagged rocks and climbing closer and closer to the river, whose roar became more distinct as he neared it.

Through a split in the huge wall so narrow as to be almost a crevice, the trail led him quite suddenly to a narrow shelf set sheer above the river. Crude steps cut in the rock went down the cliff at a slant. He heard the water worrying over something unseen at the bottom, and began to descend, his right hand steadying himself against the granite wall. He was curious, somewhat mystified. Neither Peter nor Nevada had mentioned any possibility of reaching the water's edge in the canyon.

He found himself in a tiny cove which had been formed when some primal upheaval had split the granite wall at the base, throwing the outside into the river. No more than a wide crack, it was, but it was serving well a purpose. A small, rock landing filled the shore end of the slit completely. Riding quietly in the slack water of the small anchorage, a squat, powerful looking launch sat bow to the landing, secured there by a heavy chain.

A great deal of labor had gone into the making of that landing and the steps leading down to it. His trained eyes could see where an inner portion of the jagged point had been cleverly blown off in such manner that the huge fragments formed a most natural appearing breakwater, making quiet water within instead of a moiling swirl. If the Cramers wanted a secret landing on the river, here was one ideally suited to their needs.

But the Cramers had another landing, in plain sight of the flat rock at the rim of the basin. At that landing also a launch was tied; a very ordinary launch of a type sufficiently sturdy to combat easily enough the strong river current. It was that other launch that was out of repair so that a trip to Needles had been declared impossible. True enough, this launch might also be out of commission, but Rawley did not think so. Stopping and looking in at the engine, he judged that it was in very good working order indeed, and from certain little, indefinable signs, he believed that it had been lately used. By whom he did not know, although he remembered now that Young Jess—who was not so young as he sounded, since he was well past forty—had not been in evidence lately among his family.

He saw all that was to be seen and retraced his steps up the rock stairway. It could not matter, one way or the other, if the Cramers kept a dozen secret landings on the river. Nevertheless, Rawley was frankly puzzled. He thought he could guess why his Uncle Peter had not wanted to take them to Needles in this large boat. If he really meant to keep this boat a secret, it would scarcely do to run it down to the house landing, alongside the smaller, crippled launch. Rawley and Johnny might come back, some time, and they might ask about the second launch, seeing only one down there at the other landing.

Some one must want absolute freedom to come and go by the river without observation, he decided. With the smaller launch innocently swinging in the eddy at the lower landing, the Cramers would naturally appear to be at home, or ranging in the hills; whereas one or two of them might be absent in this boat here. It was very simple—and very mystifying as well. The rock landing stage was built to make safe anchorage in high water as in low; which proved conclusively that this was an all-year landing.

At the top he hesitated, in some doubt as to whether he should return to the house or follow the path on up the canyon. He yielded to the unknown trail, which was singularly well-traveled for a trail that apparently led directly away from any logical destination. He had not gone far when he came upon the flat, level space of a dump. Close beside him the black mouth of a tunnel opened into the cliff rising a sheer hundred feet above his head. He stopped, astonished at this unexpected ending of the trail. The solid face of granite gave no indication whatever of carrying mineral of any kind. There was no logical reason, therefore, for all this evidence of development work.

The ethics of his profession forbade his prowling underground without being invited. He would as soon open an unlocked door and go spying through a man's house and personal belongings. From the size of the dump he judged that the workings extended for some distance underground, and from the look of the rock that had come from the tunnel he knew that any hope of reaching mineral was likely to remain long unfulfilled. Instinctively he picked up a piece of rock here and there, looked at it and threw it aside. If they were driving in to a contact, he thought, the Cramers must have sharp eyes indeed for surface indications. Knowing mineral formations at a glance was a part of his trade, and he had seen absolutely nothing that would lead him to the point of advising any man to lift a shovelful of muck.

He turned back. The afterglow was purpling across the river, and he did not want to be too long away from Johnny Buffalo. He reached a turn in the trail where a jutting crag thrust out and overhung the river—and there he stopped short.

Perched on the point of the crag like the vulture his grandfather had named him, Old Jess Cramer leaned and looked down upon the hurrying waters, a full six hundred feet below him. The distance between them was mostly a matter of altitude, for Old Jess had climbed considerably to reach that particular point. Staring up at him, Rawley was struck with a certain weird resemblance to that predatory bird. There was something sinister about him as he sat there; something rapacious and purposeful. It was as if he meant to seize the river and wrest from it something which his greed desired. While he looked, Old Jess stretched out his arm and shook his fist at the roaring stream.

Rawley turned away. Something within him revolted at the sight, though even to himself he could not have explained why. As his gaze dropped from Old Jess to the trail, there was Peter standing looking from one to the other. Peter's face was stern, his eyes cold with disapproval. It seemed to Rawley that he was purposely blocking the trail.

"I see you've done quite a lot of development work back there," Rawley remarked to cover a vague embarrassment.

"Yes. Quite a lot. Did you go in?"

Rawley smiled at what seemed to him a needless question. "Certainly not. I never go underground unless I'm hired to do so."

He thought he saw relief in his Uncle Peter's eyes.

"Well, I never saw any particular fun in it, myself. It's all work, to me." He turned and seemed to be awaiting Rawley's pleasure. "If you want a view," Peter hazarded drily, "you ought to go down to where the river swings east, below the basin where we live. You can look straight up the canyon here for a long way. Cliffs are too jagged here to get much of a view; there's a bulge in the canyon that interferes."

"It's better down at the landing in front of the house than it is here," Rawley agreed carelessly. "I see now why Nevada always heads straight for that big, flat rock."

He caught a swift, questioning side glance from Uncle Peter and knew beyond all doubt that the big launch, the hewn-rock stairway and the tunnel in the cliff were things which he was not supposed to know about. But the reason for the secrecy he could not guess.

CHAPTER 14

THE VULTURE SCREAMS

A high-keyed snarl brought the two sharply facing the crag. Bearing down upon them with his fists flailing the air in a kind of impotent fury came old Jess Cramer, like a vulture fighting for his feast. Rawley had seen the old man at a short distance, but he had never before stood face to face with him. He would cheerfully have missed the meeting now. Old Jess craned his long neck toward him, his bleak, blue-gray eyes venomous. But it was Peter to whom he spoke—screamed, rather.

"Told ye it'd come to this, didn't I? You *would* take 'em in and pet 'em up, and treat 'em better'n you do your own kin! Think so much of 'em you had to go and show 'em what we're doing and why! Reckon when we touch 'er off and git the damned river penned back, you'll beg 'em on your knees to go down and claw out gold till they wear their fingers to the bone!

"What have I slaved for and worked for and hoarded for, all these years? To let you give away the gold when we git it? Is this the kind uh thing I raised ye for? Take in the first stranger that comes snoopin' around the place, and bring him sight-seein' up here to our dam! You—!"

Rawley had thought the miners he sometimes worked among could curse, but he stood agape before the blistering vituperations of this gray-bearded old man. He looked at Peter, wondering how any man with the King blood could have endured his fancied father's vile tongue all these years. Peter stood with a face of iron, his eyes terribly blue and hard, and listened impersonally to the frenzied outburst.

"That's enough, now. Shut up and listen to me!"

It was like snapping a whip in the face of a roaring lion. Old Jess had stopped merely to gasp fresh air into his lungs so that he could go on. He glared at Peter, weakened and cringed. The fire that had flared in his eyes died as suddenly. He looked toward the river, looked at Rawley and his glance slid away from the two of them.

"What'd yuh want to go and let it all out to him for?" he half whimpered. "Now he'll want a share—and there might not be more 'n five or six millions in the hull damned river bed! And you know 's well as I do, Peter, that our dam is liable as not to go out, next high water. We won't have many months to work in, mebby. I—I want a word with yuh, Peter. I—I want a word with yuh, that's all. I guess mebby you know what you're up to, but—"

"Shut up!" Peter snapped the verbal whip again. His eyes turned briefly toward Rawley. "What's been let out, you did yourself, dad." (Rawley thought that Peter hesitated over the last word.) "I have never breathed one word of our plan. Slave? What have *I* been slaving for, all these years? Do you think *I* have not endured everything but dishonor, for the sake of the millions we plan to get? And Nevada—what about *her*? Hasn't she done the work of a man and slaved over her studies, so that she could help, too? It's you, letting go your tongue and raving like a fool, that has betrayed the secret. *You've* done it. This man didn't know or suspect a thing, till you let it out, accusing me of telling!"

The old man looked uneasily from one to the other. Peter stared unrelentingly at him. Rawley, stealing a glance at his face, thought that he knew now the kind of man his Grandfather King had been in his old, fighting days.

"Now, he'll have to know." Peter's voice relaxed the tension. It was as if he had suddenly determined to accept the situation and make the best of it—and the most. "He can be trusted, I think. He'll *have* to be trusted, after your blathering."

Old Jess turned his predatory eyes on Rawley, and his beard moved to a sinister smile beneath.

"You're a big man, Peter—and it ain't but a few steps to the edge!" He tilted his head backwards toward the river. There was no possibility of mistaking his meaning. But he added a sentence to clinch it: "She never gives up a body—the Colorado don't!"

Peter's grin was a withering thing to face. Again the old man cringed, and his eyes shifted like a cornered rat.

"I'll remember that, if you open your mouth again. I'm strong—and the river never gives up a dead man. You keep that in mind, will you?" Peter insisted ominously.

"He shan't have none of *my* share," Old Jess shrilled, his voice cracking with anger and fear. "It was my idee, before you was born, Peter. You shan't rob me in my old age—you shan't, now! I'll be the first one to pick up the gold—that's been understood, since you was big enough to talk. An' he better not let it out to anybody! I'll kill him if he does—you mark me, Peter! I'll kill any man that stands in my road to them millions I been watching over all these long years—scrabbling the gold together, ounce by ounce, till I've got enough to do it! A million dollars—but I'll reap a thousand dollars for one. You mark what I say; I'll kill anybody that tries to horn in—It's mine, every bit of it!"

"In that case," said Peter contemptuously, "you can go ahead and get it."

"All but your share's mine, Peter. Yours and Young Jess' and Nevada's. This feller better not think—"

"He only thinks you're a fool," Peter told him harshly. "Stay and watch your gold, then. It might float off!" He motioned with his head toward home, and Rawley obeyed the signal and started ahead of him down the trail, wondering a good deal over the encounter.

"Looks like I'm driving you off," Peter remarked after a bit. "But I'm merely bringing up the rear. Old Jess is not all there. I'll tell you all about it, now he's told so much. I had half a mind to, anyway, if I could get him and Young Jess to agree. You're a mining engineer. I kind of wanted your opinion and advice. It is out of your line, probably; but technical training helps. I never had any, myself. Old Jess is a slave driver, all right. And now he's half crazy, and I wouldn't want to go off and leave him with the women. If a stranger happened along and roused his suspicion, there's no prophesying what might happen."

"It sounds pretty wild, to me, all his talk," Rawley returned after a minute. "I can easily believe the old man's crazy. I can't seem to get any sense out of it; millions of gold—and all that. Uncle Peter, were you just stringing him along—because he's crazy?"

Peter laughed queerly. "I can't wonder at your thinking so," he said. "Sit down here, and I'll tell you the straight of it."

It was the flat rock which they had reached. The shouts of the children, the barking of the dogs and the crying of the baby came to them in one indistinguishable chorus from across the small flat. In the deepening dusk they would not be noticed and interrupted.

"Away back, before I was born," Peter began, "Jess had mining claims here. Placer, and he was doing pretty well at it, I imagine. He bached here beside the river, and an idea came to him one day that has stuck to him like a burr ever since. That idea, boy, has ruled this bunch, has driven us like dogs. It's a big one—the only big idea he ever had, so far as I know.

"Old Jess got to thinking how much gold must lie at the bottom of the river, washed down through all the centuries of time, through Colorado, even through Wyoming, where its main tributaries rise. When you think of it, the thing gets hold of you. And the more you think, the stronger it holds. He thought how tremendously rich and powerful he'd be if he could just get at that gold out there. But you see the old river; she holds what she's got. And in flood time—

"Well, it wasn't long before he began to figure out how he could get at that gold. And he got the idea of throwing a dam across the canyon here, and backing up the water. I don't think he ever told any one, but he kind of quizzed around and decided finally that it would cost a lot of money. A million dollars, we made it at a rough guess. So he began to save his gold, instead of gambling and carousing with it down in El Dorado and at the fort. For that matter, I believe the old man always was a grasping, avaricious individual. It's his nature—I've seen it demonstrated all my life.

"We're all living fairly decently now, son. But until I was old enough to assert myself a bit, he almost starved us, he was so keen on saving that million. Even now I have to have a run-in with him, every so often, about the money that goes for living expenses. But he can afford it. He's got his million, and then some."

"*What?*"

"He's been saving every grain he could scrape together, for fifty years, Rawley. And it's a good claim—group of claims, rather. No one in the country has ever dreamed that we've done more than scratch a living here. Some day, when your arm is well, I'll show you. Yes, he has his million.

"For a long time, now—several years—we've been getting ready for the dam. That tunnel you saw is part of the work. When you're better, I'd like to take you through our workings and see what we've done and what we expect to do. Maybe you can give us some advice. We've had to use our own wits, because we can't consult with experts, in the very nature of things. We are not," he said cynically, "the only vultures in the world. The country would be black with them. And when all's said and done, we have first right. Why, look at El Dorado! Men sat down there and cursed their luck—and looked straight at the richest gold mine in the world! This canyon was here, everything was here, ready for them to go to work and get the gold just as we are going to do. But nobody thought of it. Sheep—that's what men are. Not one in a thousand does any thinking outside the beaten path. Nobody *had* dammed the river to get the gold; they had no precedent to follow—no bell wether to show them the way. So nobody ever thought of the possibility of doing it. Old Jess, I must say, shot up head and shoulders above the ruck when he conceived the idea. His avariciousness and dwelling on that one thought all these years have given him a mental twist. He'd kill any man who seemed to be standing in his way. He's gone too far now—he has lived with that air castle too long. But my God, think what a castle he's built!" Peter's voice was vibrant with emotion. Here, as with Old Jess, was the dream of a lifetime revealed.

"Yes—it's a tremendous scheme," Rawley admitted guardedly. "I'm afraid it won't work, Uncle Peter. It doesn't, somehow, seem feasible."

"Why not?" Peter's voice challenged him. "Merely because you hadn't thought of its feasibility. Nobody thought of it. Why, you're like all the rest, son. You can't think constructively. You must have a precedent to hang onto with one hand, before you think out into the ocean of unguessed achievements. Fifty years ago, they would have shut you up in an asylum if you had declared it possible to telegraph without wires. How was the first telephone hooted? And history tells us that a large faction of religious people declared that anesthetics were contrary to the will of God, who meant that men should suffer.

"When I show you the canyon, back here, and explain to you how we mean to do it, you'll have to admit the simplicity of the thing. And that's it! The very simplicity of it has prevented men from grasping it." He laughed scornfully. "What a to-do about building a dam they make! They must have government backing, and political wirepulling, and they must fiddle around for years with hundreds of men building a dam up from bedrock, with cement and stone! Wait until I show you what *we* mean to do! Simplest thing in the world—since we don't want canals for irrigation and only want to get at the river below. Even if we did want to divert the water, instead of restraining it only, we could build our canals just the same, and at our leisure.

"But it's all desert, above and below. Already I've bought any little rancher out, that might have his land flooded when *we build our dam*." Peter laughed again triumphantly. "I'll arrange to get possession before we're ready to back up the water—"

"Will the government allow that?" Rawley's tone was troubled. So great a hold had Peter's argument taken upon him that he found himself *fearing* that the government might object.

Peter gave a contemptuous snort. "Give us a chance to rake the gold out of the river bed below here, and we can pay whatever fine or indemnity the government may see fit to levy," he retorted. "But why should it object? We'll be saving the folks away down below here a lot of trouble and loss from high water. They've been howling for flood control ever since the Imperial Valley began to be settled. The dams they've got don't answer the problem. Sooner or later, the government, or somebody, will have to put a dam in the river, up this way. They will be mighty grateful, I should say, if we do it at our own expense while they're talking about it.

"Then, if they want to, they can pay us for our trouble and go ahead and build their canals, or power plants, or whatever they want. All we want is the gold that has been washed down during a few thousand years." He lifted his arm and pointed down to where the river could dimly be seen moiling and grumbling over its rocky bed.

"You see how rocky it is? Figure for yourself what a perfect trap for gold every bowlder makes! And there is gold! You don't deny that, do you?"

"Why, no. I can't deny the very probable presence of gold in considerable quantity." This being rather in the nature of a professional question, Rawley instinctively leaned toward conservatism in his reply.

"Well, that's our object. We feel it's going to be worth the expense of building the dam. Other people may possibly want to make use of our dam, when they see it. In that case, we should be able to get back at least what money we are going to put into it. We'll know, to a dollar. Nevada has got the education and training the rest of us lack and can tell us at a minute's notice just what the work is costing us. That's her job. And Old Jess has signed a contract with us three. The idea was his in the first place, and the claims that produced the gold to do the work with are his—most of them. He gets half of all the gold we take out. We repay, out of our share, one-half the expense of building the dam, and the three of us share equally in the rest. In other words—I suppose I've put it clumsily—he takes half the net proceeds, we divide the other half. And since we inherit, at his death, we are all satisfied." He stood up and smiled down at Rawley in the half darkness of early night.

"So you see, son, why I won't need any of that gold you and the Injun are looking for. I expect to be pretty well fixed myself, before so very long."

CHAPTER 15

THE LAND OF SPLENDID DREAMS

For days Rawley watched the might of the rushing Colorado and wondered at the temerity of men who would calmly plan to check its headlong progress to the sea. A splendid dream, he was compelled to own; a dream worthy a better man than old Jess Cramer. But every man must have one vision of great things during his life, else he would lack the spark of immortality. He may distort the vision to baser depths, but to each life is given one dream, one glimpse into the realm of beautiful possibilities. So Jess Cramer had dreamed his dream, had seen his vision, and had held aside the curtain so that others might see.

It interested Rawley in his days of helplessness to observe the reactions of that dream upon the diverse natures that dwelt within the basin. Old Jess Cramer had become a vulture in human form, his whole soul enslaved by the greed fostered by his individual conception of the vision. Rawley could look at the river and picture Old Jess down in its slimy bed of mud bars, rocks and groping streamlets, wildly scrabbling amongst the gravel and stones for the gold his insatiable soul craved. He pictured Old Jess gloating over his gold, weighing it in his hands, stupidly goggling without the wit to give it for what pleasures his spent old life could still enjoy.

Young Jess, too, had pulled the splendid vision down to his dull understanding. Young Jess, low-browed, sullen, would like to throw the gold with both hands into the lap of brutish gratifications. Young Jess was a gambler by nature, Rawley gleaned. He must never be let loose in a town, because he would have to be hauled out in a drunken torpor, his pockets empty, his credit strained, his soul fresh blotted by vice. Young Jess had "sprees"; from Gladys Rawley learned that. So Young Jess was kept on a leash of family watchfulness.

"When we make our big clean-up," Gladys confided from the bench on the screened porch, her baby nursing desultorily in its sleep, "Jess has gotta give me half of his share fast as he rakes it in. I'm going to have Peter see't he does that—or we'll be broke ag'in in no time. I'm going to put it where he can't git his fingers on it to gamble, you bet! And he runs with women—that sure makes the money fly! But I guess they'll be two of us, at that!" she tittered. "I ain't so old yet I can't git up some speed—give me some decent clothes and di'mon's. I'm going to Salt Lake, an' I'm going to have me the biggest car they is on the market. My folks is got a car, down to Needles—"

Anita—Rawley was long in learning what was Anita's bright, particular vision. One day he asked her outright, since he could not lead her to talk about her expectations in a general way. And straightway he was humbled and ashamed.

Anita looked at him stolidly, turned her great bulk and stared down at the river hurrying by in the midday sunlight. She lifted a hand to her eyes and stared out from beneath the flat of her brown palm.

"Gol'—if it can buy me back—t'ings I have love'—t'ings I have los' long time ago," she murmured. "Gol'—it don't buy young body—pretty face—voice to sing like a bird. Gol' don't give back my girl—modder of Nevada. Pah-h!" She spat at the river contemptuously. "W'at I care for gol'?"

Nevada—to her the dream was a splendid vision indeed. To her it was achievement—success—the open door through which she might pass to a glorified future. Nevada, when pressed, admitted that she loved pretty things—"And then, the world is so full of people who want to be helped!"

Rawley nodded. "I know. I've felt that."

"And if there is gold to be had, so that they can be helped, I think it's wicked not to use every ounce of energy we possess to get it, so that we can use it," she declared with more enthusiasm than Rawley had ever seen her show. "When it's fought for, just for sake of self-indulgence, it ought to be fought for in the interests of good. I'd found a home for—well, almost anybody that needed it. And I want so to travel, Fifth Cousin! I don't mean to spend more than two or three millions, just myself. I'm afraid I might grow reckless and extravagant. So I shall only hold out three million, at the most, for my own personal needs. The rest I shall give away." Whereupon she laughed at him.

"You don't really expect to be a lady billionaire?" Nevada sobered. "It's such a big, untamed land," she dreamed aloud, her young eyes on the river, as Anita's had been. "If you don't dream splendidly, you somehow feel that you're too small for the desert. It's a land of splendid visions, Fifth Cousin. Never mind if they don't come true. They're like the sunsets and the sunrises. They live, and they die, and they live again, on and on—forever." She lifted a tanned, rounded arm and pointed away to the floating, hazy blue of the horizon.

"That's what I mean," she said. "Can you look at that and think small? Why, every old prospector who follows a burro along the desert trail has his visions. The dim distances promise him heart's desire. Why else would he keep going? He's a millionaire—in his dreams. The next gulch may change his vision to reality. Think how the Spaniards came dreaming up this very river, as long ago as when Washington was praying for boots at Valley Forge! What brought them, but the splendid dreams—their visions of what lay over the next hill?"

Her gaze dropped to the river. Just as every other adult member of the Cramer family looked at the hurrying water, so Nevada gazed and saw— not lost youth and lost love, as did Anita, but the splendid future that would be hers when the river gave up its hoarded gold. She smiled and forgot to speak. Her vision held her entranced.

Peter's dream was very like Nevada's. Peter, as Rawley knew, exulted over the achievement itself; the constructive thinking that left the beaten path of thought and plunged boldly into the realm of unguessed possibilities. The taming of a river that called itself untamable meant more to Peter than to Nevada, even. The gold would be his just reward for having dared to achieve the improbable.

Peter also craved emancipation from the petty round of his isolated life. Around the world Peter would sail and learn of other lands and other peoples and the problems which Fate had set them to solve. Peter was willing to divert a part of his gold to the welfare of his fellow men, but he did not dream of that as did Nevada. The building of the dam, the actual getting of the gold, the splendid hazards of the undertaking, these things set Peter's indigo-blue eyes alight with the flame of his enthusiasm.

So even the tribe of Cramer dreamed, each according to the quality of his soul. And Rawley knew why his Uncle Peter stayed and worked shoulder-to-shoulder with men whose half-relationship humiliated and embittered him. He knew why Nevada chose to remain here, in an environment ludicrously unsuitable, inharmonious. Indian and white, they held, in various forms, the same vision. There was something fine, something splendid in their even daring to dream.

CHAPTER 16

RAWLEY INVESTIGATES

Came a time when Rawley felt fit enough for work; and this investigation of the wild, improbable scheme of the Cramers would be work, with every faculty of the engineer on the alert for his clients. For the others he would not have attempted the thing he contemplated. He would have told them, more or less politely but nevertheless firmly, that the whole thing was out of his line and that he could not assume the responsibility. But for his Uncle Peter and for Nevada he would do the best that was in him.

Old Jess and Young Jess still looked at him with suspicious eyes, but they made no comment when he set off one morning with Peter to look over their work. They followed sullenly along the trail, ready, Rawley thought, to turn at the slightest indication of treachery and pitch him over the edge of the cliff—if they could—as Old Jess had naïvely suggested to Peter.

Back to the tunnel Peter led him—and within it. It was smaller than the usual mine tunnel, and fifty feet back from the portal two crosscuts ran parallel with the face of the cliff for a distance of fifty feet in either direction. In the hard rock, working with hand drills, the excavations had been made at the expense of infinite labor, Rawley could see. No car or track was there for removing the muck, which had been taken out in a wheelbarrow. At the face of the tunnel, a winze had been sunk fifty feet, and from this two other crosscuts extended, apparently directly beneath the upper ones.

Rawley saw it all, riding down the winze in the bucket, since he had but one arm of any use. With Uncle Peter at the windlass he felt perfectly secure—though he would have refused the descent with one of the others, so great was his distrust of the Cramers, father and son.

When he returned, Peter conducted him down the stairway hewn into the cliff, and into the big launch.

"This is something we don't let the world know about," he remarked. "From Nelson we pack in supplies that any ordinary miner's family would need—if they were just scratching a living out of their claims. You saw how we do it—with burros. Fifteen years ago we began to work on that stairway and landing. It was a long, hard job. But I knew that we were going to need some private way of getting supplies and material in for the dam. Now, we can slip down to Needles and get a boat-load and get back without these people around here knowing it. Early morning, just at peep of day, is the time I choose for running in here. On the far side of the river, none of the El Dorado prospectors would be apt to notice; and if they did, they would think I was on my way farther north. Now, I'm going to take you across the canyon."

Once out and fighting the current, Rawley saw at once why it was that the Colorado was not considered a navigable river. There were no rapids in the canyon, properly speaking. But the pent volume of water rushed through like a dignified mill race, and it was only Peter's skill and the power of the motor that landed them across the canyon.

Here, a small eddy, with a break in the bold, granite wall, made a fair landing. Peter tied the launch securely and led the way up a steep trail from the water's edge to a natural shelf, where another tunnel with crosscuts was being run. As far as the contour of the cliffs would permit, the workings here were identical with those on the home shore, except that they were not finished. They had just completed the winze.

"We can't work over here except when the weather and the river are favorable," Peter explained. "And Old Jess kept us at the gold diggings until we balked. He'd got that one idea so firmly fixed in his mind that he wouldn't let up when he had his million. He seemed to think a few months' work would put the dam in, and it was next to impossible to pry him away from the gold grubbing. When we finally struck and refused to put in another shift in the mine, he yielded the point. Now he's in a fever to get this done. He'll sit and watch the river by the hour, just as you saw him that night he came down on us. Gloats and grudges by turns, I suppose. He doesn't realize what a job it is—blowing enough rock into the canyon to dam the river."

"I wonder if you do, yourself!" Rawley remarked laconically and led the way out. "I want to study these cliffs a bit from the outside. I've seen enough of your underground work."

He spent two hours sitting on first one jutting rock pinnacle and then another, studying the cliffs and making sketchy diagrams and notes. A splendid dream, surely; but a dream wellnigh impossible, as he saw it.

That evening after supper, he sent word to Peter that he was ready to talk to him and would prefer to have the Cramers present. Wherefore Peter brought them over to the cabin; Old Jess vulture-like and grim, and fairly bristling with suspicion, Young Jess surly, but wanting to know what was going on between Peter and this stranger. Rawley dragged chairs out to the porch and laid a diagram sketch on the small table beside him.

"I want to say first, to all of you," he began gravely, "that I don't approve of the scheme from any point of view. Peter says that is because I think by rule; because the thing has never been done, and I therefore have nothing to work from. However that may be, I warn you at the start that I don't like it. I don't believe you can dam the river in the way you are going at it. It's a cinch you will have to alter your plans in certain ways, if you are to have any hope whatever of accomplishing the feat.

"I want to warn you that the government will probably have something to say about your performance. If the river had not been declared unnavigable, you would be in trouble for obstructing the channel, if for nothing else. What Washington will say about it in the circumstances, I can't predict. I don't know. But if you persist in carrying out your scheme, be prepared for trouble with the authorities. Red tape may wind you up tighter than you anticipate.

"With the understanding, then, that I absolutely disapprove of the idea, I am going to give you my opinion of the most feasible method of making it a success. Of course, I needn't point out to you the very obvious fact that, if you don't make a success of it, you will lose every dollar you put into it, and probably get into trouble just the same. If you spend a fortune throwing rock into the river and fail to dam the flow so that you can carry on whatever operations you have in mind on the river bed below, you will be worse off than if you had not started. Therefore, I'm going to tell you how I think you should do it."

"In other words, 'Don't do it—but if you *do* do it, do it this way,'" Nevada murmured mischievously.

"Something like that," Rawley grinned. "In the first place, your work is far from finished. You will have to put in relievers, to break the rock between your crosscuts and the face. That can be done by raising, or you can sink incline shafts from the surface. My diagram here shows approximately what I mean. Later, when my arm is well, I will, if you like, run your lines for you. I have a small instrument for my own use.

"These relievers must be shot with dynamite, of course. I suppose, having had long experience in mining, you know that you should use some dynamite for breaking the rock, and black powder to lift and heave it over into the river. Since dynamite gives a quick concussion, the whole can be fired simultaneously; the black powder will follow the dynamite.

"What you should have, of course, is the advice of expert engineers who specialize in this sort of thing. It's out of my line, and I am merely giving you my opinion for whatever it is worth—in soundness," he added, catching a miserly chill in Old Jess's eyes. "I couldn't sell advice on a matter outside my profession, and in any case I am glad to do whatever I can to help you avoid mistakes. I am trying to see it as a mining problem—the opening of a glory hole, we'll say."

"Your idea of crosscutting at different levels is a good one, but you should by all means break your rock to the surface, and so give your main explosives a chance to lift it over. You see what I mean?" He lifted the diagram and held it up for them to see. "Here are your tunnel, winze and crosscuts. Then here are your relievers. An incline to the surface—or close to the surface—as high as you wish the cliff to break. I shall have to survey that for you, to give you the proper pitch. Then these 'coyote holes' between the apex and your adit—these will be filled with dynamite. I wonder if you have formed any definite idea of how much powder and dynamite you are going to need!"

"Nevada and I have been working on that for five years," Peter said, and smiled. "We intend to use plenty."

"I should hope so," Rawley exclaimed. "Better a few tons too much, than to have all your work and money go for nothing. Make a dead-sure job of it, or—drop the scheme right here."

This brought an ominous growl from the old man and Young Jess. Peter was studying the diagram. He passed it along to Young Jess, who scowled down at it intently, his slower mind studying each detail laboriously. Old Jess reached out a grimy claw and bent over it like a vulture over a half-picked bone.

"I'm afraid you'll have trouble getting your explosives," Rawley observed. "The war is taking enormous quantities to Europe. And I'm afraid we're going to be dragged into the scrap ourselves. In which case, the government will probably shut off private buyers entirely."

Young Jess laughed a coarse guffaw. "We should worry!" He leered at Rawley. "We got a glory hole a'ready, back at the diggin's. We been five years gittin' powder in here. Gosh! We c'd blow up Yerrup if we wanted to, ourselves! Y'ain't showed him our powder cache, have yuh, Pete?"

"I didn't know anything about that. It isn't necessary that I should," Rawley broke in impatiently. "My concern is merely the engineering problem you've got on your hands. As to the details and the means of putting the idea into execution, I'm not sure that I want to know. I might be hauled up as a witness, sometime—and what I don't know I won't have to lie about."

"That's right. That's the way to talk," Young Jess approved. The diagram had evidently impressed him considerably. He stared at Rawley from under his heavy, lowering brows. Though he spoke as any illiterate white man of the West would speak, he looked like a full-blooded Indian. Rawley wondered which side of him did the thinking—if any. The worst of both sides, he guessed shrewdly.

"We ain't tellin' more'n we're obleeged to tell," Old Jess grumbled, lifting his greedy old eyes from the sketch. "We ain't sharin', neither! You're eatin' my grub—two of ye—"

"Grandfather!" Nevada sprang up and faced the old man furiously. "How can you dare! Have you forgotten that Mr. Rawlins and his partner saved my life and Grandmother's? Oh, what a groveling lot of brute beasts we have become!"

"Mr. Rawlins is my affair," Peter said sternly, catching Nevada's hand as she would have passed him and pulling her down to his knee. "I brought him here. He is doing this work for me. You two will profit by it, though it will not cost you so much as a crust of bread. Nevada is right, except that you strike me as being more like vultures. All you think of is what lies at the bottom of the river.

"The bigness of the achievement, the real significance of a lifetime's devotion to one tremendous demonstration of man's dominion over nature means less than nothing to you two. I asked Rawlins to look over our work and advise us. He's doing it. It's only by courtesy that you two were called in to hear what he has to say. It's out of friendship for *me* that he's going on with his study of the problems we have to solve.

"Why, damn you," he flared out suddenly—for all the world like King, of the Mounted—"you couldn't hire this man to do for you what he's doing for me for nothing!"

CHAPTER 17

CHANGED RELATIONS

Young Jess and Old Jess exchanged sidelong glances. Young Jess turned his head away from the group and spat out a quid of tobacco on to the porch floor, whereat Nevada frowned her disgust.

"Yeah—we know all about him doin' it fer *you*," he leered. He eyed the two through half-closed lids. "You played it slick, but not slick enough. When yuh thought up a name fer him, Pete, you'd oughta stuck to it, 'stid of changin' your mind first day he was here. Gladys knows. He told Nevada one name, an' you come along and changed it on him.

"Look at 'im, Dad! D' yuh ever see father an' son look more alike in your life? By—, you can't make a fool outa me, Pete, nor outa Gladys. Why don't yuh own up? *We* know you're his daddy. You can't claim to me an' Gladys you never throwed in with no woman! Not with that face, right there, callin' you a liar!"

Nevada started, and Peter's arm around her tightened restrainingly. She did not speak, although her lips parted in astonishment. She looked at Rawley and met his eyes fixed upon her questioningly. Nevada flushed and turned away her face, hiding it against Peter's cheek.

"Why didn't you tell me, Uncle Peter?" she whispered chidingly. "You could have trusted me—you know you could."

Peter's arm tightened again. His face was turned toward the Cramers. His lips were drawn up a bit at the corners in a smile, but his eyes were hard.

"Well, and what of it?" he asked calmly. "Suppose he *is* my son—what then?"

Young Jess was prying off a fresh chew of tobacco from a half-plug that filled his palm.

"Nothin', I guess. Only I want yuh to know we're wise to you. You mighta come out with it, 'stid of lyin' and beatin' about the bush, that's all. Any fool can see you two're close related. I seen it first thing, and so did Gladys."

"Is it anybody's business, besides his and mine?" Peter's voice was still calm, though it boded ill for Young Jess if he did not watch his tongue.

"Can't say as it is," Young Jess admitted. "Mebby his mother might think it was *her* business—whoever she is."

"Leave my mother out of this," Rawley cried hotly. "She's not—"

"Aw, what the hell do I care?" Young Jess rose and hitched up his sagging breeches. "Yuh can't fool me—that's all. And I will say I ain't afraid to have yuh go ahead and look the works over. My own *nephew* wouldn't double-cross his paw's family, I guess."

He left them, turning his head once to grin knowingly over his shoulder. Old Jess mumbled a general curse on all family ties, or anything that would interfere with his getting the gold out of the river, and followed. Ten steps away he saw what he believed to be a joke and went off cackling, "Pete's own son! he-he!"

Nevada shivered and pulled herself free from her Uncle Peter's arms. Her lips were pressed rather firmly together, and she avoided looking at either of the men.

"Well, you were the first to notice the likeness, Nevada," Peter reminded her banteringly.

"And you were the first to—no, my *cousin* was the first to lie to me about it!" Her voice was coldly disapproving. "I'm very sorry—I did think that I was worthy your full confidence, Uncle Peter. It seems that I have been mistaken all along. You have only pretended to trust me, and all these years—though that in itself doesn't so much matter, since there may have been good reason for keeping the secret, even from me. But when my—*cousin* came here, you must have known immediately who he was, Uncle Peter. It is that which hurts. You pretended to me that you never had seen him before, and that you were not quite willing that he should stay. And he—oh, I hate you both!"

Her voice broke quite unexpectedly. She gave an impatient, spurning gesture and fled.

Peter got out the solacing "makings" of a cigarette. He glanced at Rawley queerly and gave a cynical smile.

"Talk about the beautiful faith of your own people," he remarked philosophically. "Here's a sample for you. Even Nevada believes right away that I have lived a double life."

"It makes it damned awkward—this resemblance," Rawley muttered ruefully. "Young Jess ought to have his block knocked off."

"Dynamite wouldn't feaze Young Jess," Peter declared. "He and Gladys have cooked this up between them. 'Twouldn't have done any good to deny it, son. They wouldn't believe it unless it suited them. And if I convinced them, they'd want to know more than ever why we look so much alike. Poor old mother—I was thinking of her. I hope you don't mind?"

"Not in the way you mean," Rawley assured him discontentedly. "I only wish you were my father. That is, I would if— I hate to have Nevada feel that we both lied to her," he blurted helplessly.

For once, Uncle Peter was dense. He laughed quietly to himself.

"Oh, she'll get over that," he declared easily. "That's the drop of Spanish blood. Don't you worry about that, boy. On the whole, I'm rather relieved. I've caught Young Jess eyeing you; Old Jess, too, and even Gladys noticed, I think. I was waiting for one of them to mention the resemblance between us. I was braced for it. I meant to laugh it off, as just their imagination. This way, they think they have it all accounted for. It does save a good deal of dangerous speculation. I'm not guessing. I know that Old Jess used to take spells of jealousy. Anita—mother—has always been afraid of him. When I was just a kid, I threw up his gun when it was pointed at her heart, and the quarrel was over your—over my father. Something had brought up the subject, some chance remark. The Spanish in her flamed up, and she told him that she loved King. Then he pulled the gun. He may have been drunk—I don't remember that part.

"So you see, son, I know why she's in deadly fear of having him find it out. And there are other reasons why none of them must know. While he and Young Jess think I'm a Cramer, they will listen to me. I can keep things straight here. If they knew the truth, I'd probably have to leave." He lighted the cigarette, and Rawley watched his face revealed for a moment by the flare of the match.

"Boy," he went on, turning toward Rawley, "I've got to stay. I've grown up, I've spent my whole life dreaming of the dam. It isn't what we'll get out of it, altogether, though it's human and natural to want the gold, too. It's the *dam*. I've planned and worked for it so long. I've got to see it go through."

He smoked and meditated for awhile, staring down at the river, always slipping past him, always in a hurry to meet the tides; to mingle its mountain water with the salt of the ocean.

"I saw two men drown out there, once." He waved a hand toward the river. "I'd like to stop it running, just to show it who's master here." Another silence, and then he looked at Rawley. "You don't mind being thought my son?" There was a wistfulness in his tone. "If I thought you minded—"

Rawley shook himself out of his mood. He leaned forward and forced himself to smile at Peter.

"I don't mind, at all," he lied. "I hate to have Nevada think that I deliberately lied to her because I was ashamed of any such relationship. I—want to keep her confidence and respect—"

Strange words for the leaden depression that had come over him at her anger, but he was fairly sincere in their employment. He believed—because he was forcing himself to believe—that he merely liked Nevada very much, and admired her, and was anxious to preserve the friendly relations into which they had drifted. It amused him to be called "Fifth Cousin" in that whimsical tone she used for the term. He thrilled a little whenever she reminded him thus of the make-believe relationship. To be called her cousin was somehow quite different. There was a chill in the word—and any young man would rather be thrilled than chilled by a girl as beautiful, mentally and physically, as was Nevada.

"I'll tell her you didn't know you were my son," Peter was calmly planning aloud. "She'll believe it, if I tell her so. I have never lied to Nevada in my life. She'll believe whatever I tell her about this affair. She's bound to." He chuckled under his breath, still blinded by his relief at the attitude his family had taken. "A reputation for honesty comes in handy, sometimes!"

"You don't think, then, that it would be wise to tell Nevada the straight of it?" In spite of himself, Rawley spoke constrainedly. He wanted to appear nonchalant, even amused, but he knew that he was betraying himself to any man who chanced to observe him.

"I don't. The truth is not our secret, boy. It belongs to a silent, sad old woman who never speaks what's in her heart and so is not considered as having any feelings. Do you think the taint of Indian relations will do you the slightest harm? Tell me honestly."

"No. I'm young, but I have made a certain name for myself for all that. I have the name of never having been bought and never leaving a job until I have the correct data. My clients have never yet inquired into my personal affairs. They never will. They know I'm an American; that's about all that counts, these days, so far as your blood ties go."

"There isn't one chance in fifty that this will ever be known, even in this district. We keep to ourselves. The old man has made it plain, ever since I can remember, that he doesn't want his neighbors to come around the place. If you inquire amongst the miners and prospectors, you will hear that we are a tough outfit and best let alone. It is believed, as I told you, that we're just a bunch of breeds digging out a little gold—enough to support us. Dad's a half-crazy squaw-man, and Young Jess is mighty unpopular. Whatever business must be taken care of outside, I attend to myself. Or Nevada sometimes does it for me. She never talks with people except when it's necessary. Whenever she goes to Nelson, or to Las Vegas, my mother goes with her.

"Nevada would not mention the matter, in any case, but I must ask you not to tell her. Mother is almost uncanny at reading faces. She'd see at once that we had told the girl. She worships Nevada. It would break her heart if she saw that Nevada knew her secret. She's afraid of Old Jess, but that's partly because of what it would mean to the girl. She thinks Nevada would despise her for the sin of her youth. That's the way she put it, and there's this about an Indian: You can't pry an idea out of their minds, once it's firmly planted. Poor old mother broods over these things. She feels as if Nevada is her one hope of heaven, almost. To keep that girl pure and sweet is her religion. I promised her, by everything that she called sacred, that Nevada should never know; at least, not so long as her grandmother lives. So that's why," he finished gently, "I'm pleased at the turn it's taken. I don't mind anything they may hatch up about me, if it will protect poor old mother."

Rawley felt humbled. He remembered how old Anita had spat her contempt of the gold that could not buy her the things she had loved—and lost. In that gross, shapeless body, who could say how fine a soul might be hidden?

"It's all right," he said, after a minute. "I'll have to warn Johnny Buffalo, and then I'll adopt you for my dad, if you like. I can see how it simplifies matters here. But I'm afraid Nevada never will forgive—"

"Oh, she'll be proud of her new cousin, once she recovers from the shock of not being told first thing," Peter assured him gratefully. "I'm afraid I've spoiled that girl."

CHAPTER 18

THE JOHNNY BUFFALO UPRISING

Johnny Buffalo was on the warpath. Figuratively speaking, he was brandishing the tomahawk over the tribe of Cramer. The gods he worshiped had been blasphemed, the altar upon which he laid the gifts of his soul had been defiled.

In other words, Johnny Buffalo had lain in his bed and listened while Young Jess and his father jibed at Johnny Buffalo's two idols, in whose veins flowed the blood of his beloved sergeant. The blood of the Kings might not be made a mockery while Johnny Buffalo could lift one arm to fight. When Rawley returned to him, he was discovered out of his bed, braced against a table and trying unsuccessfully to load the old King rifle which he had first used to kill Mohaves on that day, fifty years ago, when King, of the Mounted, received the shot that changed his whole life.

The old Indian was shaking with weakness, but his eyes blazed with the war spirit of his tribe.

"They are dogs of Pahutes!" he exclaimed, when Rawley entered the room. "They would drag the virtue of good men in the mud. They shall retract. They shall know the truth! Or I shall kill."

With three long steps Rawley was beside him, his hand on the rifle barrel, touching the trembling, sinewy hand of Johnny Buffalo. But the old man would not yield the gun. His eyes neither softened nor lowered themselves before the steadfast blue eyes that were the heritage of the Kings.

"You better get back to bed," Rawley warned him, half-laughing. "If Peter comes and finds you up, there'll be the devil and all to pay. I guess we won't massacre anybody, Johnny—at least not tonight."

"I heard the half-breed make a mock of Peter and of you. I heard him say that Peter is your father. When he said that, he laughed. His laugh was evil. Now he shall kneel upon his knees and beg the forgiveness of Peter and of you. He shall say that he spoke a lie from his black heart that would like to see others vile, because he is vile. If he does not say that he lied, I shall kill him. And that half-breed cousin, Anita, shall own her sin and her son. It is not good that Peter should be thought the son of that old vulture, when we know that he is the son of my sergeant. He is not your father. He is your uncle. I will tell them so, and we will see then if they laugh!"

If unshakable dignity can rave, then Johnny Buffalo was raving. Rawley tried again to take the rifle gently from the Indian's grasp; but the brown fingers seemed to have grown fast to the barrel. Rawley hated to do it, but his word had been given to Peter and this unforeseen uprising must be quelled; he therefore took Johnny Buffalo firmly by the shot shoulder. The old man wilted in his grasp. Rawley leaned the rifle against the table and helped Johnny Buffalo back to his bed.

Subdued but knowing no surrender, Johnny Buffalo lay glaring up at Rawley, even while his lips were twisted with pain. With a singularly motherly motion, Rawley adjusted the pillows and smoothed the sheet.

"That's a nice way to act—start out gunning for my adopted family the minute I get one!" he scolded with mock severity. "Can't leave you a minute but you jump the reservation and go on the warpath. And here I thought you were civilized!"

He grinned, but in Johnny Buffalo's eyes the fire did not die. His thin, old lips would not soften to a smile. The immobility of his face reminded Rawley of what his Uncle Peter had just said about Indians: that it is impossible to pry an idea out of their minds, once it is firmly fixed there. Nevertheless, he sat down beside the bed and repeated to Johnny Buffalo all that Peter had said concerning Young Jess's charge. He was wise enough, however, to refrain from any attempt to rouse sympathy in Johnny's heart for that pathetic culprit, Anita. Rather, he flattered himself by declaring that Peter was pleased because the tribe of Cramer believed him Rawley's father, and he emphasized the need of protecting Peter's influence over the two men, and his and Nevada's interest in the river gold. The mocking laughter of Young Jess, he declared, was not worthy a second thought.

It took Rawley just three hours to bring about an unconditional surrender to Peter's wishes in the matter. Even so, Rawley went to his own bed fagged but feeling that he had done pretty well, considering Johnny Buffalo's first intention. But as an indemnity to the old man's pride, Rawley had faithfully promised that he would get their camp outfit up from its hiding place on the morrow, and that he would pitch their tent as far as was practicable from the tribe of Cramer. Johnny Buffalo, it appeared, would not attempt to hold himself responsible for what might happen if he were compelled to listen to further inanities from Gladys, or to hear the voices of Old Jess or Young Jess or Anita. Nevada he very kindly excepted from the general condemnation of the tribe. And Peter, of course, was a King. He therefore could do no wrong—in the eyes of Johnny Buffalo.

It was a secret relief to Rawley that the change could be placed in the form of a concession to the Indian's pride. His own pride was demanding that he should move under his own canvas roof and eat the bread—so to speak—of his own buying. He had never felt quite right about taking Nevada's cabin. He happened to know that their occupancy had forced her to many little makeshifts. Then the jibe of Old Jess had made his position as a guest intolerable, in spite of the quick championship of Nevada and Peter. He had felt obliged to consider, however, Johnny Buffalo's welfare. The old man was not recovering as quickly as he should. Rawley had felt constrained to stay on his account; but now it seemed likely that a change to their own tent would really be beneficial. He had not dreamed that Johnny Buffalo's Indian pride had been daily martyred by the presence of Anita and Gladys.

"The scion of chiefs," Johnny Buffalo had declaimed bitterly, "should not be forced to become a companion of the squaws. Anita knows the etiquette of our tribe. Yet she would humiliate me by forcing me to listen to her chatter. Bah! I am not a squaw, nor a lover of squaws. Take me to our camp, my son. There I need not submit to the indignity of their presence."

So the next morning, when Peter stopped by the porch for a minute on his way to work, Rawley told him honestly what it was that he and Johnny Buffalo had burned a light so late the night before to discuss. Peter seemed to understand and offered the burros and Nevada for his service. Rawley grinned over the manner in which Peter had made the offer, but he made no comment. The burros and Nevada would be very acceptable, he said.

"I had a talk with Nevada last night," Peter added. "You'll find she's all over her temper. And she knows all the good camping places between here and El Dorado. You couldn't stay down there in the canyon; it's too hot. There are places, like this basin, where the breeze strikes most of the day. I want you close. I'll have Nevada show you a place down the river, on one of my claims. I don't suppose you'll object to camping on my land, will you?"

Rawley would not, and he said so. And after breakfast he started out with Nevada, following the two burros which went nipping down the river under empty packsaddles. There seemed to be certain advantages in becoming a cousin of Nevada, Rawley discovered. Their chaperonage had been practically abandoned; they were accompanied by the burros and only one dog. The trailing cloud of young Cramers were sharply called off by Aunt Gladys, and Nevada drove the other dogs back with rather accurately aimed stones. Anita, for some reason which Rawley was not sufficiently acute to fathom, failed altogether to put in an appearance. It was the first time since Rawley came into the basin that Nevada prepared to set off without her grandmother.

Nevada, in her high-laced boots, khaki breeches and white shirt open at the throat, walked with her easy stride down the faint trail behind the burros. Rawley followed her, wondering man-fashion what thoughts she was thinking, how she felt about him, whether she was glad to be setting out like this with him for trail partner instead of her grandmother, and what she thought of him as a cousin.

He was not a particularly shy young man; there was too much of his grandfather in his make-up not to have had certain little romantic adventures of his own. He would have told you, with a bit of cynicism in his tone, that he knew girls and that they were all alike. But he was beginning to discover that he did not know Nevada Macalister. Now that he seemed to have become irrevocably her cousin by diplomacy and tribal belief, he was disposed to make what use he could of the relationship. But after half a mile of traveling with no more than an occasional monosyllable for Nevada's contribution to the conversation, Rawley was compelled to admit to himself that the cousin business was not working as he would like to have it.

In view of her emotional outbreak last night, Rawley could not quite bring himself to the point of asking her outright how she liked her new cousin. But the question kept tickling his tongue, nevertheless. Then he reflected that Nevada was rather generously supplied with cousins, none of them definitely desirable. From that thought it was only a short jump to the next inevitable conclusion. Nevada, he decided, had placed him mentally alongside those other pestiferous cousins, the offspring of Gladys and Young Jess. Or if she had not, she was surely according him the same treatment.

As a romantic chapter in their acquaintance, the trip was a flat failure. Nevada was businesslike—and aloof. Rawley's faint hope that some unforeseen incident would occur to shock Nevada out of her insouciant mood died of inanition. The camp outfit they found exactly as it had been left, except that a rat had rashly decided to make a nest in a fold of the wrapped tent. This did not seem to interest Nevada in the slightest degree. She helped him with the packing and did not seem to care whether he hurt his newly healed arm or not. They returned as they had gone—Nevada silent, following the burros that plodded sedately homeward under their loads, Rawley trailing after her in complete discouragement over the rebuffs his friendly overtures had received.

They did not so much as see a rattlesnake.

CHAPTER 19

THE EAGLE STRIKES

The month of inaction which followed fretted Johnny Buffalo nearly as much as the companionship of the squaws had done. In his boyhood he had been trained to serve his sergeant. For fifty years that service had been un-interrupted by ill health or accident. It irked him now to lie idle and watch Rawley burn his fingers on the handle of the frying pan, or wash the dishes from which Johnny Buffalo had been fed.

The long days when Rawley was away with Peter were lonesome. There was nothing to do but to seek sedulously after comfort, which is so rare a thing in a camp beside the Colorado in summer that every little whiff of cool breeze is prized, every little change in the monotonous diet makes an impromptu banquet. Sometimes Nevada walked down to camp with things she herself had cooked; but Johnny Buffalo had taken care to insult Gladys and Anita so definitely that they refused to come near him.

"I am well enough now to walk," he announced one evening, when he had insisted upon cooking the supper. "Today I climbed to the top of that hill. In a sack on my shoulder I carried a rock that weighed twenty-five pounds. I am well. We can go now and find the gold."

"You packed a rock up that hill?" Rawley laid his hands on his hips and squinted at the hill indicated. "You ought to get sun-struck for that. But if you think you're up to it, we can hit the trail to the mountain about day after to-morrow. I'll have to drive up to Nelson to-morrow to get more grub and the mail. You might borrow the burros from Peter and meet me at the mouth of the canyon. That will save time and give you a chance to try out your shoulder."

Johnny Buffalo actually grinned and stepped more briskly than was his normal gait, as if he would prove himself as spry as any young man of twenty-six.

Thus for ten days they wandered through rocky gorges, and climbed the steep sides of hills, and returned to their camp for fresh supplies and a day or two of rest. The "great and high mountain" in the distance had seemed to recede before them as they walked. They had been three days in reaching its base. Another two days had served to take them over the top and down on the other side westward. There their trail seemed to end, for that side of the mountain was almost entirely covered with loose rubble of decomposed rock. There were no cliffs or jagged rocks anywhere that they could see.

Since Peter had burned the code, and the list of references was in St. Louis with Grandfather's Bible, they were compelled for the present to depend altogether on memory. But Rawley could repeat the code from beginning to end without hesitation. The only explanation, then, of their failure was that either he had made a mistake somewhere in writing down the marked passages or Grandfather King had marked them wrong.

Rawley astonished Nevada somewhat by asking to borrow her Bible. But when he received it he could not remember the references, so that he was no better off than before. One thing was certain: the only great and high mountain within sight of El Dorado, looking north, with "Cedar trees in abundance scattered over the face of the high mountain" had no cliffs upon its western side. When the mountain itself failed to measure up with the description, the whole code fell flat. It was a big country, and it was a rough country. A man might spend a lifetime in the search.

"My sergeant did not lie," Johnny Buffalo contended stubbornly. "He was a great man. He did not make mistakes. When he said the gold was there, in the clefts of the jagged rocks, it was there. He said it."

"He said it—fifty years ago," Rawley retorted rather impatiently. "I didn't see any gold formation anywhere on that mountain. It's true that 'Gold is where you find it'; but it leaves earmarks in its particular neighborhood for the man who knows how to read the signs. If there is any gold on that mountain, some one carried it there."

"There is gold where my sergeant said there is gold," Johnny Buffalo insisted. "I shall look until I find."

"You will need winter quarters, then," Rawley observed grimly, rummaging for his sweater. October was hard upon them, and the wind was chill. "Tell you what, Johnny. I'll have to get out and earn some more money, anyway. I have a dandy offer that came in the last mail. It's a big job, and it ought to net me a thousand dollars, easy. You remember that spring we passed, back here three or four miles? It isn't far from the trail. There's plenty of wood, and a little prospecting there might turn up something. I noticed as we came through that the country looked pretty good. I'll help build you a cabin there and get you fixed up for winter. Then I'll go and report on this mine—and come back, maybe, after I'm through. Peter'll see that you have everything you need while I'm gone."

Johnny Buffalo nodded approval. "All winter I will hunt for the gold my sergeant gave you," he declared. "He said it was on the high mountain. I shall find it."

Rawley had long ago learned that argument was a waste of time and breath. All the while they were building the cabin, Johnny Buffalo talked of finding the gold while Rawley was gone; and Rawley did not discourage him. He was saving a secret for the old man, and he was in a hurry to have it complete before he must leave.

Rawley's mother had offered for sale the furniture and belongings of the west wing, and Rawley had surreptitiously bought them for a fair price through the friendly dealer who had known him since Rawley was a child. The things were stored ready for shipping. Rawley wrote for them; and on the day when the truck was to bring them to the end of the road nearest Johnny's winter quarters, he encouraged Johnny to start on a two-day trip to the mountain. Peter and Nevada arrived with the burros before Johnny had much more than walked out of sight.

Never mind what it cost those three in haste and hard work. When Johnny Buffalo dragged himself wearily to the cabin at dusk on the second day, he walked into an atmosphere poignantly familiar. Even the wheel chair had arrived with the rest of the things. That, however, Rawley had left crated and stored in the little shed adjoining the cabin. Everything else he had unpacked and arranged as he had seen them in the west wing.

Peter and Nevada had lingered, waiting for the old man's return; but after all they lacked the courage to follow him when he went inside. He was gone a long while. The three sat out on a rock before the cabin and watched the moon slide up from behind a jagged peak across the river. They did not talk. Splendid dreams held them silent—dreams and their conscious waiting for Johnny Buffalo.

Even when he came from the cabin there was no speech amongst them; Johnny Buffalo looked as though he had been talking with angels.

A few days after that, Rawley went away to his work, content because he had wheedled from Nevada a promise to write to him and keep him informed of Johnny Buffalo's welfare and the progress of the dam. He expected to return in a month. But instead of coming he wrote a long letter.

He had finished the mine report and was about to leave for Washington, he said. The president of the School of Mines where he had studied wrote him, asking if he would not offer his services to the government, which was badly in need of men for research work. Minerals hitherto in little demand had suddenly become tremendously important—for while the country was not yet at war it was quietly preparing for such an emergency. He told Nevada that, much as he disliked to change his plans, it was too good a chance to pass up, even if his loyalty to the government did not impel him to accept the tacit offer. He would come in contact with some of the biggest men in the game, he wrote.

In April, when war was actually declared, Rawley was already thoroughly shaken down into his job. He still wrote twice a month to Nevada, but his letters became shorter—as if they were written in stray minutes snatched from his duties. An interesting assortment of postmarks Nevada collected during the ensuing two years. Every State in the Union that could flaunt a mineral product seemed to be represented. Her replies were usually about two jobs behind him, so that letters with the Nelson, Nevada, postmark trailed patiently after Rawley wherever he went.

During the war, his mother saw him just once, when he happened to be passing through St. Louis and could stop over for a few hours. Johnny Buffalo, Peter, and Nevada saw him not at all.

CHAPTER 20

NEVADA ANALYZES

On a certain day in June, Rawley left his car at Nelson and started afoot down the trail to Cramers. Although the war was over he was still in the service of the government. A bit leaner, a bit harder-muscled, steadier of eye and of purpose, with a broader vision, too. Rawley had been making good.

After more than two years away from this particular point on the Colorado, old emotions came sweeping back upon him as he caught sight of this bold peak or that wild gorge, familiar landmarks along the trail. Halfway to Cramers, he turned aside and followed a dim trail that went climbing tortuously up a narrow canyon and so reached a bold hillside where the cabin of Johnny Buffalo squatted snugly beside the spring.

Johnny was absent—probably still hunting for the gold, Rawley thought, as he grinned to himself. After so long a time spent wholly in service to others, with the weal of his country always in the front of his mind, the search for his grandfather's gold mine seemed a shade less important than it had been two years ago. He had the Bible and the old diary with him, but that was partly to please Johnny Buffalo and because he thought the books might be interesting to Peter. For himself he had not much hope of finding the cleft in the rocks; for Johnny Buffalo the quest would be a wholesome object in life. Johnny Buffalo would continue the search from no selfish motive, but in a zeal for Rawley's welfare. There was a difference, Rawley thought, in the way you go at a thing.

He left a note for Johnny on the table and went on down the hill and back into the trail to the river. At the edge of the basin he stopped and surveyed the somewhat squalid huddle of buildings, wondering why it was he felt almost as if this were a home-coming. Perhaps it was a fondness for his Uncle Peter, and because Nevada had kept the place fresh in his mind with the letters she had written him.

Two strange dogs were added to the hysterically barking pack that rushed out at him as he drew near. Five children instead of four grouped themselves and stared. Gladys appeared in the open doorway of her cabin; a fatter Gladys, with another baby riding astride her hip. The tribe of Cramer was waxing strong.

He was sure that Gladys recognized him, but with the stolidity of the race which dominated her nature, she merely stared and gave no sign of welcome. Rawley kicked a dog or two that seemed over-serious in their intentions and kept straight on. When he reached the hard-trodden zone immediately before the cabin, he lifted his hat and spoke to Gladys.

"Hullo," she grinned fatuously. "We don't see you for a long time."

Anita came to the door, looked out and nodded with an imperturbable gravity that always disconcerted Rawley. He asked for Peter and Nevada. Peter was at work, Gladys told him vaguely. And the clicking of a typewriter in the rock dugout told him where Nevada might be found.

Rawley was amazed, almost appalled at the agitation with which he faced her. In the press of his work, of meeting strange people and seeing strange places, he had thought the image of Nevada was blurred; a charming personality dimmed by distance and the urge of other thoughts, other interests. But when he held her hand, looked up into her eyes as she stood on the step of the porch, he had a curious sensation of having been poignantly hungry for her all this while. He found himself fighting a desire to take her in his arms and kiss her red mouth that was smiling down at him. He had to remind himself that he hadn't the right to do that; that Nevada had never given him the faintest excuse to believe that he would ever be privileged to kiss her.

He sat in the homemade chair on the porch and, because looking at Nevada disturbed him unaccountably, he stared down at the river while they talked. He wondered if Nevada really felt as unconcerned over his coming as she sounded and looked. She was friendly, frankly pleased to see him— and he resented the fact that she could speak so openly of her pleasure. She could have said to any acquaintance the things she said to him, he told himself savagely; she was like all her letters, friendly, unconstrained, impersonal. It amazed him now to remember that he had been delighted with her letters. If at first he had wished them more diffident, as if she felt the sweet possibilities of their friendship, he had come to thank the good Lord for one sensible girl in the world. Nevada had no nonsense, he frequently reminded himself. She didn't expect the mushy love-making flavor in their correspondence. He could feel sure of Nevada.

Now it maddened him to feel so sure of her; so sure of her composed friendliness that left no little cranny for love to creep in. She liked him—in the same way that she liked Peter. He could even believe that she liked him almost as well as she liked Peter; that he stood second in her affections before all the world. Covertly he studied her whenever the conversation made a glance into her eyes quite natural and expected. She met each glance with smiling unconcern—the most disheartening manner a lover can face.

"You've grown, Cousin Rawley," she said. "Yes, I've got your home name on my tongue—from Johnny Buffalo, I suppose. Well, you *have* grown. I don't mean your body alone, though you have filled out and your shoulders look broader and stronger, somehow, even though you may not weigh a pound more. But you've grown mentally. There's a strength in your face—an added strength. And your eyes are so *much* different. You keep me wondering, in between our talk, what is in your mind—back of those eyes. That's a sure sign that a great, strong soul is looking out. It's been an awful two years, hasn't it?"

"It has," Rawley answered quietly, his mind reverting swiftly to several close squeaks from the enemy at home.

"Two years ago you'd have said 'You *bet*!' just like that. 'It has' wouldn't have seemed expressive enough. That's what I'm driving at. Now you can just say 'It has', and something back of your eyes and your voice gives the punch. Cousin Rawley, you can cut out all exclamatory phrases from now on, if you like. The punch is there. I've seen other men back from service. One or two had that same reserve power. The others were merely full of talk about how they won the war. It's funny."

Rawley did not think it was funny. She had lifted his heart to his throat with her flattering analysis and had dropped it as a child drops a toy for some fresher interest. He was all this and all that—and she had seen other men return with the same look. Right there Rawley silently indulged himself in his strongest exclamatory phrase in his vocabulary.

Nevada had turned her head to call something in Indian, replying to her grandmother's shrill voice. She did not see what lay back of Rawley's eyes at that moment—worse luck.

"Well, I wanted to get in and help. Gladys and Grandmother knitted sweaters and socks, and so did I. I wanted to be a Red Cross nurse—was there a girl in America who didn't?—but Uncle Peter wouldn't let me go. He said I was needed here, to help hold things together. But I'll tell you what I did do. I went into the old diggings and mined. I found a stringer or two they hadn't bothered with, and I mined for dear life and sent every last color to the Red Cross. Uncle Peter was helping, too—I mean giving all he could—but I wanted to do something my own self. And do you know, Cousin Rawley, Grandmother got right in with me and shoveled gravel to beat the cars! I didn't write you about it—it seemed so little to do. And besides, I didn't realize then the importance of living up to you. But with that—that Sphinxlike strength you've acquired, I'll just inform you that your Injuns were on the job."

"I knew it, anyway. And you did more good than your personal service in hospital could have done. It took money to keep the nurses going that were on the job, remember."

"Two years ago," mused Nevada, "you'd have called me on that Sphinx remark and for calling myself Injun. Yes, you have grown. You can keep to the essential point much better than before. Well, and how is Johnny Buffalo? I haven't seen him for a week."

"Nor I for over two years. I left a note on his table. Nevada, how long has he had that wheel chair of Grandfather's standing across the table from his own?"

Nevada looked at him studyingly until Rawley, for all his vaunted strength, found his eyes sliding away from the directness of her gaze.

"Cousin Rawley, if you have grown hard, you won't sympathize with Johnny Buffalo, or understand. For more than a year, now, he has believed that his sergeant comes and sits in that chair to keep him company. He really believes it. You mustn't laugh at him, will you?"

Rawley was staring down at the always hurrying river. He said nothing.

"Just don't laugh at Johnny," Nevada urged. "And don't argue with him. It's a *comfort* to him to believe that. He doesn't always keep the chair at the table. Sometimes it is by the window, or close to the fire when I go there. I think he moves it just as he would if your grandfather were living there with him."

"That's nonsense!" Rawley spoke sharply.

"It's a comfort to Johnny Buffalo," Nevada observed calmly. "I'm glad I saw you first, if that is your attitude. Johnny Buffalo has been brighter and happier, ever since he first thought he saw your grandfather walk in at the door and stand smiling down at him. He insists that his sergeant has his legs back, and that not a day passes but he comes and sits awhile with him. He—there's something he won't tell me, but he's very anxious to see you, especially. I think it is something concerning your grandfather."

"Oh, well, if it's any comfort to the old man—" Rawley frowned, but his tone was yielding.

"Then do, please, act as if you believed your grandfather is there when Johnny says he is there! You needn't pretend to see him. I never do. I always say I can't see him; and then Johnny Buffalo tells me just how he looks, and what he says. It pleases him so! He will be sure to have his sergeant meet you, Cousin Rawley. And you must pretend to believe. He's just waiting for you to come, so that something important can take place. He wouldn't even tell Uncle Peter what it is." Nevada leaned dangerously toward Rawley and laid a hand on his, apparently as unconscious of the possible results as is a child who picks up an explosive.

"Promise me, Cousin Rawley, that you'll be careful not to hurt Johnny's feelings." Her hand closed warmly over his.

Rawley's silence was not the stubbornness she seemed to think it. He was holding his teeth clamped together, trying to reach that quiet strength of soul she had naïvely credited him with possessing. He had tried to hold himself together, to refrain from making a fool of himself, and she had mistaken the effort for strength of soul, he thought with secret chagrin. Oh, as to Johnny Buffalo—

"I should feel very badly if I knew that I had hurt any one's feelings," he said. "Least of all, Johnny Buffalo. If he can be happy with an hallucination, I shall not disturb his happiness. But that means a mental letting go, according to my way of thinking. When he takes to having delusions, he's weakening. I don't like that. I can't be with him, you see. I have a few days to myself, and then I must be on the job again."

"Oh. I thought you would be here for awhile, anyway."

Rawley tried to extract some comfort from Nevada's tone of regret. But her regret was, after all, too candid to mean anything especial, he feared. He did not make the mistake of asking her if she really minded his going again so soon.

"How is the dam coming along?" That, at least, would be a sane subject, he hoped.

"Oh—it's coming along. I believe they're all across the river, today."

She did not seem eager to pursue that subject, either. He began to wonder more than ever what was in her mind. Something she would not talk about, he knew. But presently she pulled herself out of her preoccupation.

"Can you imagine that sliding volume of water being halted in all its hurry and made to stop running to the gulf; thwarted in its whole purpose?" she asked dreamily. "I've watched it all my life. Sometimes it's savage and boils along, with driftwood and débris of all kinds—I saw it at Needles, once, in flood time. It was awful. Then to think how three men have lived beside it and planned and worked for years and years, to stop all that tremendous movement and pen it up in the hills and—it seems to me that it's like life. It goes hurrying along, too, for years and years, and its power is devastating and awful, sometimes. And then—after all, it's so easy to stop it."

"Yes," said Rawley, his thoughts forced back again to things he would like to forget. "It's easy to stop it. Like that." He snapped his fingers. "A man standing so close to me our shoulders rubbed was stopped in the middle of a sentence. We were talking. I asked him something about the mine. He was telling me. A cable broke, and the end of it snapped our way and caught him in the head. Life stopped right there, so far as he was concerned. He wasn't given time to finish what he was saying."

Nevada was staring at him, her lips parted, the easy flow of her thoughts halted by the horror of the picture he had drawn with a few quiet words. So few words—spoken so quietly, she thought fleetingly.

"I—didn't know—right beside you! It might have—Weren't you hurt?"

Rawley lifted a hand to his cheek, where a fine, white line was drawn.

"The tip of one strand flicked me there," he said. "Made a nasty gash."

The pallor in Nevada's face deepened. She shivered as if a sudden chill had struck her skin.

"Well," said Rawley, after a further five minutes of staring at the river. "I'll be getting back. Tell Peter I'll be down again. Or if he can take the time, have him come up, will you?"

"Why don't you call him father?" Nevada asked him. "You aren't ashamed of him, are you?"

Rawley looked at her, the truth on the tip of his tongue. But he closed his lips a bit more firmly, smiled down at her and shook his head.

"Peter and I understand each other," he told her enigmatically and went away.

He quite agreed with Nevada. Even in times of peace, life could almost be called devastating.

CHAPTER 21

THE TRUTH ABOUT RICHES

"To-morrow," said Johnny Buffalo, with a transparent air of triumph, "we will go to the cleft in the rocks, by the path which no man knoweth, and you shall go down into the deep pit and find the gold."

"What's that?" Rawley looked up from crowding tobacco into his pipe after a most satisfying supper. "You found it, did you?"

"My sergeant led me to the place," Johnny Buffalo stated gravely. "There was a mistake. The great and high mountain which holds the gold was not that greatest mountain which we can see. There were cedar trees scattered over the face of the mountain when my sergeant found the gold. That was many years ago. Now there are no cedar trees or trees of any kind. That is why we could not find the place. One year ago, my sergeant came and led me to the spot."

"Is the gold there?" Rawley leaned forward, studying the old Indian through half-shut eyes.

"I did not go down into the pit. My sergeant would not permit me to go. He says that you will go, and that you will there learn the truth about riches. He told me that I must not go down and look, for it would not be good that I should see what will be revealed to you." Johnny Buffalo spoke as if he were reciting a lesson. His face was turned toward the empty wheel chair, drawn before the open window.

Rawley frowned over the lighting of his pipe. The mystical message made little impression on his mind, but he did worry over the Indian's implicit belief in it. His promise to Nevada bound him to silence on the subject of hallucinations, however, even though he had in mind several things which he would like to say.

Johnny Buffalo, sitting straight-backed with his hands spread palm down on his knees, related all the incidents of his life during the past two years. Queo had been accused of other murders, and after a particularly heinous one at the Techatticup mine had disappeared altogether. Once Johnny Buffalo had seen him and had taken a shot at him, but again the gun had kicked—or perhaps his aim was not too good. He had missed. Once his cabin had been robbed of food, and he suspected the outlaw of committing the depredation. Of the tribe of Cramer he would say little. Not once in the two years had he been in their camp, he said. Peter and Nevada came often to see him. They were good to him. His sergeant had come, and he had seen him. His sergeant sometimes spoke to him. Perhaps Rawley would see him.

Rawley did not think so, but he refrained from voicing his doubt. As tactfully as possible he avoided the subject and told some of his own adventures, to which Johnny Buffalo listened with polite attention. It was plain to Rawley that his mind was given up to another matter, and that he was merely waiting with his Indian patience until he could guide his adopted son to the secret cleft on the side of the mountain.

"No man has been before us," he declared emphatically, when Rawley questioned him. "Bushes have grown in the cleft until I could not have found it or suspected that a cleft was there if my sergeant had not shown me the spot. The cleft is there. I have seen it. The bushes are very old, and there is much dead wood. There is the great heap of stones, and there has been a dead tree. But it is gone many years and only the root is left to show that it once stood joined to the great heap of stones. When the sun comes I will show you."

He was punctiliously true to his promise, for the sun was not ten minutes above the peak across the river when Rawley stood beside the "Great heap of stones ... joined to a dry tree", or what even he could see had once been a dry tree. It had been an unmerciful trail, and he could easily believe that it was a path which the eye of man had not seen. Indeed, it was not a path at all, but a line of least obstruction through an upheaval of what Rawley's trained eyes recognized as iron-stained quartz and porphyry.

The place was almost inaccessible, and from a short distance it resembled a blow-out of granite so much that no prospector would trouble to investigate. Besides, Johnny Buffalo explained that this had been a popular habitat of snakes, and that he had spent a great deal of his time, since the location of the spot, in hunting rattlesnakes. He proudly added that he had earned many dollars in extracting the oil and in selling the skins. He feared that he had not gathered them all, however, and he warned Rawley against setting his foot carelessly amongst the rocks.

Johnny Buffalo then gathered dry leaves and started a fire in the brush. So much dead wood underlay the growth that the crevice was presently a furnace.

"If any snakes are there, they will come out," he observed grimly. "Also, light will go down, so that you will not stumble in darkness. I know what my sergeant meant in the message: 'Take heed, now ... that is exceeding deep.' You will need light."

Rawley nodded. He was watching the flames curiously.

"By Jove, Johnny, I believe you are right," he exclaimed, pointing. "Do you see that? There is a strong draught from *beneath*. There's an opening down there, sure as anything. And I'll admit to you right now that this is gold formation blown out here. The iron stain is a good mask for it. I can readily believe that it hasn't been prospected."

"My sergeant does not speak lies," Johnny Buffalo retorted imperturbably. "I know that it is so." Whereupon he gave chase to a rattlesnake that had slipped out from between two tilted bowlders and went sliding sinuously away. With a crude trident, long of handle and tough and light, he pinned the snake to the ground and neatly sliced off its head with a light ax which he carried suspended from his belt.

"Here's another," Rawley told him, and Johnny Buffalo, moving with surprising agility, caught that one also.

"For a time I gathered the venom in a bottle," he informed Rawley in his serious tone. "But now I take only the body. When you go down into the pit there will be no snakes until you reach the bottom. Then you look out."

Rawley was sufficiently impressed to borrow the trident, which was barbed and could kill as easily as it could capture. So, when the fire had died and the rocks had cooled a little, he went down into the pit.

A blowhole it was, such as is frequently found in a country so torn by volcanic action. As he descended he read the signs at a glance—signs which to a layman would have meant nothing whatever. Beneath all this, said the rocks to Rawley, there should be gold. His pulse quickened as he worked his way downward, seeking foothold precariously where he might. The thought that Grandfather King, of all the millions of men in the world, was the only one who had ever dared these depths, thrilled him with pride. Not even the Indians had known of it, he was sure. He wondered how his grandfather had managed the snakes, and then it occurred to him that Grandfather King might have discovered this place late in some season after the snakes had been overcome by their winter lethargy.

He breathed freer when his feet crunched in coarse gravel and he knew that he had reached the bottom. He had encountered no snakes, which he considered good luck, especially since he had needed hands and feet and all his great strength to negotiate the descent, and had been compelled to abandon the trident before he had gone fifty feet. As nearly as he could estimate, the blowhole was well over two hundred feet in depth, and there were places where he had no more than comfortable room for his body. The flashlight hung on a thong around his neck showed him how terrific had been the explosion that had torn this crevice open to the surface.

Rawley stood in a cavern probably ten feet high and extending farther than his light could penetrate in two directions, which his pocket compass showed him as east and west. So far the code was correct. The width he estimated as being approximately thirty feet, although the walls drew in or receded sharply, as the formation turned hard or soft. He faced toward the east and went forward, pacing three feet at a stride, his flashlight throwing a white brilliance before him.

Seventy-two strides down the high, tunnel-like cavern brought him to the "River of pure water." There he stopped and stood, turning his light here and there upon the walls, the water, the gravel. His heart, that had been beating exultantly as his hopes rose higher, slumped and became a leaden weight.

Gold had been there. Of that he had no doubt whatever. But the placer had been mined—gutted and abandoned. He apprehended at once the truth; that here was an underground stream, one of the sunken rivers for which the desert country is famous—that, or a small branch of a sunken river. There must be some other point of ingress, one of which Grandfather King had no knowledge. Some one had come in by the other route and had taken the gold. The work had been done systematically, by miners who knew what they were about. A glance at the workings told him that.

Rawley turned his light down the stream. As far as its rays could pierce the dark of the cavern, the placer workings extended. He went on, following the windings of the stream and its natural tunnel. Now that he had discovered his grandfather's potential riches, the legacy which he had confidently believed was a fortune, Rawley was determined to see just where the watercourse would lead him.

He thought that he must have followed it for a mile or more, although it could have been farther. All the way along, the gravel had been worked and the gold taken out. A suspicion had been growing in his mind, and quite suddenly it crystallized into certainty. He walked into a larger cavern, the full extent of which he could not see from that point. There he stopped and considered.

Near at hand, all around him, black cans were piled. He did not need the second glance to tell him what it was he had run into. Here was the secret hoard of black powder which the Cramers had been gathering together for years. Here was the powder that would, in the space of a breath, tear down two mountain sides and halt the flow of a great river—if what they hoped and dreamed should come to pass.

The Cramers, then, had taken the gold which Grandfather King had discovered. Here was a part of it, no doubt, transformed into tons of explosive. Rawley's grin was sardonic as he surveyed the piled cans. It would be a bitter ending for their quest that he must show to Johnny Buffalo, he thought.

He walked on slowly and halted suddenly when a light showed ahead. Some one was coming toward him, and Rawley instinctively snapped off his light and moved to one side. War habits were still strong upon him, and in any case he would not trust the Cramers.

Presently he saw that it was Peter, and called to him and went forward. Peter was astonished, but he was also glad to see Rawley.

"I meant to walk over to your place this evening," he explained. "We're so busy, right now—"

"With the dam?" Rawley sat down on a keg of powder, started to roll a cigarette and remembered that it might not be wise.

"Yes. We're loading her as fast as we can. It's a big job, and the old man is getting fractious over the delay." Peter sat down on another keg and took off his hat, wiping his forehead with his sleeve. "It's going to be a blistering day outside. Seems like an ice-box in here. How did you come?"

Then Rawley told him.

Peter listened in complete silence, his arms folded on his knees. When Rawley had finished, Peter straightened up with a sigh.

"I never dreamed we had cut into your ground," he said heavily. "I thought, as you probably did, that the code described an old, underground watercourse some miles from here. But you must be right, this is it. Old Jess discovered gold near the river, at a point where this stream back here dives under the cliffs and empties, most likely, into the river somewhere under the water line. It was rich; a heap richer than any one ever dreamed, I guess. And the fact that the stream flowed right into the Colorado may have given him his first idea of gathering the gold that had washed on into the river. If you come with me, I'll show you."

"I can't be too long," said Rawley. "Johnny Buffalo's up on top, waiting for me to come back with my pockets full of gold. It's going to be hard on the old man, especially since Grandfather's gold went into the clutches of Old Jess. I don't know that I'd better tell him. At the same time," he mused aloud, "I can't tell him that there isn't any gold; he is so firmly convinced that his sergeant told the truth. He'd have to know that some one else has beat us to it."

Peter turned and looked at him thoughtfully. "I'll give you some nuggets to take up to him," he said. "Old Johnny's pretty keen, and he holds a bad grudge against Young Jess and the old man. If I could, you know I'd replace the gold we got from under that blowhole. But I can't. It has all been spent, practically. Gone into the dam, along with the rest."

Rawley laid his hand on Peter's shoulder and left it there.

"You wouldn't do anything of the kind," he laughed. "That darned dam idea of yours is catching. I've got it, and got it bad. If that gold you beat me to will tip enough rock into the river to make a good job of the dam, I'm satisfied. All I ask is that you let me know when you're ready so I can see her go. Are you doing as I advised—preparing to shoot her with electricity?"

Peter nodded. "Old Jess kicked on the cost, but we showed him how it was the only safe way. She's all loaded, across the river. We did that during low water and carried the wiring across up to a high, overhead cable that crosses the river all ready to be hooked up to the battery. I talked with a mining man about explosives and found out some things that came in pretty handy, I guess. I got a hint not to break the ground with dynamite enough so that the power of the black powder would be killed in the seams opened up. We didn't use so much dynamite, after all. We're depending on the black powder."

"I still warn you against it," said Rawley. "But if you can't be stopped, I do want to see the fireworks. There's a pretty engineering problem there, and it will be worth a good deal to see how it works out." His thoughts returned again to the old Indian waiting up on the hill. "I'll buy some gold from you, Uncle Peter, if you have it handy. I'll tell old Johnny it's all I could find; I think I can satisfy the old fellow with the thought that his sergeant had it straight."

Peter left him for five minutes and returned, carrying a small canvas sack.

"Here's a handful of specimens I tucked into a niche in the rocks, intending to give them to Nevada for a necklace or something," he told Rawley. "But Nevada can have diamond necklaces when the dam goes in. You take these, boy. Maybe some of them sort of belong to you, anyway."

"Lord, *I* don't want them," Rawley protested. "I'll give them to Johnny Buffalo, though. It will keep him from worrying about it. More than all that, it will keep him off the warpath, the old catamount."

CHAPTER 22

GREATER THAN GOLD

Johnny Buffalo held a handful of nuggets in his hard, brown palms. His eyes shone whenever he looked toward the old wheel chair beside the window. He listened to Rawley's explanation of why there would be no more gold, but the technical phraseology went completely over his head, and he smiled abstractedly and held up first one bit of gold and then another to the light. They were very heavy. They were beautiful. They had lain, hidden away all these years, just where his sergeant had said that they were hidden.

"'There is a path which no man knoweth,'" he muttered, when Rawley had finished and was waiting to see what effect his harangue about erosions and changed currents had taken on the Indian mind. "It is so. My sergeant said it, and it was the truth. My sergeant never lied. Always the words he spoke were true. I know it without proof. Now you have the proof, and you know it also."

"There won't be any more, you understand," Rawley repeated with finality. "My work is to examine these matters and report the truth about them. After examining what lies at the bottom of the pit, I am reporting to you that there will be no more gold—"

Johnny Buffalo stopped him with a hand lifted, palm out. "What was revealed to you in the pit is not good for me to know," he stated firmly. "My sergeant has said that you should know the truth about riches. He said that it would not be good that I should know the truth as you would know it."

"That's true, too," Rawley admitted, taken aback.

"The gold was there when my sergeant said that it was there. That is good. My sergeant did not say that there would always be gold where gold has been. I think that is the truth about riches which you have learned."

"You're right, Johnny." Rawley grinned at him ruefully. "If we've had any dream of being millionaires, we may as well forget it. Grandfather gave us the straight dope, and you found the cleft in the rocks. It isn't Grandfather's fault that the millions have moved on. So that's all of that, and the next thing is something else."

"The next thing is what is given us to do," said Johnny Buffalo solemnly. "We will do our duty, whatever that may be. Now I have no more searching for my sergeant's gold. I shall live here until it is time to go. I do not think it will be long."

Rawley looked at him anxiously, but he could not bring himself to speak what was in his mind. Johnny Buffalo would not understand that to the young death is a dreadful thing, to be shunned and never thought of voluntarily—an ogre that may snatch one away from the joys of living. After all, he thought, Johnny Buffalo had outlived his love of life. No one needed him. He had only to wait. Rawley wished that he could be with him longer and oftener, but that was not possible unless he were willing to sacrifice the work he loved. Even if he could bring himself to that, Johnny Buffalo would not permit it. It would break his heart to feel that he had hindered his sergeant's grandson.

"Your work," said Johnny Buffalo, almost as if he had been reading Rawley's thoughts, "is better than the gold. A man is great within himself, or he is nothing. The full pocket makes the empty head. It is greater fortune that you have honor and youth and work to perform. So my sergeant would tell you."

"You're right, Johnny," Rawley assented again. "If we'd found a ton of gold I think I'd have gone on with my work just the same. A man my age can't stop working for the sake of seeing how fast he can spend money. I couldn't, anyway."

"Then you do not need the gold. You can earn what you need and have the pleasure twice: in the getting and in the spending. So you have not lost."

"We're a great pair of philosophers," Rawley laughed, "or else we are eating sour grapes. Blamed if I know, sometimes, just where the difference lies. Or perhaps there isn't any, and crying sour grapes is true philosophy, after all."

Peter and Nevada, coming up the path, diverted the talk to lighter channels. Nevada, spying the gold, exclaimed over the odd pieces and took them in her cupped palm to admire each specimen by itself.

"They are yours, save this one which I shall keep," said Johnny Buffalo unexpectedly. "Rawley will not take them. I do not need gold. I have three friends and the spirit of my sergeant, who waits for me. I am rich. They are yours. Put them on a chain and hang them around your neck while yet it is white and round."

Nevada looked at him a full fifteen seconds before she moved. Then she rose and kissed Johnny Buffalo on the withered cheek nearest her.

"To know a man like you is a privilege," she said simply. "I shall keep the nuggets to remind me that not all men worship gold."

"You will wear them in a necklace. My sergeant wishes you to have them. They are not so beautiful as your white throat."

Nevada blushed vividly and shook the nuggets in her two hands. "It's a good thing Grandmother can't hear you," she laughed. "An old bachelor like you!"

"An old bachelor can say what the young man dares only to think," Johnny Buffalo stated calmly.

Rawley was trying distractedly to read a letter which Nevada had brought down from the post-office, and to pretend that he did not hear what was going on. But it is reasonable to assume that there was nothing in the letter to make him blush at the moment when Johnny Buffalo said his little say. Nevada stole a glance at him from under her lashes and smiled.

"What is it, Cousin Rawley?" she asked wickedly. "You seem disturbed."

"I'm called back on the job." Rawley tried to meet her eyes unconcernedly. "I won't even have the week I promised myself. This is pretty urgent, and so I think I'll take the trail again in the morning."

Even Nevada betrayed some mental disturbance over that information, especially when Rawley could not hazard any opinion concerning his next visit.

"I won't even have time to look over your work at the dam," he told Peter. "I intended going down to-morrow. I wanted to have a talk with you about that. I've picked up a little information, here and there, and I'm afraid there will be complications. But I've been holding off until I was sure of my ground. I know, of course, that my personal opinion won't have much weight."

Peter shook his head. "You can work and pry and lift till your eyes pop out of your head, starting a bowlder down a mountain," he said grimly, "and you can give it the last heave and over she goes. Any time, up to that last heave, you can quit and she stays right there where she was planted. But once she starts, all hell can't stop her. I'm afraid we've given the last heave, son."

"*Look out below!*" Nevada cried mockingly and looked at Rawley. "I could tell a cousin in three words how he can make himself as popular as a rattlesnake with the Cramers—and the last of the Macalisters."

"And those three words?" Rawley looked her squarely in the eyes.

"Fight the dam." Nevada's eyes were as steady as his own.

"Thunder!" Rawley sat back and reached for his tobacco sack. "I've no notion of fighting the dam. It's the biggest proposition I ever saw three lone men—and a girl; excuse me, Nevada!—tackle in my life. Four of you, thinking to stop, just like that,"—he made a slicing, downward gesture, "—the second largest river in the United States! You'll be damming the Gulf Stream next, I suppose. Divert it so as to warm up Maine and make it a winter-bathing resort!"

"Do you dare us to try?" Nevada poured nuggets from one palm to the other. "That might be a good investment, when we've made our clean-up in the river bed." She smiled dreamily at her handful of gold. "That's a wonderful idea. We need some wonderful idea to work on, after the dam is in and the gold is out. You can't," she looked up wistfully at Rawley, "you can't live with a tremendous idea all your life and suddenly drop back to three meals a day and which dress shall you wear. One would go mad. It— it's like taking the mainspring out of life."

Johnny Buffalo nodded his head in significant approval. "A man can only wait, then, until it is time to go," he said with quiet decision.

"Very well. I'll speak to the Peace Conference about the Gulf Stream," Rawley assured her gravely. "In case I am unable to reserve it for you— would the Gulf of Mexico do, or the Mississippi River, perhaps?"

"We're accustomed to cracking our whip over fresh water," Nevada retorted. "I should prefer to have the Mississippi, please."

Johnny Buffalo glanced toward the wheel chair, gazed at it intently and nodded his head.

"You will succeed and fail in the succeeding," he intoned solemnly. "In the failure you will rise to greater things. It is so. My sergeant never speaks what is not true."

Eyes moved guardedly to meet other eyes that understood, conveying a warning that the old man must be humored. Johnny Buffalo stood up, his face turned toward the wheel chair. He seemed to be listening. His eyes brightened. The wrinkles in his bronzed old face deepened and radiated joy.

"It is good! I need not wait—I go now!" He took an eager step and wavered there.

Peter and Rawley, rising together, caught the old man in their arms as he went down, falling slowly like a straight, old tree whose roots have snapped with age.

CHAPTER 23

THE EAGLE LOOKS UPON
A GREAT RIVER

Rawley drove down El Dorado Canyon, now silent in mid-afternoon, with not a sound of stamp mill or compressor or the mingled voices of men at work. Techatticup stood forlorn, deserted save by one old man who bore himself proudly because he was the guardian there. The war, the labor question, the slump in metals, had done their work. It seemed to Rawley as if the nation were taking a long breath, making ready to go forward again more resistlessly than before. He missed Johnny Buffalo terribly; but if he could, he would not have called him back. Johnny would have had a dreary time of it, alone all these long months when Rawley's work had held close to the affairs of the government.

The eye of the Eagle had not been closed. His keen glance had gone to this and to that, his piercing gaze had fixed itself upon the desert land and the river that went hurrying down through flaming gorge and painted canyon, a law unto itself, an untaught, untamed giant of the wild; a scenic wonder set deep in savage walls of rock, where people came and looked down upon it, drew back shivering, ventured to look again in silent awe; a terrible, devastating thing from which men fled in terror when the giant river rose, leaped from its bed and went raging across the land.

Men called for power, for protection, for water to till barren acres that might be made fertile. Men shouted for the things which the Colorado held arrogantly within its grasp, to hoard with miserly greed or to let loose in a ferocious fury. The Colorado had power, it had water, it had a cruel habit of devouring lands and homes and whooping onward toward the gulf, heedless of the destruction in its wake.

And the Eagle had lifted his head and turned his eyes upon the great river. Here, within the borders of his domain, dwelt a powerful, savage thing that must be tamed and taught to obey the will of men. The Eagle considered this headlong defiance of all civilized restraint. The Eagle saw how men looked upon the river, drew back in awe and ventured to look again; men, who should be the masters of the river. The Eagle lifted and spread his wings. And the tip of a wing reached over the desert land and laid its shadow across the Colorado.

A great orator had painted it so, and Rawley was thinking of that picture of the Eagle as he drove down the canyon to the very brink of the river and climbed out of his car. Still desolate, more forsaken than ever was the place where El Dorado had stood alive, alert, self-sufficient. The camp was gone, almost forgotten. The river flowed past, disdainful of the puny efforts of men who died and forgot their dreams and their endeavors, while it rushed on through the ages, and played with the lives of men and mocked at their fear of it.

But three men and a girl had dared to dream of holding the might of it in leash. It was to see these dreamers, to warn and to show them the shadow of the Eagle's wing, that he had come in haste to the bank of the Colorado. For months he had heard nothing. Nevada had not written, or if she had the letter had not reached him. There was danger in delay, in their continued silence.

Rawley slung a canteen over his shoulder and started up the river, taking the well-known trail. This was the quickest way to reach the Cramers, and now that he was in their neighborhood once more a great impatience was upon him, a nervous dread that he might be an hour, a minute too late for what he had come to do.

He came upon Nevada suddenly. She was standing on the site of the old camp where he had stayed with Johnny Buffalo. Her back was toward him, and she was holding something in her two hands; something he had seen her extract from the thorny branches of a stunted mesquite bush. When his footsteps sounded close, she turned and looked at him dumbly, her eyes wide and dark. The thing she held in her hands was his pipe—one that he had lost on that first trip into the country.

Before his better judgment or his doubts could stop him, Rawley drew her into his arms and held her close while he kissed her. It was so good to see her again, to feel her nearness. But after one rapturous minute, she put away his arms and faced him calmly, though her breath was not quite even and her eyes would not meet his with the old frankness.

"Your one eighth of Indian blood should have given you more reserve, Cousin Rawley," she reproved him mockingly. "The Spanish of us must be watched. Well, I needn't ask about your health; you haven't been pining during your absence, that one could notice."

Rawley barely escaped forswearing both his Indian and his Spanish blood, but remembered his promise just in time. He did not believe that Nevada regretted his impulsiveness—for you simply can't fool a man under thirty when he kisses a girl. Nevada's lips, he joyously remembered, had not been unresponsive.

"Here's your pipe," she said lamely, when he only stood and looked at her. "I was just wondering whether it's worth saving, or whether I'd better heave it into the river and see how far it would float."

Rawley did not believe that she intended to heave it anywhere, but he passed the point.

"If cousins fell in love, they—would you consider the relationship any bar—"

Nevada went white around the mouth.

"I certainly should! You ought to be ashamed to ask a question like that. No man with any decency could think of such a thing."

"I'm decent," Rawley contended, "and I thought of it." But he did not pursue the subject further. Nevada had turned and was walking on toward the camp of Cramer, and Rawley could do nothing but follow. The path was too narrow to permit him to walk beside her, and a man feels a fool making love to a woman's back.

"Have you done anything further about the dam?" he asked, after a silence.

"I believe the work is going ahead," Nevada replied, keeping straight on.

"You must have received my letter about it; or didn't you?"

"Yes, I received a letter about something of the sort."

"You didn't answer it, did you? I never received any reply."

"I did not think," said Nevada, "that the letter required any answer. You wrote and told us to stop all work on the dam, and give up the idea, because some one else wanted to build a dam. Or was considering the building of a dam. I read that letter to Grandfather and Uncle Jess and Uncle Peter, as you requested. They swore rather fluently and went to work the next morning as usual." Then, as if it had just occurred to her, "Did you come to see about that, Cousin Rawley?"

"Oh, I wish you'd omit the 'cousin'," Rawley blurted irrelevantly. "I don't like having it rubbed in."

Nevada said nothing for a time. Then she laughed, a hard little laugh that sounded strange, coming from her.

"Certainly, if you wish. I'm very sorry I seem to have 'rubbed it in', as you put it. And I quite understand how you feel. Out among men—and women—as you have been, all your life, the—er—mixed relationship would prove rather a handicap. Poor old Grandfather and Grandmother should have thought of their children's children, before they fell in love. And Uncle Peter should either have brought you here and raised you with the rest of the tribe, or never told you the truth. I'm not blaming him; I'm merely sorry for the mistake. I know what it means. I've been out in the world, too."

Rawley stared at the proud lift of her head and wondered just how much of that she meant. She must be quite aware of his reason for disliking to be called her cousin, but he would not argue with her. Except about the handicap.

"You're mistaken, if you think the mixed blood is an objectionable feature," he said firmly. "Indian and Spanish have the same essential characteristics of race that the straight white blood owns. Besides, there are mighty few Americans who couldn't trace back to something of the sort. Character, culture and environment sweep a few drops of red blood into the background, Nevada. You wouldn't feel bitter over it, if you didn't live right here and see the Indian predominate in Young Jess and Gladys—and your grandmother."

"*Your* grandmother, as well as mine," she flashed over her shoulder with a very human spitefulness. "Don't deny it—to me."

Rawley did not deny anything at all; wherefore, conversation languished between the two. Since first he had known her, Nevada had frequently withdrawn into an unapproachable aloofness discouraging to any lasting intimacy, but she had never before betrayed resentment against her blood.

He had hoped that she would be glad to see him and would let him see that she was glad. He had hoped to win her complete confidence in his devotion to their interests and welfare. He needed to have both Nevada and Peter on his side, if he were going to be successful in his mission to the Cramers. But he was extremely doubtful now of ever winning Nevada's confidence. It began to look as though he may as well count her an opponent and be done with doubt.

CHAPTER 24

ANITA

Life seemed to have moved sluggishly in the basin, save in the increase of the tribe. Six young Cramers now walked upright, though the smallest walked insecurely and frequently fell down and lay squalling with its eyes shut and its nose wrinkled until one of the older children picked it up and dusted it off, remonstrating the while in Pahute. The seventh was not yet old enough to ride the well-upholstered hip of Gladys, but wailed in a cradle which some one must be incessantly rocking.

Gladys was more slatternly than ever she had been, and her vacuous grin had lost a tooth. Anita had aged terribly, Rawley thought. She moved slowly, with a long stick for a staff, and her eyes held a dumb misery he could not face. Nevada informed him that Grandmother had not been very well, lately, although there was nothing wrong, particularly.

"She doesn't sleep at all, it seems to me," Nevada detailed. "Often she's up and prowling along the river bank in the middle of the night, and I have to go and lead her back. I think she's getting childish. She will sit and watch me by the hour, when I'm working, but she doesn't seem to want me to talk to her. She just sits and looks, the way she's been looking at you."

Nevada went away then to some work which she said was important, and Rawley wandered down to the river bank. In a few minutes he heard a sound behind him and turned, hoping that Nevada had yielded to his unspoken desire and was coming to join him.

But it was Anita, walking slowly down the uneven pathway, planting her crude staff ahead of her in the trail and pulling herself to it with a weary, laborious movement. Her gray bangs hung straight down to her eyelids. Her wrinkled old face was impassive, her eyes dumb. Rawley bit his lip suddenly, thinking of his Grandfather King sitting, "a hunk of meat in the wheel chair." Life, it seemed to him, had dealt very harshly with these two. He was no longer swayed by the stern prejudice of Johnny Buffalo. He did not believe that Anita, in her lovely youth, had been merely a whimsy of love. His grandfather had loved her, had meant to return to her. He did not believe that King, of the Mounted, would have loved one who loved many. The King pride would not have permitted that.

Anita came up to him and leaned hard upon her stick, her eyes turned dully upon the river. Never before had she sought him out; rather had she avoided him, staring at him with a look he interpreted as resentment. She looked so old, so infinitely tired with life, and her eyes went to the river as if it alone could know the things she had buried in her heart, long ago when she was a slim young thing, all fire and life.

With a sudden impulse of tenderness he put his arm around her, leading her to the flat rock and seating her there as gallantly as if she were Nevada, whom he loved. It was what his grandfather would have done. Rawley felt suddenly convicted of a fault, almost of a sin; the sin of omission. Here was the love of his grandfather's youth, the mother of his grandfather's first-born. And because she was old and fat, because the primitive blood had triumphed and she had yielded to environment and slipped back into Indian ways, he had snobbishly held himself aloof. He had ignored her claim upon his kindness. Had her beauty remained with her, he told himself harshly, his attitude had been altogether different. Now he wanted to make up to her, somehow, for his selfish oversight. He sat down beside her and patted her hand—for the Anita who had been beautiful, the Anita whom King, of the Mounted, had loved.

"You love—my girl—Nevada?" The old squaw spoke abruptly, though her voice held to a dead level of impassivity.

"How did you know?" Rawley took away his hand.

"I know. I have seen love—in eyes—blue. Eyes like your eyes."

"Nevada doesn't care anything about me, Anita."

At the word, the old squaw turned her head and stared at him fixedly. "You call that name. Where you know that name? Jess, he call me Annie."

Rawley flushed, but there was no help for it now—or, yes, there was Johnny—

"Johnny Buffalo called you Anita," he parried.

Anita shook her head slowly. "Jawge—your gran'fadder—he call me Anita too," she said wistfully. "You ver' much—like Jawge. I firs' think—you are ghos' of Jawge, when you come."

"Grandfather was crazy about you," slipped off Rawley's tongue. "He spoke of you in his diary—a book where he wrote down things he did—things he thought."

Anita stared down at the river.

"You tell me," she commanded tersely. "All those things—Jawge think—about—Anita."

Rawley's hand went out and closed again over her wrinkled, work-hardened knuckles.

"The first was when he came up to El Dorado on the *Esmeralda* in '66. He was leaning over the rail, watching the miners crowd down to the landing. He wrote, 'I saw a young girl—I think she is Spanish. She has the velvet eyes and the rose blooming in her cheeks. She's beautiful. Not more than sixteen and graceful as a fairy.' What more he wrote of you I don't know. He cut the pages from the book so no one could read it."

Anita raised a knotted, brown hand and smoothed her bangs, tucking them neatly under her red kerchief.

"I was little," she said complacently. "Ver' beautiful. Every-body was—crazy—about—me." She halted, choosing the best English words she knew. "I was—good girl. I love—nobody. I jus' laugh all time—when them so'jers make the love. Then I see—Jawge—my Sah-geant King. He is king to me. Tall—big—strong—all time laughing—making love with blue eyes—like you—all time make love—with eyes—to Nevada. I know them eyes—I have lived—to look—in them eyes."

"I don't do anything of the kind," Rawley protested, confusion crimsoning his face. "I've always tried—"

"Eyes like them eyes—no tell lies. Woman eyes see—things they tell. Jawge—he write more?"

"Most of it was cut from the book. He called you '*el gusto de mi corazon*,' and his '*dulce corazon*.' Do you know—?"

Beneath his palm Anita's hand was trembling. She pulled it free and lifted it to her face, her withered fingers wiping the tears that were slipping down her wrinkled cheeks. Rawley could have bitten his tongue in two. Awkwardly he patted her on one huge, rounded shoulder.

Like a lonesome dog, the old woman whimpered behind her brown palm, from beneath which a tear sometimes escaped and splashed upon her calico wrapper. Rawley sat silent, abashed before this forlorn grief over a romance fifty years dead.

"Now I love Nevada, Peter." She mastered her tears and became again impassive. "You leave me—Nevada? Lil time—I want Nevada. I die—then you can love—many years. You do that?"

"Of course. I promised Peter, a long time ago. But it doesn't matter, anyway. Nevada doesn't care a rap about me."

The old woman looked at him stolidly.

"You not tell Nevada—you not Peter's boy," she said. "Nevada think that. You not tell Nevada—that's a lie. You tell Nevada, I kill myself."

"I've no intention of telling Nevada," Rawley said, chilled by her manner. "It doesn't matter, anyway."

"You not come—for Nevada? You not think, marry Nevada—take Nevada 'way off, I no see any more?" Anita peered into his face.

"No. I came to see Peter. About the dam."

Anita took some time over this statement. Then she rose stiffly and hobbled away, leaving Rawley to stare morosely into the river.

CHAPTER 25

THE EAGLE AND THE VULTURE

"You may as well listen to me," said Rawley in the incisive tone which big responsibilities had taught him. "I am your friend. My only object in coming here is to be of service to you. If you do not listen to what I have to say, you will have to listen to the Federal Reclamation Service, acting under the Secretary of the Interior. That may be more convincing to you—but believe me, it will be less pleasant!"

"You were keen for the dam, last time you were here," Peter reminded him drily. "You called it a big idea. You've had a change of heart, son."

"I have. I have come to tell you that there are other ideas bigger than yours, and a power behind them that will make yours look like building a toy dam in the sand, like kids. You must have read of it in the papers. There's been all kinds of publicity given to the project."

"You're right. There's been a heap of talk," Peter retorted. "The papers have done the talking, and we've been sawing wood and keeping our mouths shut. While they're still talking and arguing and speechifying, we'll put 'er in. There's nothing the matter with that, is there? Take the wind out of their sails, maybe, especially the fellows that have their speeches all written out, ready for the next banquet. But—*the dam will be in*! They'll have some work, trying to get around that point.

"You ask if we've read the papers. I have. They've been talking about spending a hundred million dollars. We've spent one. They've been fiddling along the river, looking to see if it's feasible. We've kept right on digging. They thought we were *mining*—the only party that discovered our diggings. They were very patronizing, very polite, and they talked about the wonderful things a dam would do for us. Is that what you came to tell us, son?"

Rawley leaned back against the wall and laid one foot across the other knee, tapping his boot with his finger tips. He was facing them all. He must convince them, somehow, and he must batter down the dream of a lifetime to do it.

"No, you've read most of the talk," he told Peter. "I admit the thing has almost been talked to death. It begins to look as though the general public is tired of reading about damming the Colorado. If that were all there is to it, Peter, I'd never say a word. But there are some facts we can't get around with talk, or defiance. I came here to show them to you—just plain, hard facts—and let you see for yourself what they mean.

"In the first place—and this is probably the hardest fact you have to face—the Colorado is an international stream. It flows through a part of Mexico. The Constitution of the United States has decreed that such rivers must at all times and in every particular be under the control of the Federal Government. There are seven States bordering this river, yet not one of them dare build a dam without the consent and supervision of the government. Get that firmly planted in your minds, folks."

Young Jess turned his head an inch and slanted a look at Old Jess. Old Jess crossed his legs, folded his arms and trotted one rusty boot, waggling his beard while he chewed tobacco complacently. No one could fail to read his mind, just then. He was thinking that what seven States were afraid to do, he, Jess Cramer, had dared. The joke was on the seven States, according to Old Jess's viewpoint.

"Arizona," Rawley went on, after a minute of contemplating the complete satisfaction of Old Jess, "Arizona wants water for irrigation. One hundred and fifty thousand acres of desert land can be made fertile with the water of the Colorado, properly diverted into a system of canals."

"They kin have the water," the Vulture conceded benificently. "We don't want it. Glad to git rid of it. You kin tell 'em I said so."

Young Jess laughed hoarsely.

"Sure. Glad to git it off'n our hands!"

"The State of Nevada wants power for her mines. The copper interests are after a dam up the river here, so that they can resume the output of copper. They want a smelter, operated by power from the Colorado. Two million brake horse-power of electric energy is slipping past your door, worse than wasted.

"California wants more power for her industries—"

"She's welcome," Old Jess stated smugly. "We ain't hoggin' no electric energy 't I know of."

"You are, if you interfere with the building of a dam of sufficient size and strength to conserve that power."

Young Jess leaned forward, grinning impudently into Rawley's face.

"Hell! There's thousands uh miles up river that we ain't doin' a thing to. They kin build dams from here to Denver, fer all we care! That's all poppycock, our interferin'. Everybody with ten cents in his pocket is talkin' about buildin' a dam in the Colorado. Why the hell don't they go ahead and *do* it? We ain't stoppin' nobody!"

"You may be, without knowing it," Rawley explained patiently, determined to educate them beyond their single-track idea, if possible. "I see how it looks to you, of course. But I'll explain how it looks to the greatest engineers in the country, Jess. You remember I was rather keen for it, myself. It was out of my line, and I didn't know.

"Now the fact is, you are attempting, with a certain amount of rock blown into the river from the sides, to dam a river second only to the Mississippi.

"I know, the Missouri is wider, but I am speaking now of the volume of water that passes through this canyon right here. It is a swift river, and it is a deep river. You don't realize, any of you, just how deep and how swift it is, though you have lived beside it all your lives.

"Peter has spoken of the amount of money they are talking of spending to build a dam at Boulder Canyon, up here. The canyon there is as narrow as this; perhaps narrower. And to hold back the tremendous volume of water that flows past your door, engineers have said that they must go down one hundred and fifty feet, to bed rock, and start there to build their dam. They say that the dam will—must—to hold back the terrific pressure of water, rise something like six hundred feet above low-water mark. It will keep several thousand men working for eight or ten years to complete the dam, its spillways and main canals. It will cost around one hundred million dollars, and it will bring both protection and prosperity to thousands and thousands of people. That," he declared, leaning forward, "is what it means to dam the Colorado."

"It don't mean that to us," Old Jess stated, turning his quid to the other cheek. "We aim to show 'em something about buildin' dams." He grinned and showed yellow snags of teeth.

"Yeah. Wait till they see how *we* aim to do it," snickered Young Jess. "We'll be rakin' in the gold whilst they're still standin' around with their mouths open."

Peter had fallen into a taciturn, grim mood, staring somber-eyed at the river. Beside him, Nevada leaned chin upon her cupped palm and stared also. Several thousand men, working for eight years! That was as long as the years back to her first sight of the convent where Peter took her to be educated. Thousands of men working all that time—thousands! Was it, then, so deceptively vast, that river? Would the cliffs they had undermined fall in and be swept disdainfully away? Did it really belong to the government, that river, so that no man living all his life on its bank might say what should be done with it? Had Uncle Peter, and Young Jess and her grandfather been children, playing all these years beside a stream they must not touch or tamper with?

"It sounds as big as the stars," she observed vaguely. "As if we had been waving a handkerchief at Mars, down here by the river, and then some one comes along and pushes us back and says, 'Here, here, you must stand back. You are obstructing the view. The President wants to wave his hand-kerchief. You annoy him.' Do you think," she flashed at Rawley, "it is going to make any difference to the river—who dams it first?"

"You don't get the point," Rawley protested. "I am not responsible because the undertaking is so stupendous that it is beyond any private en-terprise. You *can't* shoot a lot of rock into the river and call that a dam. And if you could, you must not. Don't you see? The welfare of too many thousands of people are involved. It's a job for the government. You can't take it for granted that, just because you have lived beside it all your lives, and because it doesn't seem to belong to anybody, any more than the clouds belong, that you can claim it, or even claim the right to do as you please with it. There's a right that goes away beyond the individual—"

"The gold down there is ours," Old Jess cried fiercely. "We own placer claims on both sides of the river, and the lines run across. We've got a right to placer the gold in the river bed. It's *ours*. We got a right to git it any way we kin! The gov'ment can't stop us, neither."

"Oh, yes, it can!" Rawley rashly contradicted. "When you come down to fine points, the government owns this river. It owns the river bed and whatever gold is there. By 'right of eminent domain', if you ever heard of that."

"Right of eminent hell!" Young Jess got up and stood over Rawley threateningly. "Tell *me* a bunch uh swell-heads back in Wash'n'ton, that never *seen* this river, can set and tell us what we can do an' what we can't do? We own claims both sides the river, and we got a right to what's *in* the river. You can't come here and tell us, this late day, 't we got to quit, and lose our time an' money, because the gov'ment or somebody wants to build a dam. Hell, *we* ain't stoppin' nobody! They better nobody try an' stop us, neither!"

CHAPTER 26

"TAKE THIS FIGHTING SQUAW AWAY!"

Never before had Rawley seen Young Jess in a rage. A surly, ignorant fellow he knew him to be, and not too intelligent. A dangerous fellow, Rawley believed him; quite capable of killing any man who thwarted him or roused his fury. But Rawley did not move or attempt to placate him. He had learned that some natures must blow up a great storm before they can yield. He hoped that this was the case with Young Jess.

The old vulture craned his neck forward, his eyes piercingly malevolent.

"Think I've waited fifty year fer that gold, t' be robbed of it now? They ain't no gov'ment on earth can step in an' take what's mine! I'll blow 'em to hell first! I'll—"

As once before, when he thought his gold was threatened, Old Jess ran the full gamut of anathema. Nevada fled from the sound of his cracked voice shrieking maniacal threats and maledictions. He shook his fist under Rawley's nose and stamped his feet and raved. Young Jess was over-ridden, silenced by the old man's insane outburst.

As once before, Peter said absolutely nothing until Old Jess had reached the zenith of his rage. Then he rose deliberately and without excitement, took the old man by the collar and headed him toward the door.

"Go and cool off," he advised dispassionately. "You old vulture, you can't scream any louder than the Eagle. You, too, Jess," he added, turning harshly upon his half-brother. "You're a pretty good man when it comes to swinging a single-jack, but you're a damn poor hand at thinking! This thing is away beyond your depth. You can't holler the government down. Get out!"

Young Jess blustered and threatened still, flailing his fists and mouthing oaths.

"That's about all from you," grated Rawley, stung to action by some vile threat against the government.

"Is, hey?" Young Jess advanced upon him.

Then Rawley went for him, the blue eyes of the Kings gone black with fury. The fight, if it could be called that, was short and undramatic. No tables were overturned, no glass was shattered. Young Jess aimed a sledge blow at Rawley, got one on the jaw that spun him so that he faced the other way, and Rawley forthwith kicked him off the porch. Young Jess rooted gravel, looked over his shoulder and saw Rawley coming at him again, and started off on all fours. When he regained his feet he went away, blathering blasphemy. He was going for his gun—so he said.

Peter stood looking after Young Jess, his brows pulled together. A slim figure slipped past him and went straight to Rawley, who was pulling at his tie, which had gone crooked. She was pale, breathless with the fear that looked out of her big eyes.

"Oh, you must go—*now*," she breathed, clasping her two hands around his arm. "You think he's just like any other bully, all bluster. He'll kill you, just as sure as you stand here. Grandfather, too. Uncle Jess will shoot you in the back—oh, *anyway*! He's the worst of the Indian blood; once you rouse him, there's *nothing* he'll stop at! Get him away, Uncle Peter! It isn't brave, to stay and be killed. It's the worst kind of cowardice; the kind that is afraid to show itself. Uncle Peter!"

"We're going, Nevada. I know Young Jess. A rattlesnake's a prince alongside him when he's mad. Son, you should have left him to me. I can handle him pretty well, no matter how mad he gets. Come along; he'll not be above potting you from ambush, Injun style."

He left the porch at the farther end, pulling Rawley after him; and much as Rawley hated the thought of retreat, he was forced to believe that Nevada and Peter, neither of them timid souls, must know what they were talking about.

Nevada disappeared, with no word of farewell to Rawley. Young Jess could be plainly heard bawling at Gladys because his "shells" had been misplaced.

Peter chuckled.

"One of the kids shot himself through the hat, a month or so ago," he explained his amusement. "Since then the guns are kept unloaded. Jess is hunting cartridges; God bless Gladys for a poor housekeeper!"

He still held a firm grip on Rawley's arm, leading him down the path to the river. But suddenly, keeping an ear cocked toward the sounds behind him, he swung away from the trail toward the bluffs.

"He's found them, from the way things have quieted down, back there. He'll be hot on your trail, now—unless Nevada can stop him, which I doubt. He's Injun enough to hold women in contempt when it comes to a show-down. Here."

He pulled Rawley down between two great, upstanding bowlders standing black against the stars. Rawley felt a movement of Peter's arm, and knew that Peter had pulled a gun from somewhere and was aiming it across a ridge of rock. Rawley himself could hear nothing but the crying of the wakened baby in the shack, the yelp of a kicked dog.

For a long time, it seemed to Rawley, they waited. He could not hear a sound. But Peter still held his gun leveled across the rock before them, and Rawley could feel how Peter's muscles were tensed for a struggle.

Two greenish lights showed faintly as a star-beam struck the eyeballs of a dog. A shuffling sound approaching through the weedy gravel, a sniffling at Peter's hand. Rawley felt a crimple down his spine, though he did not think that he was afraid.

A pebble plunked into something close beside him, and the dog shied off with a faint, staccato yelp. Young Jess, then, was close. A muttered curse reached the ears of the two between the bowlders. Immediately afterward, Nevada's whisper came distinctly.

"I think he's hidden here, somewhere in the rocks. His car is down in the canyon, but he wouldn't go that way—he'd expect you to follow. Watch the dog. He hasn't any gun—I know. Can you creep back toward the hill—"

"Sh-sh. You call him. Quiet, as if you was scared. Make out you're sweet on him—"

"I can't. He knows—I hate him. We quarreled today. I hate his snobbish ways—I told him so."

"Call his name if you run onto him. Then duck. I'll—"

"Sh-sh—he may be near!"

The two were standing close together, just beyond the bowlder that reared its bulk beyond Peter. Rawley bit his lip, straining his ears to hear more.

"You call him. He won't s'spect—" Young Jess urged in a whisper.

"He'd be a fool if he didn't. I tell you he knows—"

"He's stuck on yuh. That makes a fool—"

"Sh-sh. He's not—"

Inch by inch, Rawley was drawing himself backward, until now he was free of the bowlder and Peter. From the sounds, he knew that the two were standing close to the rock. He thought that they were facing the river, though he could not be sure. It did not greatly matter. He inched that way until he could faintly distinguish two upright blots in the darkness of the bowlder's shadow.

Upon the taller of the two he launched himself, reaching instinctively for the gun he knew was there. His hand closed on the cool steel of the barrel, and he gave a mighty wrench as he went down. Young Jess, caught unawares from behind, had no chance to save himself. Rawley landed full on his back, his chest forcing the face of Young Jess into the gravel. His left hand gripped the back of Jess's neck.

"Peter, please take this fighting squaw to the house and lock her up somewhere. Then come back here. I want to have a talk with you before I go," he said hardly. "I can handle this vermin, but I leave the squaw to you."

"As you like," Peter's voice was noncommittal. "Come, Nevada."

Rawley had expected some outburst from her, some bitter reply to his taunt. But she went away with Peter and spoke no word to any one. So Rawley pulled off his necktie and tied Young Jess's hands behind him, and made himself a smoke while he waited Peter's return.

"I'll git you, and I'll git you right!" gritted Young Jess, when Rawley had his cigarette going. "You better kill me now, or you'll see the day you'll be begging me to kill yuh. I'll ketch yuh and take yuh back in the mine, an' I'll—" He amused himself for some minutes, making up the programme of his revenge. He would finish, he decided, by building a bed of powder kegs and placing Rawley full length upon it, with a ten-foot fuse spitted just before Young Jess bade him good-by.

"You ought to have lived fifty years ago," Rawley commented indifferently, and blew smoke in his face. "Why don't yuh squeal for that old buzzard of a dad? Maybe he could help yuh out, right now."

Young Jess, having just made up his mind to shout for Old Jess to come, shut his mouth so hard his teeth clicked like a dog cracking a bone.

"Any fool can plan the things he'd *like* to do," Rawley taunted. "What counts is the fact that you're on your back, right now, and that I put you there—and you with a gun in your hands! I could kick you in the slats and make you howl like a kicked pup. I could drive your teeth in, so you'd feed yourself in the back of your head the rest of your life! Don't talk to *me*—about what you'd like to do! I'm liable to experiment on yuh, just to see how it works."

Then Peter returned, and further social amenities were postponed to some future meeting.

CHAPTER 27

"YOU TELL HOOVER I SAID SO!"

Las Vegas awoke one morning to find itself in the public eye. Destiny had so decreed when it permitted Las Vegas to become the town nearest to the proposed dam site at Boulder Canyon—the largest governmental project undertaken for many a day. The Panama Canal, said the orators (and no doubt they spoke the truth), had not cost so much as it would cost to dam the Colorado River, to conserve its tremendous power, to control its flood waters and put the river to work tamely watering long rows of cotton, potatoes, great fields of grain. Long enough had it gone leaping down through the wildest, most gorgeous scenery in the country. Now it must be harnessed to new industries and become the servant of plowboys, the friend of prospectors. It must pull trains across the desert which it was to transform into tilled farms. It must keep several States vibrant with the hum of machinery. It must make of the town of Las Vegas a city worthy the name. One can't blame Las Vegas for being particularly interested in that phase of the project.

The town lay fairly under the eye of the Eagle—and of the sun, whose light the magic alchemy of the desert transmuted into soft tints on the mountains, into a faint lavender glow on the desert. The air was still, with a little nip to it that would later soften to a lazy warmth. A stranger to the desert, standing on the depot platform, would have thought that he might walk quite easily to Charleston Mountains, standing bold and stark against the western sky line.

Down the flag-draped main street, coming from the side door of the little post-office, a huge, good-natured negro leaned against a pushcart piled high with dingy, striped canvas mail sacks. When he passed, certain belated citizens swung out to the edge of the pavement and took longer steps, knowing that the train was on time, and that the crowd would already be edging out upon the platform. Automobiles with flags standing perkily from headlight braces went careening past, to swing up into the parking space, trying their nonchalant best to look as if they were not going to hold governors and high officials of the Federal Government and carry them safely down to Boulder Canyon, the most popular dam site on the Colorado.

A group of small boys dressed in white came marching down the street, stubbing toes over the uneven places because they must keep their eyes on the music while they played the uncertain strains of a march. They were very sleek as to hair, very shiny as to cheeks and very solemn, those boys. Their mothers and their fathers and their teachers were going to detect any false note or flatted sharp and tell them about it afterwards. Besides, there aren't many boys who ever get a chance to stand on the platform and play when the Governor's train comes in—and be the only band on the job. They felt the deep responsibility attendant upon the honor and thought feverishly of certain spots in the music where they weren't quite sure they could make it; not with the whole town standing around listening.

They fumbled their instruments, stood hipshot and consciously unconcerned while they waited for the train. Their leader glanced around the group, encountered certain anxious pairs of eyes fixed upon his face, and made an impulsive change in the programme. "The Star-Spangled Banner" was appropriate and customary for such occasions, but there were treacherous high notes which a certain scared boy might play flat, and other places where the slide trombone was in danger of skidding. He gave them a piece they could play with their eyes shut and was rewarded by hearing long sighs of relief here and there among the musicians.

So it happened that when the train had slid into the station and the Governors and high officials had descended from the private car, Rawley caught the familiar air, "I'm forever blow-ing bubbles" floating out over the heads of the assembled citizens of Las Vegas. If the tune wabbled here and there, what matter? Governors and high officials can hear better music anywhere—but they never will hear a more sincere effort to please, made by more loyal hearts than skipped beats under the white jackets of the "kid band" of Las Vegas.

> I'm dreaming dreams, I'm scheming schemes,
> I'm building castles high—

Rawley caught himself humming the words to himself and thought, in a heartsick way, of Nevada, only twenty-five miles from him, so far as miles went—a million miles away in her thoughts.

"I've talked Boulder Canyon Dam until I wonder sometimes if it isn't Bubble Canyon, maybe," a certain governor confided to him under his breath. "Do you reckon this is a civic confession the kids are making, or what?"

"The civic air castle—nearest the kids can come to it," Rawley grinned. "Wait till you hear this town stand up on its hind legs and tell you how they feel about it. They talk Boulder Canyon in their sleep, I reckon. It's no bubble to *this* bunch! If the rest of the country had half the enthusiasm this town has got, they'd be hauling concrete to the river today!"

"Instead of the Commission, huh? Well, I wish they were."

A man pushed out of the fringe of common citizens who came merely to look upon assembled greatness and faced Rawley, smiling with his eyes.

"Uncle Peter!" Rawley gripped his hand and did not know that his eyes searched the crowd, wistfully, seeking a face—

"No, she didn't come," Peter informed him. "I want to get a chance to talk with the men in your outfit who count the most. Not on paper, but with the government. Can you fix it for me, boy?"

"Has anything happened?" Rawley drew him anxiously aside.

"No—I just want to get at the right men. I want you there, of course." Peter glanced here and there at the men who were smiling, shaking hands, speaking pleasant phrases.

"All right. Of course every minute is mortgaged, I suppose, to the town. But I'll get you—"

"An hour will do me," Peter stated modestly, and Rawley suppressed a grin.

Looking him over surreptitiously, Rawley decided that he could be very proud indeed of Uncle Peter. Even amongst governors and such, Peter could hold his own with that quiet dignity which nothing seemed able to ruffle, that poise which came of being very sure of his own mind and of what he wanted. A great man looked from one to the other curiously, and Rawley immediately introduced Peter to him. Then he caught the eye of another, and presently that man was shaking hands very humanly with Peter Cramer, who looked so much like George Rawlins King, of the Reclamation Service. Before he quite realized what was taking place, Peter was absorbed into the party of great men, and a flustered waitress in the depot dining room was hastily making room at a table and laying another knife and fork purloined from the lunch room outside.

The reception committee probably revised at the last minute their arrangements for seating the party in the decorated automobiles. Some one must have been crowded; but Peter rode in comfort in a big car in company with some of the nation's important men, though this was not what he had gotten an early haircut for. He had seen the river in all its moods and under all conditions; it seemed strange to him now, no doubt, to be sight-seeing it with men who had heretofore been no more than names to be read in headlines in week-old newspapers. But no one suspected it—unless perhaps some member of the reception committee wondered how he had broken in. However, as a guest of the Colorado River Commission, seven governors and railroad presidents, no mere local committee dared flicker an eyelid.

"It has to be done this way—whatever it is you want to do," Rawley muttered once in Peter's ear at the river, when he caught Peter looking boredly at the bold cliffs of Boulder Canyon. "You couldn't get a look-in, just coming up and trying for an interview. As soon as we get back, and before the banquet up town, I've arranged for you to talk to the Commission. I told the chief," he added drily, "that it was more important than anything else he'd hear. I gambled on that, because I know you. And a little nerve goes a long way, sometimes. We're going to cut this short as possible and get back to the car early. Then—you'll have to boil down your hour, Peter. There won't be more than half that much time for whatever it is you want to say."

"It may pay this Colorado River Commission," said Peter laconically, "to miss their supper tonight, and even cut out some of the speeches they've got ready to hand out to Vegas citizens. As I understand it, the Commission was created for the purpose of investigating claims, collecting all data and adjusting rights pertaining to the Colorado River. They'd better take a piece of bread and butter in their hands and eat it while they listen to what I've got to say." He paused and added significantly, "You tell Hoover I said so."

CHAPTER 28

THE VULTURE MAKES TERMS
WITH THE EAGLE

Rawley had them rounded up in the private car—governors and high officials and newspaper representatives—lighting cigars, cigarettes and pipes and eyeing, their curiosity politely veiled, the big, broad-shouldered man with the brown skin and piercing blue eyes, who stood at one end of the car waiting for them to settle themselves into easy, listening attitudes. This was informal—but if they were to believe that keen young man, George Rawlins King, it was going to be pretty important; and, what appealed to most of them like a window opened in a stifling room, fresh and untalked. It is impossible to eat, sleep and live with one subject for months without feeling a tingle of relief when some entirely new angle crops up—something that hasn't been argued, weighed and considered a hundred times. The Colorado River Commission was on the job—heart, soul and mind. But that did not preclude secret sighs of anticipation when the Commission faced something wholly new to every member.

Not a man among them knew Peter Cramer. Not one had ever heard the name. He looked a man of the desert, every inch of his six-feet-and-something-over. He might turn out to be a bore; he did not look like a boor. He did not wear his hair in the prevailing fad; it grew thick to the nape of his neck and was trimmed there neatly by some barber who remembered how they used to cut hair. His dark suit was incontestably made to his measure—but it had been made before the War. You don't get such material nowadays. At least, men of the desert do not get it. His hands, as he shuffled a few slips of paper, showed how hardly they had been used. They were the hands of a laborer, scrubbed meticulously clean, the nails trimmed painstakingly—with a pocket-knife, one could guess. So there he stood, towering above them all, with pre-War clothes, the hands of a laborer, the eyes of a thinker.

The car became very still. Every man there looked at Peter. And one man's eyes held love, sympathy and a shade of anxiety. To this moment, Rawley King could only guess at what his Uncle Peter was going to say. There was a little prayer in Rawley's heart, in his eyes. A modern, youngman prayer, "God, don't let him pull a boner!" It would be well if all the prayers in all the churches were as sincere.

"Gentlemen of the Colorado River Commission" (Peter began in his deep, even voice that carried far) "you do not know me, and I do not know you. I thank you for consenting to listen to me. When I am done, you may thank me for consenting with myself to talk to you. In the words of a certain wise man—whose wisdom I wish I might borrow as I borrow his words— 'I am not a clever speaker in any way at all; unless, indeed, by a clever speaker they mean a man who speaks the truth. You will not hear an elaborate speech dressed up with words and phrases. I will say to you what I have to say, without preparation and in the words which come first, for I believe that my cause is just. So let none of you expect anything else.' If I could better that statement, make it more forceful, I should hesitate. Gentlemen, they stand for absolute honesty of purpose. Let them stand for me now, as they stood for Socrates—but I hope with happier effect.

"Fifty-four years ago, I was born within sight and sound of the Colorado River and within sight of the cliffs of Black Canyon. The river has been a part of my life. The wilderness hedged me in, mile upon mile. When I was ten, so long ago as that, I was taught the use of a rifle that I might help defend lives and property from hostile Indians and renegade white men. My mother is the granddaughter of a chief, and the daughter of a Spanish nobleman who voyaged up from Mexico before white men had seen this country. I am therefore one-fourth Indian—a son of the desert. My father was a white man of good blood.

"When I was a boy and helped in my father's mine at Black Canyon, I was urged to greater labor by the great plan my father had conceived in his long labor at the placer claims. He would save his gold until he had enough and more than enough. Then, when he had gold enough, he would dam the flow of the Colorado River and get the gold that lies in the river bed, washed down through the ages.

"That plan became the splendid dream of my life, Gentlemen of the Commission. The stupendousness of the idea took root in my very soul. I would stand and watch the river hurrying past, and I would think how best it might be done, and I would picture the river held back, halted in its headlong course to the sea.

"When I was fifteen I was studying, in a small, groping way, the engineering feat of damming the river at Black Canyon. I knew that I had a tremendous problem before me. I knew that the problem was doubled by the need of secrecy, which had been impressed upon me from the time I was a child. No one had thought of getting the gold from the river bed. The river was too swift, its currents too treacherous. I used to watch the steamboats warp up against the sweep of that current, to make the landing at El Dorado. That gave me an idea of the giant strength we should have to combat, to conquer. No one ever suspected the purpose that grew within the minds of the 'squaw man' Cramer and his breed boys, mining at Black Canyon. Deliberately we fostered the belief in our commonplace lives, our lack of ambition, our ignorance. That belief, gentlemen, was a necessary factor in our ultimate success.

"Studying alone—for my younger brother avoids thinking when possible, and my father gave himself up wholly to the thought of getting the gold—I felt the need of help from our great engineers. I could not take the time for college, for studying in the schools that turn out engineers. I am a man of the desert, as you see me. What I know I have learned by reading when others slept. I could not give my working hours to study, for they were sold to the need of getting gold to build the dam in order to get more gold! I alone realized the magnitude of the undertaking; to me they looked for the wit to accomplish their desire. And I remembered, gentlemen, the engineering problem solved by half-savage peoples; their power is gone, but their engineering feats remain to testify for them. I remembered the pyramids, some of the wonderful old cathedrals of Europe, the marvelous ruined cities of the Incas, the Aztecs—I counted myself a savage who must think for himself, and I went at the problem of making the splendid dream a reality.

"Gentlemen, when I was yet a boy I was experimenting with explosives. I was studying the resistance of granite, the lifting power of black powder; I was preparing to build the dam. Before I had books on the subject, I had measured so many cubic feet of granite and had heaved it a certain distance with so many pounds of black powder. Over and over again I did it, in spare time when I was not working in the underground placer claims by the river.

"I will be brief, gentlemen, but I want to be understood by each one of you before I stop talking. I told my father, when I was in my teens, that we must have a million dollars before we could hope to carry out his idea. I told him that we must have enough, or lose what we had. I showed him where failure to dam the river would mean a total loss of time, money, labor. I convinced him that I knew what I was talking about. I hope that I can convince you.

"Gentlemen, in order to dam the Colorado River and mine the gold in its bed, for a distance of, say, a mile or two, you must make sure first of all of the means, second of the secrecy of your plan, and third of the practicability of the project. We had placer ground of unsuspected riches; an underground watercourse with gravel bed, carrying placer gold. This gave us the means. We simulated poverty and ignorance and a paucity of ambition, which gave us immunity from suspicion that we had a secret to keep.

And I made it my business, gentlemen, to study the practical engineering problem.

"I had long ago chosen the spot for the dam; a point in the canyon where the granite cliffs rise highest. I drew charts—" Peter glanced toward Rawley, and his eyes twinkled "—of a system of underground workings which, when filled with black powder augmented by light charges of dynamite, would break the granite walls and heave them into the river. I worked upon the principle that it would be better to use too much than not enough, and for fifteen years—yes, for longer than that—I have been buying and storing black powder. Today, gentlemen, I have in place explosives which, with hush money that I was compelled to pay for the secret, have cost approximately one hundred thousand dollars. *In place!* Wired, tamped with heavy cement, ready to go. *Ready to shoot!*"

He looked from face to face, smiling while he waited for the information to sink in. He saw certain newspaper men poise pencils before they set down the sum, then scribble furiously.

"You didn't know that, did you? No one has told the Colorado River Commission, until now, when I am telling you, that twenty-five miles from here, in the cliffs beside the river, there is at this moment peacefully reposing a giant ready to rise up and fling rocks into the river, and lie back again when all is done, to watch the Colorado halt in its headlong rush to the sea! I will be more explicit, gentlemen.

"In the cliffs, *ready to shoot*—bear that always in mind—I have five hundred thousand pounds of blasting powder, and fifty thousand pounds of forty per cent. dynamite, so disposed that, fired simultaneously on both sides of the river, the volume of rock will meet midway and drop into the channel. Some distance up the river, I have an auxiliary dam built, ready to blow at a moment's notice if the main dam seems in danger of not holding against the terrific pressure of the Colorado's flow.

"Incidentally—I had nearly forgotten to tell you—I have perhaps the oldest, most complete private record of the flow, rise and fall of the Colorado River in existence. The record goes back thirty-nine years, gentlemen. I still use a gauge which I invented when I was about fifteen, and I find that it is practical, though crude.

"I have planned the auxiliary dam, as I call it, to check and help hold the pressure against the main dam, if necessary. In flood time the force is terrific; I have provided against that. The auxiliary dam, if thrown in, will give me time to strengthen the main dam. I have not expected that one big blast will end the matter. Once that is in, and further secrecy impossible, I shall be prepared to rush one hundred men, whose names and addresses I have on file, to work with compressors (two on each side of the river, each one portable and capable of running three drills each—with jack hammers and expert men behind them). These will rush another system of undermining, so that a second installment of Black Canyon can be heaved in upon the first.

"You will bear in mind, gentlemen, that we are first in the field by a good many laborious years. I grant you that the idea was born in greed. The eye of the vultures have dwelt upon the gold in the river, these fifty years. But even the vulture must give way to the Eagle. I have seen the wing of the Eagle spread, and its shadow has touched our dam in Black Canyon. Gentlemen, the vulture has come to make terms with the Eagle."

That, for reasons best known to the Commission, was applauded. A great man asked a question.

"How much, approximately, have you spent in this undertaking?"

Peter glanced down at a slip of paper in his hand.

"It is something I have waited to tell you. I divided our capital into budgets, as follows:

"A dredger, now waiting at Needles to be towed up the river, four hundred thousand dollars. (That, of course, is our personal property and need not be considered in our negotiations, if any are carried on.) Fund for payment of damages to property caused by blasting, one hundred thousand dollars. (That, I thought, should pay for all the windows and crockery we may break, and that remains in bank until such time as we need it.) Property bought along the river above the dam site, which may be inundated, fifty thousand. Incidental expenses covering a period of years, fifty thousand. Explosives, wiring, battery and cement—with hush money paid out—one hundred thousand dollars.

"The explosives, gentlemen, I should expect the government to buy, if you take over our dam; which I hope that you will do. I have no desire now to infringe upon the rights of the government, even if I could. The project has been my life's work. The achievement in itself has been the big dream of my life. If it will be of any service to you, if your engineers find my idea a practical one, I shall feel that my life so far has been well-spent. I had an idea that our dredger might still be used in the river bed to extract the gold. We have claims on both sides of the river. I have hoped that we might still be able to operate our dredger, paying a royalty to the government on whatever gold we may take out. If that is impossible, then we shall be obliged to unload our dredger for whatever we can get for it.

"Finally, gentlemen, I must urge you to extend your stay in Las Vegas, so that you may see our dam, and understand more fully what I have been trying to make plain to you: That we *have a dam*, ready to shoot within an hour's notice—yes, in fifteen minutes from the time you say the word. I believe that it will hold. You may find that, by reënforcing it, by building spillways and preparing for your canals, our dam will be of real, practical benefit to you—put you that much farther along the trail. Give you something concrete to work to, something besides politics, talk, theories, factions. It's there. It's ready to speak its little piece to-morrow, if you like—though I am not so ignorant as to speak seriously of that. I merely wish to point my information, make it definite. You, or you, or you, could go down to our place, and if I told you just where I have hidden the battery, you could hook it up to our wires and dam the Colorado—like that." He snapped the fingers he had pointed and stood waiting. And while he waited, no man in that car did more than breathe, and look at Peter, and think rapidly, with some consternation, of the significance of his information.

"Gentlemen, I have finished. I should like to show you the Cramer Dam, to-morrow. It may upset your schedule, just as I am making you late for the banquet, which is probably waiting and cooling at this moment. But, gentlemen, it will pay you to upset your schedule. It will pay you to take the time and walk the two or three miles between the nearest road and the dam. Until you do see the Cramer Dam, which I now publicly announce as being completed, you are not fully qualified to make your report, if report you must make, to the Secretary of the Interior, or whoever receives and passes upon your findings in the matter. Gentlemen, I thank you."

CHAPTER 29

FATE HAS DECREED

"I should like to say just here, if I may, that many of the astonishing facts as Mr. Cramer has placed them before you I can vouch for from my own personal knowledge." Rawley was on his feet, turned toward Peter's audience. "Just before the war, I was permitted to look over the work on the Cramer Dam"—privately, Rawley liked the way Uncle Peter had dignified the dam by giving it a name which would hereafter identify it to the public—"which at that time was uncompleted. I did not approve of their project, but I will say that I was personally in sympathy with it.

"In considering the facts which Mr. Cramer has presented to you, I am taking the liberty of asking you to bear in mind that I am willing to vouch for their authenticity. And in explanation of my silence on the subject, I will say that I went to the Cramers and urged them to abandon their project, since it would interfere with the reclamation plans of the government. I did not know, until he stated their position in the matter just now, what stand they meant to take."

He sat down, and his chief nodded approvingly. It was perfectly apparent to Peter that his cause would be none the worse for Rawley's championship. He glowed to see how friendly they all were with Rawley. Also, it surprised his unsophisticated soul to observe the ease and familiarity with which these men comported themselves. Headliners in the newspapers, every one of them save the reporters themselves, he had half expected them to retain their platform manners in private. They were just men, after all, he decided, and turned to answer the questions of a great man as easily as he would have answered Rawley.

The committee of entertainment waited a bit for their guests of honor, that night. From the manner in which the talk slid into other and more accustomed channels the moment others entered the car, Peter gathered that Las Vegas would continue for a time in ignorance of what had been going on under its nose for so long. It tickled him to picture the amazement and incredulity when the Commission should make its announcement. Or perhaps Las Vegas would read it in the city papers first. They would be slow to believe that the obscure family of Cramers could put over a thing like that and keep it under cover all these years.

At the banquet in the town hall, Peter listened to Rawley's dazed enthusiasm calmly while he watched the crowd. This was the first banquet which Peter had ever attended—a man confessing to fifty-four years and quoting Socrates!—and he was interested. But Rawley would not let him enjoy himself as he would like; instead, he must tell why and why and why; a tiresome job for Peter.

"Oh, I didn't lack confidence, boy. I wanted your opinion without any influence from me. If I'd told you all I knew, that wouldn't have helped *me* any. I wanted to know what *you* knew about it. Then I compared your ideas with mine.

"No, Jess and the old man don't know what I'm up to. I talked to them, some, after you left. But they can't see beyond the gold in the river. They'll be mad, I expect. But we couldn't go on the way we planned. You can't fight the government, boy. The old Eagle is a real scrapper.

"Yes, Nevada knows I intended to fly a white flag. She's willing. She sees, as I do, that you were right—"

Peter's neighbor on the other side claimed him then; an engineer who wanted further details of just how Peter had planned to move a mountain and cast it into the river. Two men across the table left off eating and their talk to lean forward and listen, and the man next Rawley was frankly stretching his hearing across and catching as much of Peter's elucidation as he could. So Rawley was obliged to content himself with his pride in Uncle Peter, who was plainly making an extremely favorable impression on certain governors and high officials. And it amused him secretly to observe Peter's complete unconcern over his growing popularity and his childlike interest in the commonplace incidents of the banquet.

An ambitious reporter slipped up behind Rawley and asked him for the love of Mike to arrange an interview with Cramer. His tone was imploring.

"New dope—and oh, boy, it's a hummer!" he confided in Rawley's ear. "You know we pencil pushers are just about goofy, trying to get a fresh punch into this thing. This man, Cramer, is worth a million dollars to the project, just for the publicity there is in him. A dam under our noses—oh, *boy*!"

"He won't talk," Rawley discouraged him. "Taciturn is the word that describes him."

"Taciturn? With that talk he put over this evening? I've got every word of it—it's priceless. Arabian Nights ain't in it. And believe me, King, it's going on the wires complete, the minute we get the word to release it."

"Let's see," Rawley mused. "You're an A. P. man, aren't you? Well, I'll try and run Peter into a corner for you—but I won't promise he'll give you anything."

"You, then! King, you're wise—I can see it in your left eyebrow. You've got some ripping dope on this, and I know it. Say, if you'll—"

The toastmaster had risen and was rapping a spoon against his plate. The ambitious scribe and the human beehive subsided, but Rawley observed that the reporter had pulled up a chair and was preparing to camp at his elbow and Peter's. Well, why not? he thought headily. A man like Peter could go far in the world, give him a chance. And this might be the chance. A desert man who spoke calmly of budgeting a million dollars, the savings of a lifetime for three men, to spend in secret upon a project over which the whole nation was arguing, and who could make a talk like that the first time he ever faced great men was, to say the least, unusual.

He glanced sidelong at Peter, who had straightened and folded his arms, gravely prepared to give his full attention to the speakers. There would be no word out of him now, Rawley knew. As well expect a devout old lady to divulge her recipe for piccalilli in church. He turned his head and whispered behind his hand to the reporter:

"Stick around. I'll do what I can."

The reporter patted his shoulder gratefully, and Rawley came to attention, stifling a yawn. It was so like every other banquet, and the speeches were so like all the other speeches on the same subject! He listened with the same bored loyalty with which the workers in the Liberty Loan drives and all the other drives toiled through their patriotic programme night after night, day after day. It did not lessen their patriotism that the workers sometimes wearied of the same old arguments, the stereotyped appeals to the patriotism of the public. He wished that Peter might rise and say what he had said to the Commission, a couple of hours ago. That would open their eyes!

However, the speeches which were so old to the visiting great ones were not old to Las Vegas, and they were not old to Peter. There was the usual appeal for sympathy with the project under the direct supervision of the government, to which Peter listened closely, his head turned a bit sidewise so that he would not miss a word of it. The reporter was quietly sketching his profile on a small pad, but Peter never guessed that.

A tall, lean man from California was speaking. He was the fourth or fifth on the programme, and the audience was restive under his voice, wanting to hear from the greatest of the great men there. The greatest of the great men was listening courteously with half his mind, while the other half was divided between an aching desire to crawl into his berth and forget the whole darned thing for a few hours, and recasting a certain story which might be used with effect at the beginning of his talk—unless Las

Vegas was too familiar with it. His colleagues knew the thing backward; but then, when one has traveled much with a certain group, speaking valiantly at every stop in behalf of one's cause, one's colleagues are going to be bored anyway when one starts speaking, so that their desires are never considered. The same old stuff is always new—provided one has always a new audience before one.

"Ladies and gentlemen," the speaker was crying enthusiastically, "you can't get away from the fact that progress is ever marching onward. The hand of Opportunity is lifted, knocking at your door! Whether you open or not—upon that rests your future. You can't get away from it. One day (and that day is not far distant, ladies and gentlemen), you will awake to find yourselves in the midst of great, growing industries. The mighty river at your very door, ladies and gentlemen, will be at work for the Nation! The full measure of her might, ladies and gentlemen, will be *at your service*! Can such a stupendous thing as that, ladies and gentlemen, be placed in the hands of private interests? I say, *no*!" (The tall, lean man did not say it, he thundered the words.) "I say, no man, no group of individuals, can do a thing like that! No man—"

A queer, sickening lurch of the building, forward and back, a shattering of windows drowned his voice completely. You know how it is when an earthquake intrudes upon your little thoughts, your infinitesimal activities. You suddenly know that you are nothing at all. Your very soul sickens before a mightier than thou. So it was at the banquet.

The tall, lean man's plate leaped at him, and a custardy dessert which he had not touched—on account of dyspepsia—was deposited on his clothing in splotches. He started for the door, enraged because every one else was also starting for the door.

Came a terrific, booming roar like the rolling up of the heavens into a scroll—done carelessly and in haste. Women shrieked. Men shouted unintelligibly under the impression that they were doing something to quell the panic.

Peter, stunned for a minute, jumped upon the table, one heel crunching a dish of salted almonds devastatingly. His great voice boomed above the tumult and stilled it, while each person looked to see what and why he was speaking.

"Ladies and gentlemen, that's all. There won't be any more. Folks, like it or not, you've got a dam in the Colorado River! She's dammed, right this minute. It's an accident, a slip-up in the plans, but—*she's there*. You just heard a chunk of Black Canyon go into the river. The man that made the last speech said it couldn't be done. It *is* done. Now, the government will have to do whatever else is to be done. Ladies and gentlemen, you have just heard the Cramer Dam go in!"

That stopped the panic automatically. Men and women waited to hear more. They were accustomed to blasting, if that were all. They accepted Peter's statement that this was all of it, though the women were still white, still inclined to clutch their husbands and sweethearts and wonder if they were going to faint. Las Vegas was dazed. The Colorado Commission was collectively looking at Peter through narrowed lids.

Peter glanced down into the measuring, weighing eyes of the greatest man present. He flushed at what he read there, and he answered the look.

"It's my fault," he said simply. "I ought to have tied 'em up, or brought 'em with me. I should have placed a guard over that dam. I did hide the battery—but they must have found it."

At a sudden thought he threw out both hands in the gesture with which a strong man meets the inevitable.

"Gentlemen," he cried, and his voice was a challenge. "Fate has decreed that the thing should go through! I had no knowledge of this, but—" his eyes darkened and twinkled, the endearing King smile softened his face suddenly "—gentlemen, if you will stop over a day, I should like to show you the Cramer Dam, *completed*!"

He looked at the great engineer who had questioned him during dinner.

"*You* said it couldn't be done! I'm not a gambling man, Mr. Brown, but I'll bet you fifty thousand dollars against fifty cents, that *she's there*!"

The man he challenged looked up at him. Slowly, as his thought crystallized, the blood drained out of the engineer's face, leaving it dead white. He turned to his chief, but his voice went to the farthest corner of the hall.

"My God! What if she holds a while! Warn Needles, Yuma—send out a general warning below! Tell the people to hunt the highest points they can reach! Gentlemen, if that damned Cramer Dam holds for forty-eight hours, there'll be the greatest disaster in the history of the West!"

The A. P. man leaped chairs, bowled over men on his way to the door. After him came the banqueters in a senseless rush.

CHAPTER 30

DAWN AND THE RIVER

On the street men were guessing wild. An explosion had taken place—every one knew that. The majority guessed that the powder magazine at Searchlight had blown up; though as a matter of fact they were not certain that Searchlight had a powder magazine.

The more impulsive were already tearing down the road in automobiles, without any very definite notion of where they were headed for. As is customary in such cases, every man who had a tongue had also an opinion which he was eager to impart to somebody, and was unable to find any one who would listen to him.

Into this confusion the A. P. man burst like a rocket shot off accidentally. He was on his way to the telegraph office on the second floor of the depot, and he meant to arrive there ahead of the others so that he could be sure of a clear wire to cover the story. Besides, he had been impressed with the need of haste in warning people below. Yet he found time to shout the news to a group of men as he passed them.

"Colorado's dammed!" he cried, and did not wait to explain how it should be spelled. Wherefore Las Vegas guessed harder than ever until men less hurried arrived from the banquet hall and told just what had happened. Immediately thereafter, every man who owned a car cranked up and got going in the direction of Black Canyon. The Governor of the State stayed a while to give certain orders and to make sure that they would be promptly obeyed.

Peter laid a detaining hand upon the arm of a shrewd young lawyer whom he knew slightly, and who had studied him intently while Peter explained to the banqueters the commotion. The young lawyer instinctively drew aside from the throng, to a clear space where confidences might be indulged in. But Peter was brief.

"Here's a check. It's good for ten thousand. You advertise that people with smashed windows and so on can have the damage made good. Get a contractor, have him investigate all complaints, and then fix things up. I'll see you in a day or so. I'm going to the river to see what's happened. You attend to the damages here."

He did not wait until the lawyer consented to accept the job, but left him standing there, the check in his hands, an unlighted cigar in his mouth. Peter was just climbing into the big car that drew up to the curb for him, when the A. P. man—his name was Jerry Newton, by the way—sprinted a half-block and landed on the running board.

"Sent out a general alarm," he puffed, "and got the news to headquarters. Cramer's speech—wrote it during the feed. Had a hunch I might have to make it snappy. Needles and Yuma will get word to the ranchers—if the big splash holds off a couple of hours they think they can reach everybody, practically. Anybody got a cigar? Never had time to eat a bite."

"You're out of luck, then," Peter informed him. "No chance till breakfast, now."

Rawley swung round upon them from the front seat, where he was to pilot the driver. His voice was strained and unnatural.

"The—folks would know enough to get out of danger, wouldn't they, Uncle Peter?"

"They would," Peter said grimly, "if they had any warning."

"You don't think it was an accident, surely!" As Rawley spoke, others leaned to listen for Peter's reply.

"I know I found a doctor—he's going to follow at our tail light. I hid the battery where Jess and the old man couldn't find it. The rest we'll know when we get there." Peter's exultation had left him completely. He sat back in a corner of the wide seat and said no more. And by that, Rawley knew that Peter was worried.

The reporter was saying that Needles had reported every window in town broken by the concussion.

"Of course they counted, in the five minutes they must have had before you wired," Rawley exclaimed irritably. If Peter was worried over the folks in the basin, then Rawley knew that there was cause. He told the driver to "hit 'er up, the road's good", and thereby gained some minutes and gave some great men a jolting.

They left the road to Black Canyon and went on to Nelson. They could drive to the river that way, and one glance would tell them whether the dam was holding. That was important. The Governor of the State having called for help, it was necessary to see first of all what the river was doing below the dam—if dam there were.

Several cars fell in behind them, no doubt cognizant of the fact that the Governor, Peter and the great engineer were in the first automobile, and that they knew where they were going. So it was a swift procession that swung up over the summit and down into El Dorado Canyon.

The September moon was lingering upon a mountain top, loath to withdraw its gaze from the crippled river he had watched over all these ages long. Peter was first out of the car, which, for reasons readily apprehended, he had stopped well up the wash. If the dam was holding so long, there would be a great, engulfing wave when it broke, and the longer the dam held, the greater the flood.

"The river's high for this time of year, on account of the storms in the mountains," the chief engineer of the party informed them superfluously, since the occurrence was sufficiently unusual to have excited comment before now. "She's running close to fifty thousand second feet—or was, when we left Needles yesterday." He turned to Peter with courteous criticism; not for him was it to censure or judge, but he ventured a remark nevertheless which betrayed his own personal belief.

"You should have waited until the edge of winter before you let that charge loose. This is an unusual year, I grant; but with your knowledge of the river, you must know the danger of attempting to dam it while there is so great a discharge."

The group hurried its pace to listen, but Peter, in the lead, seemed wholly unconscious of criticism and listeners alike. He was absorbed by his own thoughts, his own fears.

"It was madness to do it now, in any case," he agreed simply. "For years we've talked of shooting it during September, when the water begins to lower definitely for the winter months. That would give us the longest possible time for strengthening the dam. If this wasn't a sheer accident, it was done by a madman—the vulture who feared the Eagle would snatch away his feast. I know of no better simile. Gentlemen, I fear you will have to cope with a madman who ran amuck when he discovered my absence and feared that I would betray the whole scheme to the government. He could see nothing but disaster in that. If he deliberately blew up the dam, it was with a crazy notion of forestalling the government. I don't know; I hid the battery."

He was leading them up on the high bank on the north side of the wash by a narrow trail he knew. Even in his haste he remembered that the lives of great men must not be placed in danger, and he had not needed the reminder of the engineer that it was a risky proceeding, blowing in the dam at the height of this sporadic high water. Not so high as to overflow its banks, it is true, but with not too wide a margin of safety, either.

No man there knew better than Peter what an unexpected breakage would do, no man there felt more keenly the elements of disaster, once his first exultation over their disbelief had passed; a flare of triumph over the wise ones. Peter had been on that river just yesterday. His launch was still at Needles, where he had left it to take the train for Barstow. He had arrived in Las Vegas on the train which brought the private car of the Commission. He had planned it so, to be sure of seeing them, and also to conceal his errand from the two Cramers, whose rage would not have stopped at murder, it is likely, had they known what was in his mind.

When Peter had embarked in his launch, the river was running forty-three thousand second feet. He had looked at the gauge. He had not known how the government gauge had read at Needles when his train left there, but he did not doubt the word of the engineer. There had been unusual, heavy storms in Colorado, Wyoming, Utah. An edge of it had swept his own State. To attempt to dam that sweeping flood was, as he had named it, madness.

Once up the bank they walked rapidly. Rawley, glancing back, saw other automobiles stop behind their car, and men trailing after them up the bank. It was a somewhat circuitous route; he wondered if his party would follow Peter so patiently if they knew that they could have driven to the water's edge. They were walking half a mile when they might have ridden. But Peter was taking no risk.

They reached the high bank of the river just as the moon slipped—like the face of a boy who has been peering over a stone wall and who has lost his footing—dropped suddenly out of sight, and left the river dark, the far hills gilded tantalizingly with its white light. The party halted.

"She's dammed," Peter said tersely.

"I can hear it running," some one objected.

"I know every sound of this river," said Peter impatiently. "I've listened to it all my life. You hear a seepage fighting the rocks in the channel. It's no bigger than a trout stream now. This way, gentlemen."

In the blackness before dawn, made blacker to them by the sudden desertion of the moon, Peter struck into the burro trail Rawley knew so well.

The familiar path brought a sharp longing for Nevada, whom he had left in anger some months before. Of course she had not been plotting with Young Jess against him! Once his hurt pride let him think clearly, Rawley knew that she had been trying to save him. She would naturally suppose that they had gone straight toward the canyon, and she was encouraging Jess to waste time looking among the rocks, never dreaming that they were there. Many a time Rawley cursed the King temper for letting him taunt her with her Indian blood. He had wanted to hurt. His instinct had led him to the words that would sting sharpest, even though she believed him as much Indian as herself.

Men before him and behind were talking—short-breathed over the pace Peter was unconsciously setting them—of the dam, its probable strength and the danger of a disastrous flood if it held a while and then failed to hold. Rawley walked among them, thinking of Nevada, wondering if she would ever forgive him for what he had said to her. Strangely enough, of Young Jess's hate and promised revenge he did not think at all. Nevada's resentment, her forgiveness—these were the things that mattered. The dam was an incident, a job for others to handle. Rawley's whole thought was of persuading a girl to forget a dozen words which he had spoken in blind fury.

Then, looking across at the piled hills beyond the river (the hills of Arizona), the white radiance faded, chilled, merged into the crepuscule that threatened to deepen again to darkness. The moon was retreating before the coming of the sun.

The twilight brightened, pulled lavender and rose from the dawn and spread over the hills a radiant, opal-tinted veil. The great men stopped and faced the dawn, and forgot the problems set by the great Teacher for human minds to solve, and, in the solving, grow to greater things. The Governor removed his hat and stood, head bared, waiting for the coming of the sun. The heralds flung banners of royal purple and gold. The hills laid aside the thin veil of enchantment and spread a soft carpet of gray and brown.

The King appeared, a ruddy disk with broad bars of purple cloud before his face. The heavens blazed with the glory of a new day. Somewhere behind them, in hidden mesquite bush, a mocking bird began singing reverently its morning aria.

Eyes left the savage wonder of the wilderness greeting the dawn and dropped to the crippled Colorado.

In a dark canyon drab bars of silt stretched like gigantic crocodiles upon the river's bed, with the shiny humps of moss-slimed bowlders in between. Rosy pools of still water reflected the barbaric dawn clouds above. Ridges of water-worn gravel. A thin swift current was fighting the huge rocks in the channel with a great splutter and turmoil of spray flung up. Smaller streams were worming impatiently aslant the river bed to join the stream fighting so valiantly in the channel.

Already the main current was yielding, choked by the neighbor mountain that had suddenly assailed it from above. Against the rocks the sun painted inexorably the mark of its surrender.

Peter looked down upon the river bed and saw his splendid dream come true. For a moment his exultation returned. He looked at the Governor.

"I believe, sir, that the Cramer Dam is a complete success!" A ringing note of pride was in his voice.

CHAPTER 31

THE VULTURE FEASTS

They walked on, heads turned toward the spectacle. The sun, rising higher, splashed a mellow light into the deep crannies between the bowlders, set the bald pates of smoothed granite rocks a-gleam—rocks never before uncovered in the history of man.

Rawley turned and looked curiously at Peter, whose eyes were upon the river bed while his feet stumbled along the trail. They were anxious to reach the dam, every man of them. The engineer was stepping out briskly, keen glances going to the cliffs up-river; but for all their haste they could not forebear to gaze down at the stark, denuded canyon bottom, where a great river had been halted in its headlong rush.

"Well, Uncle Peter, you've had your wish," Rawley said at last. "You said you were waiting for the day when you could show the Colorado who was boss. You wanted to stop it. It's stopped."

Peter looked at him, smiling faintly.

"I was just thinking of Johnny Buffalo, that last night," he said, speaking so that the others, straggling along the trail, would not hear. "What was that he said? 'You will succeed, and fail in the succeeding. And from the failure you will rise to greater things'—or something like that. It just struck me. I wonder if he meant—this." He tilted his head toward the river. "I've succeeded. I've stopped the Colorado, and shown it who's boss. But it isn't like I dreamed it, after all. I've got a hunch, boy, that we'll never work that dredger. Maybe the government will have other ideas about that. It was a self-centered plan, I admit that now. It had no right to succeed. The folks below need the river. I hadn't figured them into the calculations at all."

Jerry Newton overheard that last observation and stepped faster until he was just behind them.

"Did you ever see a flood, Mr. Cramer? I covered Pueblo and several other places; was down South, that last big one. Families down below here are getting out—and believe me, they are making it snappy! I'll bet you couldn't find a breakfast cooked in its own kitchen, down below here, to save your life! They know what a flood means, and this is going to be like the crack o' doom when it comes. Sudden, what I mean. They've been tickling the gas levers, believe me, since that blast went off."

Peter turned and looked at him, frowning.

"What makes you all take it for granted the dam won't hold?" he queried resentfully. "It would, I'd stake my life on it almost, though it should have been shot in low water, or falling water. This high water is not going to last. It's the run-off of a big general storm, and I believe the peak is past, anyway. You don't realize the size of the Cramer Dam. And you seem to forget altogether the auxiliary dam that can be thrown in, any time it seems necessary."

Jerry Newton saw the point, but he saw something else, and being a blunt young man by nature, he blurted a retort.

"If you're so sure of its holding, Mr. Cramer, what are you so worried about?"

Peter's eyes hardened.

"Lives, young fellow. Two of them dear to me."

The A. P. man was silenced. He looked contritely at Peter's back, but he could not think of anything to say.

"Look there!" The engineer, hurrying along in the lead, stopped and pointed. "That's what I call enterprise. But it's taking a chance I shouldn't care about, myself."

The party pulled up, facing the river. They had reached the lower edge of the basin, about where Rawley and Johnny Buffalo had camped. The bank here was high and rocky as the canyon opened slowly its mouth. The river had been forced to a narrower channel, and it held therefore a deeper bed.

Away down there in the middle of it, almost at the edge of the channel fighting still to hold its own, a bent figure was groping, bent almost double, eyes to the ground. Now and then it knelt and clawed in slimy pools. Then it went on, inch by inch, like a child picking pretty pebbles on a beach.

"Old Jess!" cried Rawley. "Peter, it's Old Jess! Call to him! He'll step into a hole—there's quicksand—or if the dam breaks—"

"He's crazy!" several of the party spoke the words at once, as sometimes happens, unconsciously forming an impromptu chorus. "Call him out of there!"

"He wouldn't come!" Peter was starting toward the edge, seeking a trail down. Rawley, running ahead to the place where he used to bring up water, was down before him.

"Go back! I'll get him," shouted Peter, scrambling after, and those left at the top gesticulated and shouted.

"You go back," Rawley cried over his shoulder. "One's enough!" Then, having reached the bottom, he started out.

The vulture saw them, and flapped his arms and screamed vituperations in a reasonless rage, greed-mad, thinking they were come to rob him.

Slipping, sliding among the bowlders that piled the river bed in places, the two ran out, instinctively avoiding the treacherous bars of engulfing mud that lay upstream from some larger obstruction, the deep pools where fish were leaping. Neither would turn back. Both men realized that.

The vulture picked up a rock as big as his fist and threatened them with it. They went on, straight for him. Old Jess gave a maniacal scream, hurled the rock and fled. Rawley ducked. But Peter, coming just behind him, was caught in the chest. He lurched, slipped on a slimy spot and went down backward on a rock.

Rawley did not see. He was hot after the old man, who ran awkwardly, his pockets weighted so that they sagged the full stretch of the cloth, a sample bag over his shoulder knocking heavily against his back. He headed straight for the current that boiled, a miniature Colorado, in the channel.

He meant to jump it and gain the other side. He had lost all sense of proportion. He did not see that a horse could scarcely clear the racing flood. Rawley shouted a warning just as Old Jess reached the brink. The old vulture gave a scream, sprang out, and the current caught him and dragged him down.

Rawley ran for a few steps down the plunging stream, put one foot in the quicksand and hurled himself back just in time. The black, tumbled object that was Old Jess whirled on.

"The river never gives up its dead; he said it himself," Rawley exclaimed in an awed tone to Peter, and turned. But Peter was not behind him, as he had supposed. Then he saw him lying among a litter of small, mossy rocks.

Up on the bank men were shouting, pointing upriver when Rawley heaved Peter up on his back and started picking his way toward shore. Rawley glanced up, saw the stretched arms, looked, and began running.

Up the river, close against shore, looking as if it were hugging the rocks for protection, a narrow, white line came leaping down upon him. The Colorado was not a river to submit tamely to the will of man. It had found a weak spot close inshore, and in the few hours that it had been fretting against its barrier, it had eaten a way through. Now a slim skirmisher came surging down through the tunnel the water had made.

Men scrambled down the bluff toward him; well-groomed men with patent leathers that slipped on the steep bank. They could not help, but neither could they stand up there with their hands in their pockets and watch.

Rawley did not see them. He did not see that gamboling white line, after the first glance. He did not see anything, save the next place where he must set his foot, the next mud bar which he must avoid. His shoulders were bent under the two-hundred-pound weight of a man he loved as he had never before loved any man, and he knew that safety might lie in a second—in one long stride.

The rocks seemed to grow more slippery, more slimy as he went on. The mud banks seemed to slide in upon him. He had to turn back once, just in time to avoid a patch of ooze. He imagined that the shore receded, or that he stood still and moved his feet in one spot. But he fought that notion and forced himself to believe that he was making time against the small, devouring flood that was racing down at him. He kept telling himself that the water had twice as far to travel in order to engulf him as he must go to escape it.

He was right. The water had farther to travel, and he made time. Indeed, the spectators swore that he made a new record for speed. Running with two hundred pounds on his back was a feat for any man on smooth going, they told him. Over that course, it was not an achievement at all; it was a miracle.

However that may be, Rawley used his last ounce of energy to reach the bank. A gloved hand reached down and caught him. Its mate seized the other wrist. He gave a final dig with his toes and a scrambling wriggle, and crawled up as some one pulled Peter off his back and the small torrent swept past.

On a shelf of rock above the watermark he lay back for a minute to breathe before he essayed to climb the high bank. He looked down at the rush of water, his eyes wide.

"Lord, I thought it was the whole river coming at me!" he panted disgustedly, looking up into the face of the Governor, whose hand had reached down to him. "Why, I could jump that—almost."

"Hardly, with a load," the Governor retorted. "And then, the whole dam may give way at any moment, now it has started."

Peter stirred and struggled to sit up. His dazed eyes went down to the new torrent. The sight stung him to full consciousness. He came up like a lion wounded but full of fight.

"Come on! We've got to shoot in that auxiliary dam," he shouted thickly. "I—was going to—anyway. And let this flood down—easy."

CHAPTER 32

ANOTHER RESCUE

"Going to try for a rescue of the—body?" Jerry Newton looked up from fussing with one of the best small cameras on the market today. He had "got" that dramatic race with the flood, and he made no apologies for his enterprise. It was his business to get such scenes.

The Governor pressed his lips together and pointed downward.

"We're going to save the living," he said. "Where's that doctor?"

A shrewd-eyed, tanned man was already feeling of Peter's skull with finger tips that seemed to own a detached intelligence.

"Just a simple contusion," he announced cheerfully. "Put you to sleep for a minute, though, didn't it? Here. I'll fix you up in two shakes so you'll feel like new. Let's have a look at your chest."

In five minutes Peter was standing steadily on his own feet, ready to go. Rawley caught his somber glance at the place where Old Jess had disappeared and shook his head, unconsciously aping the Governor.

"No use, Uncle Peter. I tried to get him. It's running like a mill race. He landed square in the middle of it."

"He did this." Peter swept his arm out toward the bared river bed while his eyes sought the Governor's. "Crazy—you saw that. My half-brother would have more sense. The old man did it, to get the gold before the government could beat him to it."

He looked from one face to another trying to choose who stood highest in rank.

"I want permission," he said more firmly, as the doctor's stimulant took hold, "to go ahead now and carry out my plans. I warn you, gentlemen, that if that is not done there may be a great flood. Let me go ahead and shoot in that auxiliary dam *now*. That will relieve the pressure until we can shoot in more rock here. If I hold back the flood for you, at my expense, you can do as you think best with me afterwards, and with the river."

He threw out a hand toward the mutinous inshore stream.

"That dam is all rock; tons upon tons of it. Inshore is where a channel could eat through. The cliffs overhang and would prevent a full drop there of broken rock. I counted on this. It was my natural run-off. If it broke through anywhere, it would break here. Nature's a pretty good engineer, gentlemen. But we'll make it a safe proposition. We'll shoot in the auxiliary dam. I want a free hand in this, or—I can't answer for the consequences. I warn you."

The Governor lifted his eyebrows at the great engineer of the party. The engineer looked at the Chairman of the Commission. He looked at the river. Plainly, he disliked to give his word, which would carry much weight and which might lead them astray. Peter walked steadily along, between the Governor and Rawley, who held him solicitously by the arm.

"You will bear in mind that I have studied this problem all my life," Peter added urgently. "I've been spending a good deal of money on it. I have laid my plans very carefully, so as to risk neither lives nor money. The people below us will be safe, if you let me go ahead. In spite of the high water the Cramer Dam will hold—if you let me go ahead and finish the job."

The engineer shut his technical eyes and listened to his common reason. The Governor was still glancing his way between steps, wanting his opinion.

"There's a good deal in that," the engineer said at last. "I should advise that under the circumstances we permit Mr. Cramer to go ahead and make his dam as safe as possible. It will not render the present danger any greater. The longer the Cramer Dam holds, the better chance we will have of averting disaster. Give me a little time, and I can, I think, promise to get the river under control without any disastrous flood condition arising."

Peter's eyes darkened at the inference, but he had won at least one point. That, he reflected, was more than might have happened. These were truly great men; they were greater than their training of keeping well within the red-tape fences.

"Very well, Mr. Cramer," the Governor said. "I appoint you to take charge of the safeguarding of the river against a flood. I cannot promise immediate funds, however—"

Peter dismissed that point with a gesture.

"I expected to finance the Cramer Dam from start to finish," he said bluntly. "I still expect to do that. All I ask is to be left alone."

They had reached the flat rock, on the river bank opposite the shacks. Peter sent a glance that way, saw that the shacks were standing, apparently unharmed, and dismissed from his mind the thought of danger to his family. With the engineer beside him, the Governor and others behind him, he kept straight on to the dam site. He was wondering if that maniac, Old Jess, had thought to remove the big launch to a safe point around the bend above. If not, they might not be able to cross the river, should they want to do so. There were a few ticklish little points in the situation, he was bound to admit.

Rawley let go his arm and turned away toward the camp, and Peter called after him.

"Have Gladys and Nevada cook a big breakfast, son. We'll be back in an hour or so. And look out for another blast. But it will be a lot farther off than this one was. Have plenty of hot coffee."

"You bet!" Rawley promised, his heart curiously light. Angry or pleased, Nevada was very close. In another minute or two he would see her. There would be plenty to talk about, besides themselves. Just to hear her voice, he thought exultantly, would be a panacea for his loneliness.

As he neared the place he stopped as though some one had thrust him back. Then he went on, running as he had not run from the small flood in the river. The shacks stood, unharmed save for gaping window sashes, splinters of glass sticking like flattened icicles to the edges. The porch of Nevada's rock-faced dugout cabin stood upright, though slightly twisted. But behind the porch the rockwork was tumbled in a confused heap.

At a certain place in the ruins, Anita was whimpering and tearing at the rock with her fingers. Two of the older children were trying to help. It was the sight of these which filled Rawley with a cold fear. They would not tear at the wreck of an empty cabin.

Anita turned and stared at him dully. Then she pointed, her hand shaking as if she were stricken with palsy.

"In there—Nevada," she quavered. "My girl die, mebby! Lil time ago, speak to me. Now don't speak no more. Mebby die."

"Get back, out of the way." Rawley went up, looked at the place where they had been digging, and caught his breath.

"A little more, and you'd have had the whole thing in on top of her. Don't you see that wall just ready to topple? Kid, go get a pick and shovel. I'll try the roof."

He recalled the construction of the place, thanking God that he had spent many days there. The rock cabin had been set back into the hill, against a rock ledge of the prevailing granite. That, he felt sure, would hold against anything but a direct charge of explosives. In the far corner a dark, closet-like recess had been cut, and roofed with poles, corrugated iron and the dirt. It was used, he remembered, as a storeroom. It had never been finished like the two rooms in front. The rock walls were bare, the poles and iron showed in the low roof.

With pick and shovel he began digging at the roof, which had remained intact. As he worked he cursed Peter's thoroughness in constructing the place. The poles were set rather close together, and they were spiked down to heavy beams. The oldest boy brought a pinch-bar for that, and Rawley, throwing back the iron roofing, pried up a pole and let himself down into blackness.

The heavy curtain that hung in the doorway of the storeroom was slit. Beyond, the room seemed at his first dismayed glance to be completely filled with rock and débris. Then, quite close, he saw her.

She was sitting before the homemade desk that held her typewriter. Spread out before her were the books wherein she kept the records of the Cramer Dam. She had been working on the books when the blast wrecked the place. A beam from the ceiling had fallen, caught upon another beam, and pinned her down, bowed over her desk. Perhaps she had been leaning upon her folded arms to rest, when the shock came. But the beam was lying against her back, holding her down, and upon that, around it, rocks were piled.

Rawley set his teeth, carefully removed the rocks between him and the girl, and crept closer. Hesitating, afraid, he reached out and touched her fingers, still closed around something which she had been holding in her hand. Her fingers were cool, pliable—alive, he could have sworn. So his heart, that had seemed to stop altogether, gave a great jump.

Very gently he released the thing she was holding and drew it toward him. His old, weather-scarred, briar pipe! He looked down at it dumbly, looked at Nevada and very carefully laid the pipe back, against her fingers. His eyes were very blue and bright; his face was very pale. He steadied himself. He would get her out; he *must* free her and bring her alive to the safe outside, where—

A fear stabbed him. They were going to shoot in the other dam! He hadn't much time, then. Another shock—Peter had told him to look out for a blast. It was perhaps a matter of minutes.

He raised himself, looked at the beams. They seemed to be solidly braced, for the present, though another concussion would be likely to throw them down. He looked down.

Nevada was sitting on a reed stool, with two cushions upon it to give her height. He crept closer, raised himself and set a shoulder against the beam that lay along her bowed shoulders. He steadied it so while he took firm hold of a cushion and pulled it from beneath her.

Nevada's body sagged a bit. Rawley could see daylight now between her shoulders and the beam. He waited a breath, felt no settling of the beam, and pulled out the remaining cushion. Still the beam held fast. Nevada, then, was not being crushed; she had been pinned down without bearing the weight of the beam.

Rawley went back, crouching under the caved roof. His arms were round Nevada when he stopped and picked up the pipe, slipping it into the pocket of her blouse. Then, pulling her gently to him, he drew her out from under the beam and into the granite-walled storehouse. As he lifted her in his arms Nevada groaned.

Anita's arms were uplifted to receive her when Rawley came up head and shoulders through the gaping hole in the dugout roof. But he shook his head, stepped out with her in his arms and dug heels in the soft bank, working his way down to the level.

He still held the girl in his arms, looking for a place where he might lay her comfortably, when the earth shook beneath his feet. The terrific boom of the explosion deafened him. The jumble of rock shook and fell, tighter packed.

The auxiliary dam was in.

CHAPTER 33

THE EAGLE'S WING

Nevada was lying on the bed in Anita's shack, trying to convince Rawley that the doctor knew what he was talking about. The doctor had declared that Nevada's injuries were mostly superficial bruises and the nervous shock of sitting cramped in one position for hours, expecting every moment to be crushed to death. Nevada had seemed rather crestfallen when Rawley told her how simple a matter it had been to free her from the beam.

"The whole thing caught me unawares just when I had stopped a minute to rest," she explained defensively. "I think I was half asleep when it happened, and of course my lamp was smashed too flat even to think of exploding. It was black dark, and I suppose it was natural to imagine that I was being crushed when I was merely held fast. I did not try to move. I was afraid the whole thing would come down on me. Of course, I should have thought of the cushions—"

"You'd be a wonder if you had; even more of a wonder than you are." Rawley took her hand in both of his and patted it, in a sublime disregard of the circumstances of his last visit to the basin. "I believe in omens, Nevada. Fate gave me a splendid one when I found you." Rawley smiled at her mysteriously, his eyes twinkling.

"In the general wreck, my old pipe had landed from some cranny right on the desk beside you. You can't make me believe that Fate didn't mean something by that! The way I interpret it—"

"A freak accident," interrupted Nevada, her cheeks showing alarming symptoms of a sudden attack of fever. "That old pipe! You didn't take it, and I must have tucked it up somewhere until you came again. I suppose it rattled down."

Rawley's eyes had never been so blue. They were like looking down upon a sunlit sea. He dipped his fingers into the pocket of Nevada's blouse and produced the pipe, turning it tenderly in his hands.

"God bless the day I learned to smoke!" he murmured, his eyes still dancing. "It may have rattled down—but I know it's a good omen. It means—"

"Yes?" Nevada's big eyes were upon his face. A faint tremor was in her lips, as if laughter and tears were fighting for the mastery.

"The omen says that you and I are going to get married within a week. Well within a week." He was studying the pipe as a mystic studies the crystal. "It tells me that the hatchet is forever buried. This is the pipe of peace, and it passed from me to you. That means that you and I go through life together. Our trails never separate. It means—"

"Oh, hush!" Nevada cried sharply and struck at the pipe in his hand. "Our trails can't lie together. We can't marry, ever—ever! You know that as well as I do. We're cousins." She turned her face to the wall.

Rawley did not speak. He looked up from the pipe, straight into the eyes of Anita, sitting in a corner like a bronze Buddha disguised as a squaw.

Anita met his look with stolid obstinacy, never blinking, never a quiver in her face.

Rawley's jaw squared a little as he continued to look at her. His body swayed forward, his eyes boring into her very soul. So had King, of the Mounted, looked when he demanded that Anita should choose between himself and Jess Cramer. Rawley did not know why he stared at her so. He only knew that the truth was there, hidden behind those unreadable eyes. He knew that the truth would give him Nevada the moment that truth was spoken. No lips but Anita's might speak that truth; other lips were sworn to silence.

The old squaw whimpered under her breath. Her eyes flickered and could no longer look defiance into those terrible, commanding blue eyes—the eyes of King, of the Mounted. Her hand went up to shield her face from the stare of them. She stirred uneasily in her chair. She spread her fingers, peering fearfully between them. The terrible blue eyes looked at her still. Slowly, painfully, scarce knowing that she did so, Anita pulled herself up from the chair and went forward as one goes to the bar of justice.

As a flame shoots up suddenly from dying embers, so did a flame dart out from the ashes of her youth. The stooped, gross old body straightened. Anita's head went back. Her eyes glowed with a little of their old fire. Her voice rang clear, proud with the pride of ancestry unknown.

"Nevada," she cried imperiously and spoke rapidly in Indian. "It is not true that you are his cousin. He is the grandson of a man I loved in my youth. He is the grandson of Sergeant George King, who was the father of Peter. I have been ashamed that you should know the truth. Now I am not ashamed, for I know that stolen love is more noble than a lie. The father of Peter, him I loved. He was a soldier and he went away. He promised to return in one month. In three months he had not come, nor sent me word. I was angry and I let the man he hated think that I loved him and not my soldier man. Then I went away, for my heart was sad. I would not follow my soldier man. I was proud. After a long time—after more than a year had passed I returned to El Dorado and I brought my child, who was Peter. I sought for news of my soldier, but there was none. He had not come, he had not sent me word. So I went to the man I hated. I told him that Peter was his son, which was a lie. I was very proud. I thought that some day my soldier would return and would see how I laughed at him and loved another. But I did not love. And Peter was not the son of the man my soldier hated. Now the young man comes and loves, and I am old. Soon I go to my soldier man. It is not right that others should have sorrow because of my lie.

"So now I speak what is true. I say that this young man is not of your blood. He is the grandson of the father of Peter, and Peter is his uncle. You are not his cousin. Now you will be his wife, and you will hate Anita for the sin of her youth."

Nevada lay listening, gazing fixedly at her grandmother. She caught the gnarled old hand of Anita in both her own. She fondled it, kissed it, laughed softly with tears in her laughter.

"You will not hate Anita?" Tears spilled over the fat lids and trickled down the cheeks of the old squaw.

Whatever Nevada said, she spoke in Indian, stealing a shy glance now and then at Rawley. But her voice crooned caresses. Now and then she kissed the old hand she held in both her own.

Anita tucked in her bangs, drew two fingers across her cheeks to dry her tears and smiled. She turned heavily toward Rawley.

"My girl say, loves you more—I love your grandfadder. My girl make you good wife."

"Hush, Grandmother! He doesn't want a fighting squaw—"

"Don't, eh?" Rawley got up and made for her.

At that moment Peter walked in upon them, unconscious of the fact that he was interrupting a very interesting conversation. Peter's face was grave.

"Nevada, do you and mother know anything about Young Jess? Gladys is all upset over him. She thought he was down in the river with his father. She heard them talking about getting gold, and then the dam went, and she hasn't seen him since. If he's hiding," he added sternly, "he may as well come out and show himself. I think it can be fixed up. The Governor wants to ask him some questions."

"How could I know? I was penned in when the cabin fell to pieces," Nevada countered. "They certainly said nothing to me, either one of them. I didn't see them all afternoon or evening."

Anita slowly lifted her hand to her face and gropingly tucked in her bangs. Her eyes were fixed dumbly on Peter's face.

"Young Jess—by river," she said reluctantly. "I walk in moonlight, no can sleep. Comes big shootin'. I fall down. Bimeby I hear Nevada—she call me come quick. I no see Jess no more. I come." She recapitulated slowly. "Jess by river, look on river. Comes shoot. No see Jess no more. Nevada call loud. Jess no come."

The eyes of the two men met significantly. Peter turned and went out, and Rawley followed him.

"Concussion," Rawley said succinctly. "If he were on the edge of the bank, it would throw him off, very likely. It's high, out here, and pretty steep. He went into the river, in that case."

"Yes—some folks upriver came near getting it when we shot in the second dam," Peter said tonelessly. "I sent a man up on a hill to wave back any stragglers, but the doctor had to do some patching on the crowd, nevertheless. Well, I'll go and look along the river. He may be hurt, under the bank."

Rawley did not think so, but he went with Peter and searched the bank thoroughly. Halfway down, caught behind a bowlder, he found Young Jess's hat. He managed to retrieve it and bring it to Peter. Peter turned it over in his hand, looked at Rawley and nodded.

"It's his," he said shortly. "It's all we'll ever find."

He turned away toward the shack, swung back suddenly and faced the tremendous heap of broken rock visible from midstream to the farther shore. He lifted both hands high above his head, his face twisted, his eyes black with sublime fury.

"Damn you!" he cried. "Curse the thought, born in greed, fostered in rapacity, that put you there! Curse the bitter years that brought you to pass! For the greed of the gold they would have filched, for the vulture's eye that watched and waited all these years, to swoop down and snatch and grab, with never a thought for the rights of other men, I curse the thing I helped to make!

"Born in selfishness, you have defiled a mighty river that God meant should flow through the land and one day be a blessing to mankind. You have made of the river a monster. It is *you* that is driving women and little children from their homes! *You*, God damn you! You have been a traitor to the mind that brought you forth. You have destroyed the two who worked and waited, that you might pander to their greed. You have tried to destroy the dearest thing I have on earth, because I saw in you something big and beautiful—because I was fool enough to think that an idea spawned in devil-greed could live in noble achievement.

"Look at the slimy thing the vultures have made of the river! The leprous thing over which the vultures croaked—for a little while—croaked and went down and died! The Eagle would never stop the river, leave it a naked, stinking thing under the sky. For the good of mankind, the Eagle would have tamed the river, without destroying it. The Eagle would have had it run peacefully within its banks, helping without hurting. Now the river lies shamed in its bed—that magnificent stream!—and men flee from it in terror. The two who thought to feast in the slime—yes, and I, too, could stoop so low as to root for gold like a hog in the mire!—you have swept them to destruction, have cheated them at the last of their prey.

"But you have done your worst! I, who helped to make you what you are, who created you thought by thought, I will tear you down. For the thing you are, a monument to greed and self, I shall tear you down stone by stone until the river is once more sweeping majestically down to the sea. As God is my witness, this thing the vultures have created shall be forgotten. The Eagle's wing shall shadow the Colorado, a river undefiled."

His voice ceased. He stood, hands clenched beside him, jaw squared, staring at the dam that had been his dream. A dream fulfilled—and hated in the fulfillment. His lips moved, muttering the prophecy of Johnny Buffalo:

"'You will succeed, and fail in the succeeding. And from the failure—'"

A gloved hand was laid in friendly fashion on Peter's shoulder. He turned and looked into the eyes of his Governor.

"It takes a big man, a man of broad vision, to look upon his life's work and dare to say what you have said," the Governor told him kindly, the look of understanding in his eyes. "Don't be down-hearted because your success has proved a failure. The Cramer Dam would hold, I believe, if we wanted it to hold. But you are right. It is not for the vulture, but for the Eagle to say what shall be done with the river. The country needs more men like you, Peter. You shall help to build another dam—and build it under the Eagle's wing."

Peter lifted his right hand and laid it upon the shoulder of his Governor. His eyes were very blue and very deep. So they stood for a space and looked into each other's eyes.

"'—And from the failure rise to greater things,'" Rawley repeated under his breath, his eyes shining.

www.ingramcontent.com/pod-product-compliance
Lightning Source LLC
Chambersburg PA
CBHW020644180626
46816CB00003B/1122